NO ESCAPE

It seemed like a nightmare—but it was most definitely happening. One moment Regina had been safe and sound in her London lodging. The next, she was in the carriage of the Duke of Torquay as it rolled along the deserted midnight streets.

Across from her sat the Duke himself. Against Regina's will, her heart quickened at his almost incredible good looks, his splendor of dress, his perfect ease of manner and charm. Against all her efforts, her courage faltered when she heard his amused voice assuring her that she had no choice but to yield to his desires, and that soon she would thank him for pleasure past all her imaginings.

Regina did not know what she could do next. She only knew that the infamous Duke had her at his mercy—and that he had a notable reputation for having none. . . .

The Duke's Wager

The Duke's Wager

Edith Layton

A SIGNET BOOK

NEW AMERICAN LIBRARY

NAL BOOKS ARE AVAILABLE AT QUANTITY DISCOUNTS WHEN USED
TO PROMOTE PRODUCTS OR SERVICES. FOR INFORMATION PLEASE
WRITE TO PREMIUM MARKETING DIVISION, NEW AMERICAN LIBRARY,
1633 BROADWAY, NEW YORK, NEW YORK 10019.

SIGNET TRADEMARK REG. U.S. PAT. OFF. AND FOREIGN COUNTRIES
REGISTERED TRADEMARK—MARCA REGISTRADA
HECHO EN CHICAGO, U.S.A.

SIGNET, SIGNET CLASSIC, MENTOR, ONYX, PLUME, MERIDIAN
and NAL BOOKS are published by New American Library,
1633 Broadway, New York, New York 10019

First Printing, February, 1983

3 4 5 6 7 8 9

PRINTED IN THE UNITED STATES OF AMERICA

For Orson, my constant companion.

I

It was not a fashionable night to be seen in the streets of London. Oh, the moon shone as brightly as ever an autumn moon did, and the air carried the light crisp taste of autumn windfall apples; the freshening breeze carried away the usual stale stenches of the city, and the woodsmoke from many fires added to the clear tang of the night. But then the month of September was never a slave to the fashions of men, so she could be excused for putting on such a show on a night when no other lady of good taste or family would dare to parade the streets of town. But she was obviously only a baggage, so she displayed her charms generously and spread her gifts lavishly and never seemed to mind that no female of repute would savor them this night. No matter, if she was not a female of discretion, why then, neither were any of the other ladies abroad this night.

But that was not to imply that there were no others in the streets. London was no ghost town, bereft of pedestrians and coaches, riders and lackeys, strollers and theatergoers. No, the city was as crowded as ever, the fashionable made up only one facet of its usual throngs. And if the ladies of the town were safely at home, or snugged at several respectable house parties, the gentlemen of their class suffered no such inhibitions. They were free to enjoy the night as they chose.

As were the beggars, warming themselves over scant alley-edge fires, waiting for some more substantial citizens to cross their paths so they could ply their practiced pathetic pleas; as were the sharpers, eyeing the passing crowds for any hint of possible gain; as were the street women, in readiness now that evening had come, to sell their flowers, chestnuts, or bodies at reasonable fair-trade prices. So if the ladies of immaculate breeding were not abroad, it hardly mattered, for the several

enjoyments offered this evening were not for them
anyway.

Even the Opera, where so many of the select disported themselves on proper evenings, was filling to
capacity this evening. For if the finer ladies would not
grace their seats, why then, there were an assortment
of other members of the gender who would gladly do so.
But if these were not ladies who were prime articles on
the marriage mart, even the most dispassionate observ-
ers would have to admit that they were prime articles of
their species. Still, there were few dispassionate ob-
servers in their company; it was not, alas, an evening
notable for opera lovers, although lovers there were, in
great numbers.

The beggars and loiterers and running boys and flower
ladies who congregated in front of the Opera did not
mind the lack of Society's finest females, rather they
knew there would be many young blades with free fingers to toss loose coins to impress their latest conquest.
For the street people knew, with their survivor's instincts, that a night such as this, a night of the demimonde, was far more of a profitable time than a night
when a gentleman had to properly escort his lawful wife
or dutiful daughters. And they watched as the colorful,
blatantly beautiful ladies, peacocked in with their
gentlemen.

The street girls would have to be content with waiting in the shadows for the final curtain to fall, so that
they could have the chance to accommodate those men
of fashion who had not brought their own ladies, and
who were either too inept or too luckless to have encountered a friend to invite them to a revel, introduce
them to an unattached beauty, or take themselves off
with them to a fashionable house of delights. These
disappointed blades would be available to invitation for
a few moments of less exalted play. The girls were not
impressed with the high-flown style of the young women
giggling into the Opera house. Some had been in their
places at one time, some dreamed of it, all knew that
without a masterstroke of luck, these same ladies would
be standing at their side in the shadows one day, wait-

ing for the last "Bravo," to compete with them for the stragglers.

Each new carriage that approached was greeted by the assembled crowd, avidly ploying their separate industries, with great anticipation. The war, though far off, was still on, there was a scarcity of the young military men who were so free with their pay, and money was hard to come by. But when the magnificent carriage bearing the insignia of St. John Basil St. Charles, Marquis of Bessacarr drew up to the curb and a large gentleman alighted, sweeping his impassive stare over them, even the hungriest among them did not press any further forward. Here was a knowing one, they thought, and a hard one, who would not need to dazzle his lady-bird with careless largesse to strangers. When the flame-haired woman alighted and preened herself for a moment, allowing the crowd to admire her finery and letting their eyes linger on the dazzling necklace which peeped through the open cape, as did the equally dazzling expanse of bosom she exposed to the September breeze, they looked for only one moment and then waited for the next carriage to discharge its passengers. There was money here, but not for them.

"Annabelle!" came the gentleman's amused voice. "Shall I have to rent a stage for you to display both my and nature's gifts? Or would you prefer to accompany me now?" Simpering, she raised her rosy face to his and, taking his arm, allowed herself to be borne off to the theater. "As I once was," thought a drab who peeked out from the side of the wall where she patiently waited. "As I shall be," vowed the young girl who stood beside her.

The Marquis looked neither to the left nor to the right as he escorted his lady up the winding staircase to his private box. Yet he knew exactly how his companion disported herself as she clung to his arm. He knew, without having to watch, how she swung her hips, as no lady he would escort on a more fashionable night would, how she alternately smiled or snubbed the other women she encountered, how she let her eyes promise or deny the young blades who eyed her flamboyant beauty. As no proper young woman would dare, he thought, but then, he smiled to himself, no proper young woman would have earned that necklace she wore in quite the way that Annabelle had. And, he admitted, she had certainly earned it.

Once settled in the ornate box, the Marquis allowed himself to glance over the program of the night's promised delights. But he was not a lover of Opera, and the delights he had promised himself would only come after the performance upon the stage. Annabelle fanned herself and looked out over the audience with great interest, noting old rivals, new contenders, and the vast possibilities of future protectors she might have to beguile should the languid gentleman next to her tire of her. For her, it was both good business and a good diversion to be seen tonight at the theater.

The Marquis, watching Annabelle coolly scrutinizing the murmuring crowd, felt a vast impatience with himself this evening. In truth, it had gone on too long. But, he had to admit, he was growing lazy in the pursuit of his pleasures. It was perhaps simpler to visit those special houses of assignation on a hit or miss basis than it was to fund, feed, and entertain a female such as Annabelle. But it was also more chancy. There was always both the possibility of finding a female who was deft and accomplished, or discovering that one had given up an evening to an unknown who was unacceptable or, at best, marginal. At least Annabelle was a known quantity and, on the whole, reliable.

But there was this necessity of taking her out every so often and showing her off to the town. Or else, she would sulk and whine, and accuse him of being unsatisfied with her services. At first, he remembered—was it only two months ago, then?—he had been well pleased with her. But as the novelty of her talents, and the familiarity of her face and form, had increased, he found himself noticing her personality, her intellect, and her habits—none of which pleased him. For though she could be said to have that most agreeable of traits, "a good heart," it was undeniable that she was ignorant, avaricious, and common. He sighed, if only women could be folded up into a closet until one took them out for the natural pleasure they provided. No, it would not be long until the Marquis of Bessacarr would be hunting a new companion.

He would not find one among his social equals. He would not find one among the dewy misses so dutifully served up at such fashionable places as Almack's, or the diverse watering spas or house parties where the fashionable amused themselves. No, those young women were, firstly, seldom as beautiful as Annabelle, and more importantly, never as accessible. They were there only for a titled gentleman such as himself to choose a wife from. Someone who would dutifully lie down, in a most civilized fashion, upon a duly sanctified and sanitized marriage couch, for the sole purpose of producing another being to carry on his exalted name. They were never, the Marquis thought, even to be considered in the same context as Annabelle. They were not, he thought with real amusement, even to be precisely considered as "female" in the same sense that she was. Certainly that was not what they, or he, had been brought up to expect. In fact, he often wondered if many of them precisely knew what sort of marital horrors their noble husbands would eventually require of them.

And those other ladies of his class, those who were not quite so newly-sprung, who had already presented their husbands with the required number of descendants and who had been given indirectly to understand that they might discreetly pursue their pleasure where they may, were little better in his eyes. For after all the courting, all the poetic flights, and subtle hand pressures, and interminable weeks of light flirtation and secret messages, and painstaking arrangements for a site acceptable for dalliance, still he inevitably found them disappointing. It stood to reason: They had once been those same demure little debutantes, they had once had the self-same expectations. The infrequent and required usage by their noble husbands had not prepared them for a life of erotic delight. Even the most willful and passionate among them, the Marquis thought, could not hold a candle to Annabelle's practice of the

art. She was born to it, he smiled, bred to it and
accomplished at it. But still, she was becoming a bore.

As for other women of his class, the ones who had
found happiness, who lived in accord with their husbands, who found their enjoyments with them alone and
sought no others, why, the Marquis had no experience
with them. The life he led was that of a hedonist, as so
many of his fellows were. As his was expected to be. He
was eight and twenty, wealthy and fashionable, and not
at all interested in perpetuating his line at the moment,
however much that fact must disappoint the general run
of young women available to him this season. They must
pass on the torch to their younger sisters, he was not in
the market for a wife this season. But looking at Annabelle inflating her already considerably inflated chest so
that his spider's net of diamonds could be seen by an
acquaintance of hers seated in the orchestra, whose expression of exquisite envy could be read even from this
distance, he knew that he was definitely in the market
for a new companion.

"Sinjin," she pouted, "it's ever so hot in here, could
you procure me an ice, or a sip of something more
fortifying?" He eyed her with annoyance, this drinking
of hers was no longer the discreet thing she thought it
was. All the oil of cloves and mint she ingested could
not disguise the ever-present miasma of gin that hung
over her. But he rose, and bowed and brushed aside the
curtains that enfolded the box. He'd be glad to stretch
his legs, and glad for the opportunity to evaluate the
other women present tonight, the other women from
among whom he'd possibly find her successor. While
she, he knew, would certainly be glad of the opportunity to drink deeply from the flask she concealed in her
wrap.

He stood in the outer hallway, tall and immaculate in
his evening wear, his broad shoulders encased in a close-
fitting jacket, his slender waist tapering down to muscu-
lar legs, his black hair swept back and cut expertly to
accentuate the fine high planes of his face, every visible
carefully designed part of him signaling the epitome of
the man of wealth and fashion. He stood at the top of

his world, by birth, by sex, by fortune and education. And his world was the only world that he cared about.

"Sinjin, by God, it's Sinjin," the rotund, balding young gentleman of fashion to his left cried, dropping his quizzing glass and hurrying over to him. "By God, sir. You thought I was dead, confess it? Did you not?"

"Not dead, James," the Marquis taunted, "only married."

"Ah well," mumbled the shorter man, "and so I was, but you were there, Sinjin, so don't quiz me. But married's not quite the same as dead, sir. I went the round, you dog, I traveled wherever I could where that cur Nappy was not, and then I came back to town. Only arrived last week. Only settled in t'other day. Only been on the town a day or so and hadn't seen you anywhere. Heard that you were cuddled up with a new friend, you dog, and never thought to lay eyes upon you so soon. How good it is to see you, Sinjin, how good it is to be back in town. Museums, Sinjin, cathedrals! Flower exhibitions, by God! None of you chaps ever told me what sort of things to expect when I made the leap! No, no, don't deny it, Sinjin. Only offered me felicitations and gave me a pile of silver and punch bowls that I could never use if I lived to be a Methusalah. Confess it, Sinjin, you never warned me about all the blasted cathedrals I'd have to trek through once I started married life."

"I never married, James," the Marquis said, "so how could I give you the benefit of my advice? And how is Lady Hoyland?"

"Breeding," his companion said briefly. "Quite a good thing."

"So you did not spend precisely all your time in cathedrals, James," the Marquis noted with a little smile.

"Sinjin!" James replied, his eyes wide with shock. "No, not a thing to jest about, my man, the lady is my wife. I can't have you saying such things about the Lady Hoyland, my man."

"Do you wish to call me out, James?" the Marquis asked, his usually fog-gray eyes admitting little sparks of icy light. "It's only that I can't conceive of how the thing could be conceived in a cathedral."

"No, really," James said hastily, looking up at his friend. "Don't jest about such a thing. It's my wife you know, not a joking matter. You know I couldn't call you out, wouldn't want to, but as you are a friend, Sinjin, don't make me a sacrificial victim to whatever sulks you've fallen into."

"Forgive me, James," the Marquis said in an unrepentant tone, bending into an insolent bow, "I had forgotten how pious you married fellows are."

"Well not exactly pious, Sinjin," James confided. "It's just that a wife's one thing, and a woman's another. Actually, I came here tonight to see if I couldn't set up something more befitting to my present station. . . ."

"I understand completely," the Marquis said, remembering suddenly the spring wedding he had attended, with James standing on the receiving line and little Lady Eleanor, her dark plump little person clinging to James's sleeve, shyly acknowledging his towering presence.

"James," he said, a wry smile springing to his lips, "I might have just the thing. Go procure an ice, my boy, a lovely lemon ice, and take it to the . . . companion . . . I have seated in my box. Tell her I am detained. She'll be glad of company, for I shall be a while. And perhaps, James, you'll be glad of the company as well."

"What?" asked James. "That lovely red-headed creature? You wouldn't mind . . . you wouldn't take offense?"

"Not in the least," he replied. "Consider it a belated wedding gift. But I'm afraid you'll have to provide the packaging and the wrapping yourself. And it will not come cheaply."

"Wouldn't expect it to come cheaply," James said eagerly, "but it would be worth it?" he asked in a whisper, like a conspiratorial child.

"I would not suggest it otherwise," the Marquis said airily, as he watched his friend rush off in search of a vendor.

He felt fractionally taller, and freer than he had a moment before, as he strolled off down the corridor, acknowledging old acquaintances and carefully watching the arrival of latecomers.

He had spent the first act of the Opera out in the corridor, reacquainting himself with an old school chum who had the latest bits of gossip to impart, and he had been feeling so free and relaxed that he was a bit surprised when the doors swung open and the promenade of Opera-goers exited for their intermission. This informal parade he knew was by far the most important reason why most of them had come to begin with.

He saw James with Annabelle on his arm as they walked toward him. She looked up at him for a moment as they walked past, and allowed a rueful grin to touch her rouged lips. He remained still, for if she chose, now was the moment that she could create an unpleasant scene. But gin-bold as she was, she was foremost a woman of business, so she merely allowed herself one last regretful look at the Marquis and then turned her attention to her small, plump companion. James, seeing the marquis standing there, took this opportunity to take one of her cool hands in his moist grip and raise it to his lips. St. John said nothing, so they passed by. "Well done," the Marquis thought, noting that the transfer had been made as correctly and formally as any ceremony he had ever witnessed.

Quite a clutch of unattached gentlemen now stood against the walls of the corridors, watching the other Opera-goers stroll by. St. John noticed a few old friends, a few older gentlemen, a few young sparks out to make their mark on the town. He felt relieved to be one of their number again, and pleased himself by watching the women of the demimonde self-consciously flirt past his raised quizzing glass. A slight stir in one group to the corner of the hall brought his attention to the entrance of the Duke of Torquay, his presence signaling the beginnings of muttered gossip. St. John smiled, and saluted the Duke with his quizzing glass.

"Sinjin," the Duke greeted him in his soft hoarse voice, "don't tell me you didn't feel the urge to tell the latest *on dit* about me to your friends the moment you saw me? What, you still stand here just to have a word

with me? Do you think I can impart something new and
exciting that they haven't yet told you?"

"I don't need to dine out on your exploits, Your Grace,"
St. John answered, looking coldly at the slight figure
beside him.

"No, no, you at least do not," the Duke acknowledged.
"You are commonly acknowledged to be my successor,
these days, aren't you? When my dissolute ways bring
me down to the worms, it will be you who replaces me,
will it not, Sinjin?"

The Marquis did not acknowledge the hit by so much
as a lift of his shoulders, but still he felt a cold chill at
the words.

Jason Edward Thomas, Duke of Torquay, was already,
although he had not entered his thirty-fifth year, acknowledged to be the supreme pleasure-seeker of his
day. The joke that made the rounds was that if the
Duke could find a way to fit it in his bed, he would bed
it. The stories told about him and his exploits on the
town beggared the imagination, and although the more
sensible of listeners discounted half of what they heard,
the half they accepted was shocking enough. Still, he
was of impeccable birth, title, and position, and many of
the gentlemen who listened avidly to stories of his scandalous exploits, would still have gladly handed over the
choice of their eligible daughters to him in wedlock,
should the elegant widower ever seek marriage again.

And the same young women whose eyes rounded at
the abbreviated tales that filtered down to them of his
doings, would still have found themselves eager to be
wed to him. For his appearance belied all the gossip and
scandal that followed him. Of medium height and slender as a boy, his pale gold hair fell softly upon a white
brow. His large clear blue eyes and tender mouth seemed
more appropriate to a romantic poet than to the sort of
man whose name had become synonymous with license.
But St. John had seen the Duke at his play. And the
Marquis had known some of the women who had known
him intimately, and did not doubt most of the stories
that he heard. Something deep within the Marquis bri-

dled at being dubbed the Duke's successor, but still he acknowledged the truth of the jest.

"Well then, Duke," he drawled, "it is most fortunate for our audience that we stand here together. It saves them a great deal of effort and eyestrain if we stay here thus, in tandem."

"It does," the hoarse sweet voice acknowledged. "It might, dear Sinjin, save you a great deal of trouble, too, for then I could not make a move you could not emulate immediately," he remarked, glancing up through his long lashes at the tight face next to him.

The Marquis pretended not to have heard, as he felt the unease spread through him, but he was spared any rejoinder as the Duke's head turned.

The wide china eyes flew open and the slight body almost visibly trembled, like a dog at the hunt. "My God!" the Duke breathed in hushed undertones. "Who is she?"

The Marquis looked with relief toward the woman whose presence had stirred his companion so. Yes, he admitted, she was worthy of the attention.

Even at this distance he could see that she was young, almost pitifully so, although many of the other women might have been of an age with her. She wore no rouge, no paint, and so her face looked more vulnerable against the background of this gathering. She was dressed simply and elegantly in a high-waisted blue velvet gown that accentuated her high breasts and slender figure. Her gleaming chestnut hair had been drawn up tightly, and only one long curl brushed against her shoulder. Her eyes were large, wide, and frightened, and a strangely vivid grass-green color which accentuated the clear whiteness of her skin. She was innocent of jewelry, of paint, but it was the innocence in her face that troubled St. John. She could almost pass for a woman of quality. But then, what would she be doing here on this night?

She stood, wide-eyed, her cloak thrown over one arm, as she realized the attention she had drawn to herself by exiting from her box. She turned and spoke in a low voice to the other woman who emerged from behind her, another young woman, but this one all frizzy ginger

hair and freckles who wore a plain serviceable dress. A
maid? St. John frowned. What the devil would a young
woman with a maid be doing here at the Opera on such
a night, when the courtesans flirted and vied for new
liaisons? Unless she was a shrewd wench who had discovered a new ploy. But the look of fright in her eyes
dissuaded him from that flight.

But his former companion, the Duke, had not waited
to speculate. With the swift grace he was famous for, he
had already achieved her side. She looked up at him in
incomprehension. St. John could not hear a word that
the Duke spoke so softly into her ear, but he could see
the color drain from her already white face. She gripped
the other woman by the arm and then almost ran to the
top of the long stairs.

For only a moment the Duke stood still, as if bemused, and then he signaled swiftly to his man, who
came to his side to listen to the quick, soft instructions
and then, nodding, was gone. The Duke strolled back to
St. John's side. "Not quite flown," he whispered in that
intimate voice. "My man will wait to see her coach, to
get her direction. It's a shame that her courage deserted her. She will be quite a success. I think that the
stir she caused quite overset her plans. And as to your
plans, St. John? I noticed that you have so generously
given over your seat to your friend. Would you care to
share my box for the duration of the performance?"

"Thank you," St. John bowed, "but I seem to have
already achieved my plans for this evening, and so must
be off to more profitable sport."

"It will do you no good," the Duke smiled. "I have
already set my sights upon her . . . unless you care to
vie with me for the honors?"

"I am not quite so exacting in my requirements this
evening, Your Grace," St. John retorted. "I'll leave that
field open to you. Remember, I am marked to be your
successor, not your equal." And, smiling pleasantly with
a humor he did not feel, he left.

Emilie Loring

and you've no right a great respectable dress,
at you long deserved. With that I would g—ne

II

Regina Analise Berryman was in a rage. When she had returned from the Opera, a combination of shame and shock, coupled with the lateness of the hour, had sent her into an unaccustomed state of subdued self-recrimination. She had lain awake for many long hours, until the sheer weight of the night had sent her drifting off into a restless sleep. But when Belinda had drawn back her curtains to admit the shallow morning light, she had awoken to a healthy sense of fury.

She drew the belt on her morning gown and, unable to find her slipper's mate, sent the orphaned partner flying to the wall. "Why," her first words to Belinda were, "did you not tell me *exactly* why last night was not a proper night to attend the Opera?"

Belinda eyed her new mistress warily. This was not at all like the quiet, amiable, green young girl she had been serving for the past weeks.

"Aye, but I told you, miss. I said and I said that it would be more fitting for you to wait for your uncle to return afore you went to the Opera. I did say that, miss, I did."

" 'Aye,' " mimicked the infuriated Miss Berryman, looking like a proper witch, Belinda thought uneasily, with her long gleaming hair tousled and wild, her odd emerald green eyes shining like a cat's. "But, Belinda my dear, you did not, repeat *not*, tell me that only . . . courtesans and their protectors would be there, now did you?"

"That's not true at all, miss," Belinda gulped, backing toward the door as Regina rounded upon her. "Why there was ever such a sweet old couple there, miss, and anyway," she said in a rush, "how was I to know who all else would be there? I'm only a poor girl, miss, and never been to the Opera at all, and only heard below

13

stairs that it wasn't the best idea for you to go . . . and I told you so, miss. Indeed I did. And you only said. . . ."

" 'Pooh!' I said," Regina admitted regretfully. "Yes, that's so. I said it wouldn't do any harm and it was a shame to let the tickets go to waste. But why didn't you stop me, Belinda, before I made such a fool of myself?"

"Ah, miss," cried Belinda, seeing and pressing her advantage, "but it isn't my place to stop you. I'm only your maid, miss, and. . . ."

"Only a poor girl," interrupted Regina, deflated. "I know, Belinda. Excuse me."

Regina turned and sank down again upon the bed. She tossed her heavy hair back from her face. Her own fault, she thought miserably, of course. No matter how poor Belinda had influenced her, it was, indeed, still her own fault. She had wanted to go to the Opera. That was undeniable. Only a few weeks in town and she had already made a cake of herself. For when the invitation had come, even though her uncle was away from home and would not return in time for the Opera, she had been determined to attend. She would not sit at home childishly, for lack of an escort. After all, she had reasoned, back at home in the country, when her papa had been alive, they had gone to the local theater as often as possible to see some of the infrequent Shakespearean productions presented by traveling troupes of players. And when Papa could not come with her, there had been no shame in attending with only her governess, Miss Bekins, as her escort.

But, she thought, as usual incurably honest with herself, she *had* wondered if the same manners obtained in the great city of London as did in her little corner of England. She had heard of how glittering and fashionable the theaters were here. Even more, she had thought of all her new dresses, hanging unseen in the closet, and no matter how often she rationalized that she wanted to actually hear a first-rate opera company, that had been the major reason she had so wanted to attend. And who, she thought, furious with herself, would have been mutton-headed enough to take the advice of a little lady's maid on matters of rules of society? Even if there were no one else she knew whose opinion she could have asked, why hadn't she waited for Uncle's return? There would have been other operas, other nights.

Because she belatedly understood, if there had been no harm in her going unaccompanied by a gentleman at home, it had only been because there were few people in the audience who did not know Miss Berryman, the schoolmaster's daughter. And they would no more have thought her fast for attending the theater without her papa than they would have thought her scandalous for attending a lecture without him.

So even if Belinda's eyes had narrowed slyly when she asked if going by herself was "done," and her answer had never been a direct "no" but rather a tangle of "Well, miss, it depends . . ." and "Some ladies do go by themselves, I hear tell . .," she had only half listened. She had not really wanted to be persuaded to stay home. Once she had made up her mind, Belinda had been in ecstacies, thrilled with the chance to see the upper classes at play first hand for the first, and probably last, time. And Regina had caught fire from Belinda's enthusiasms. She had rigged herself out in the first stare of fashion and sailed forth with an eager Belinda in tow, only to discover what she really should have guessed all along: that London was as far in miles as it was in attitudes from her home. And that no one could have guessed that she was only the schoolmaster's daughter from Dorset, gawking at their splendid world; rather they had taken her for a trollop, bent on advancing herself. Regina sighed to herself. She was, she felt, well served for her self-deception and rashness.

She glanced at Belinda, whose hands were twisting under her little white apron, and felt she ought to let the matter drop. As well chastise a cat for stalking a pigeon as to condemn Belinda for seizing her chance for a little excitement, even if it were at her new mistress's expense. My fashionable career, Regina thought glumly, shall go right back where it belongs—between the pages of a book, and in my mind. What a rustic she must take me for, she thought. And, she thought ruefully with a

little sad smile that made Belinda's hands steady themselves, what a rustic I am, indeed.

"Never mind, Belinda," Regina said. "It's over, and
you shall not bear the blame. We'll forget it. We'll avoid
the haunts of the fashionable and we'll rub on together
well enough in the future. But," she said, eyeing the
laden tray Belinda had set up on a little table near the
window and embarrassed that the whole staff likely
thought of her as a milkmaid fresh from the country,
"could you please tell Cook that although I do come
from the country, I do not eat like a yeoman and do not
require a breakfast that could easily feed five strong
men?"

"Oh yes, miss," Belinda said eagerly. "I do hear that
all the young ladies just drink a cup of hot chocolate and
have a bit of bread for breakfast."

"I'm not that fashionable," Regina laughed. "An egg
or two might be pleasant as well."

"Oh yes indeed, miss." Belinda curtsied, grateful to
make an escape. "I'll tell Cook at once."

The Master might have my skin, Belinda worried, as
she went down the stairs. But it wasn't my fault, not
really. She did want to go. And when would I ever get
such a grand chance again to go to the bloody Opera, I'd
like to know? So if my fine lady from the country wanted
to go, why shouldn't I go with her? I'd never get such a
chance again, once he came home, no I wouldn't. Didn't
she cause a stir, though? Only think, the Black Duke
himself making a proposal to her! Wouldn't I like to
have heard what he said to her? Just wouldn't I. So
handsome he was, too . . . it's a thing to tell my grand-
children, that is. I know what my answer would have
been to him, if he'd asked me, she thought. Did you
ever see such eyes on a gentleman, though? Took her
clothes right off with them, he did. Now if it had been
me. . . . And she entertained herself with thoughts of
operas, and dukes, and magnificent offers of finery and
jewels, as she took herself off below stairs to regale the
others with a highly colored account of the night's events.

But Miss Berryman was not entertaining herself with
similar imaginings. She was, instead, sulking in a very

unladylike fashion as she sat at the table and sipped her coffee. "What a fool thing to do," she sighed in disgust, "flying off like a true clothhead, decked out like what I thought was a London lady, only to find myself taken for the Queen of the Cyprians."

"Ah well," she sighed, putting down the delicate cup and rising to stare out the window, "I do have a lot to learn in this new life, and I must teach myself not to be so impetuous . . . but . . . it did seem like such an . . . unexceptionable idea. But then, after all, what do I know about the customs that prevail here?"

Regina Analise Berryman had only been a resident of the city which so perplexed her for a scant three weeks. Before that, she had spent the whole of her two decades (except for one brief whirlwind tour of Bournemouth, where an aquaintance of her father lived) in a small house in a small village on the southern edge of the kingdom. Her father had been a schoolmaster at a boys' school of little fame, and less distinction. But he, a large, gentle, and quietly unambitious soul, had been well pleased with his lot in life. True, he might have regretted the fact that few of his students would go on to a life of erudition—most were resident at his school only long enough to receive the rudiments of education. But since they were the sons of merchants, they expected no other fate and indeed chaffed at their lot while they were under his tutelage.

He himself was a younger son in a family of the merchant class. And his perplexed family soon realized his scholarly bent and, more importantly, understood that his nonaggressive ways, his lack of interest in financial dealings, and his incurable honesty ("The day John Berryman tells a lie," his family grieved, "will be the day the King kisses a pig.") made him eminently unsuitable for the freewheeling family business of business. The day he took an unsuitable wife, a girl of no surviving parents and French descent, the two beleaguered families put their heads together and soon were able to ship the changeling son and his portionless wife out to the school where a position had been found for him.

There they lived in undemanding bliss, until the birth of Regina Analise had put an end to her mother's existence. There John Berryman, with the aid of a governess that the family sent down posthaste, had raised his daughter in tranquillity and peace. Hearing no terrible thing from the provinces, the family assumed that no further evil would befall their strange kinsman and allowed themselves to forget him. Only George Berryman, the schoolmaster's brother, remembered their existence with any regularity. Indeed, it was his frequent gifts, discreetly made on special occasions, that supported the odd trio that now resided in the little house.

And it was an odd trio. John Berryman, having had very little to do with females until his besotted eye fell upon his future wife, had no idea of how to raise a young girl. Thus, the feeding, clothing, and moral training of his young daughter he gladly left to Miss Bekins, the angular lady of indeterminate years that his family had engaged for him.

Regina's formal education, he took care of. And this he found a great pleasure. It could be said that over the years, she was his only consistently interested student. And so he filled her head with all the knowledge that the squirming young future captains of industry rejected. It would have been useless to ask him why he drilled a young female in the intricacies of Latin, German, and French. Or to inquire as to why she required such a wide knowledge of mathematics, history, and literature. And it would have been impossible to try to explain to him that a young woman really only needed skill with a needle, a pleasant singing voice, a dab hand with watercolors, and a little talent on the pianoforte.

Miss Bekins certainly would not have told him so. The present situation had suited her right down to the ground. For the family, unknowingly, had hired a serpent to lie in its bosom. The plain-faced, sensible-looking woman had been a bluestocking, and a woman of radical opinion. If they had lived with her for a week, they would have seen it. But they had only interviewed her for an

hour before sending her out on her mission. And John
Berryman, in his vague, myopic fashion, had not per-
ceived anything amiss with Miss Bekins in all the years
she lived with them.

And so, Regina Analise Berryman had grown to adult-
hood with very little real idea of what life in her world
was actually about. Oh, she could recite history chapter
and verse; she could discourse at length on the deterio-
ration of Ancient Rome, she could argue politics with
force and intelligence—but she couldn't say why a lady
should never sit with her legs crossed, or why a female
should blush demurely, or why any woman should consider her husband her lord and master. Or why she
required a husband at all. Which would have been suitable if she had grown up to feel as her father did, or
look as her governess did. But she had inherited her
mother's graceful good looks, along with her father's
vivid coloring, as well as some forgotten ancestor's spirit
and thirst for adventure.

How she would have fared if fate had decreed that
she stay in the gentle countryside of her birth, there is
no saying. She had few aquaintances of her same age,
none of her class. For in truth, she had no class to which
she belonged. She had the manner and grace of a lady,
the education of a young gentleman, and the family
background of sober, strict bourgeois merchants.

On Regina's eighteenth birthday, Miss Bekins had
announced her retirement. With a brief good-bye embrace, Miss Bekins had taken her savings and herself
off to Canterbury, there to help a distant cousin set up a
school to enlighten the minds of other young females.
Two years later, John Berryman paused in the middle
of a lecture on the Trojan Wars to cough apologetically
and collapse suddenly in easeful death. For several
months after her world had collapsed as surely as her
father had done, Regina had lived by herself in a torment of indecision. She could volunteer to teach in Miss
Bekins' school, but she had no idea of whether the
venture had been successful, and whether her arrival in
Canterbury would be a genuine help or a further strain
on her former governess's finances. She could apply for

a position as governess, but she had been given to understand that she had neither the references nor the background to suit the genteel families who required such services. Perhaps, it was gently implied by the local vicar . . . if she set her sights lower, to consider working with a lower class of family.

Her letter requesting the direction of a London family of merchants who would require her services resulted in a sudden, unprecedented visit from her Uncle George, whom she had not seen in the whole of her life. In one brief flurry, overriding all her protestations, he had packed her belongings, such as they were, paid a visit to his brother's grave, and trundled her into a coach back to London. En route to the city, he had firmly informed her that he had never taken the time to marry, but had he done so, she would have been just the daughter he would have chosen, and so that was the only position she had to bother her head about filling.

In the weeks that Regina had lived in her uncle's house, she had received new clothes, her own well-appointed room, and the services of a maid. Not to mention what was to her the bewildering services of a cook, a housekeeper, and two undermaids. She had no way of knowing that her uncle, rather than employing a vast staff of servants, was actually by all contemporary standards simply scraping by. He traveled so frequently that he did not feel the need for a more elaborate staff. Her uncle had taken care of all of her needs in a breath-takingly swift fashion, and then, bowing apologetically, announced that he must depart for yet another business trip.

It was the arrival of a pair of tickets to the Opera, sent by a grateful business acquaintance, that had sent Regina off on her ill-fated excursion. She had no way of knowing that her uncle would have simply let the tickets lie till dust covered them enough to signal the housekeeper to throw them out. She had only been thrilled at the idea of attending the famous London Opera house and, dressing herself in her new finery, she had taken her maid as escort, as her uncle had told her she must whenever she ventured from the house.

The stares, the whispers, the attention she had received at the theater had seemed odd, but not exceptional, at first. But, once seated in the box, the appearance of the other women present had startled her. If this was current London fashion and behavior, she felt sure she would never fit into the scheme of things in her uncle's city. But as the evening progressed and she watched the audience more closely than the stage, she began to get an inkling of the situation from the way certain couples behaved toward each other. Surely, she realized, it cannot be the fashion for a true gentleman to rest his lips upon his companion's throat in public, in a theater! Or for the lady to stroke her escort's hair. Or for a gentleman to ogle a female so openly, or for a lady to smile in pleased pride when being so encountered.

It was only when she left the box at intermission, however, that she had known without doubt what the situation was. The snatches of speculation about her presence that had come to her ears had driven her out, in search of a carriage to return home. But when that elegantly tailored gentleman, the one with the beautiful face of a fallen angel, had seen her and come to her side as naturally as if she were an old acquaintance, and whispered his husky-voiced suggestion into her ear, she felt as if the world had suddenly ended.

For he had stunned her. He had made all the others pale to insignificance and become merely background blur. The first moment she set eyes upon him she had thought he appeared out of a childhood tale of princes and castles. All thoughts of embarrassment and flight had themselves fled as he made his way gracefully through the throng to her side. Those clear azure eyes had sought hers out and had lit with real pleasure, as if he were overjoyed at finding her. His smile had welcomed and warmed her and drawn her answering smile. She could have basked all evening in the glow from that smile. And then, he had, still smiling, bent and sweetly whispered the impossible into her ear. What sort of female had he imagined her? She flushed in shame, just contemplating it. But since it seemed only a courtesan went unaccompanied to the theater on such a night, she could scarcely blame him, in all fairness, for his incredible proposal. In retrospect, his invitation had, surprisingly, secretly disappointed her rather than shocked her.

Belinda's prattle all the way home had assured her of her surmise. The little cat, she had thought with uncharacteristic spite. She knew all the while, and never bothered to inform me of it. What a fool I've been, she mourned. But, she told herself with a little of her old spirit, what difference does it make after all? I shall certainly never encounter such people again, at any rate. Uncle does not traffic with dukes and noblemen, and neither shall I. Who she would be expected to befriend in her uncle's house, she had no idea, for her uncle seemed to have few real friends and no social life at all.

She gazed out the window at the silent morning street of gray houses. Even though this was not, her uncle insisted, a fashionable street, it was firmly middle class and, to her eyes, most pleasant. She noticed a carriage standing still at the curb, its horses at rest, and noted with interest that its sole occupant seemed to be at rest as well. But no other thing on the streets stirred, except for the horses' languid tail-switching.

Ah well, she thought. I shall dress and take Belinda with me to the book shop. I surely will encounter no evil nobleman there. And both cheered and inwardly a little flattened by her rationalizations, she began to dress, forgetting once again that no fashionable woman would have done so alone while her maid lolled, gossiping and unoccupied, below stairs.

When she had drawn her hair back neatly and robed herself in the new elegant green garment that her uncle had insisted was a walking dress, she rang for Belinda and began to descend the stairs. Belinda greeted her breathlessly as she reached the front hall.

"Oh, miss," cried Belinda in a conciliating voice, "you do look ever so elegant, you do indeed!"

Regina did not feel particularly flattered, since Belinda greeted each new dress that she wore in much the same tones. But now, she noticed, Belinda's eyes seemed to sparkle, her freckled face seemed flushed, and she appeared to have an exciting secret. I had no idea, Regina thought, that this was such an extraordinary dress.

"Belinda," she said calmly, "get your bonnet, for I wish to walk to Mr. Hughes's bookshop, and I'm afraid you'll have to accompany me."

"Oh no, miss," Belinda gasped. "You cannot go, miss."

"Why can't I?" Regina bristled. "No one at the shop is likely to have been at the Opera last night. Don't be a goose, get your bonnet."

"Oh no, miss," Belinda repeated stubbornly, and with the swollen breast of one who carries a message of dramatic import, Belinda walked to the window and pointed out. "There, miss, is why you cannot go."

"What the devil are you talking about girl?" Regina blurted, forgetting again that a proper young lady did not speak in her father's accents.

"The Duke's man, miss . . . Sedgly, the Duke's man. That's him to the life, miss. And the coachman, Tom Highet, he's a fellow we all know for his past deeds. He's a big fellow, miss. And up to no good even when he's sleeping, we say."

Regina peered out through the parted curtain. There was a large, evil-looking fellow behind the horses all right, but she couldn't get a glimpse of the man who sat back in the interior of the closed carriage.

"What is any of that to me, Belinda?" she asked in puzzlement.

"Oh, miss," Belinda burbled, her high excitement giving her freckles a splotchy, rashlike look. "It's plain as the nose on your face. We all have been talking about it downstairs. They're waiting for you, miss, they are. You ran away from the Duke last night, and he don't take to that. He sent his man and Tom Highet to abduct you, he did. Just take one step out and they'll truss you like a goose, they will, and deliver you up to the Black Duke."

Regina began laughing. She laughed so hard, she brought tears to her eyes and had to grasp Belinda's shoulder to keep from swaying over. Belinda looked at her in astonishment, which only made her laugh the more. Finally regaining some composure, she asked through little hiccups if she had heard Belinda's words aright, for, she said, "A greater mess of fustian, Belinda, I have never heard. You've been reading too many romances, girl. An evil duke abducting young women in broad daylight on a city street . . . no, not an evil duke . . . a black duke!" She almost sobbed with laughter. "Oh Belinda, you've been dipping into too many romances."

"Oh no, miss," denied Belinda, much affronted. "For I don't even read, miss. Never have. But I know what I know. And it wouldn't be the first time, neither. What of Emily Ketchum then, miss? Eh? What of her, she that worked for the Robins? Abducted she was, and by him. And when her family found her again, she was properly ruined. They had to turn her out. Even if he did give her a sum of money, she couldn't find a respectable job again. And abducted right in the daylight, as you say. And there's tales of others too."

"Emily Ketchum?" asked Regina, sobering.

"Right, miss," nodded Belinda.

"But, even if that's so," Regina said, a little more quietly, "you say she was a servant. Even evil dukes don't abduct . . . proper young women, Belinda."

"Well," said Belinda, choosing her words carefully, "you being from the country and all . . . miss, here in town, there's proper and there's proper, you see. Not saying that you're not proper, miss. But who's your family, after all? Mr. Berryman has money, miss, but not . . . position, you see. He's not an important man, miss. There's no . . . well, miss, you and he aren't of the ton, you see. If a duke was to do you wrong, what would your word be against his? A member of the peerage, miss? No, even your uncle couldn't do much except blacken his name more . . . but it's so black, he wouldn't even notice the more. And where would you be then? You'd best stay here inside the house until your uncle comes home. In time . .," Belinda said, letting the curtain fall back, "he'll forget he saw you, he'll find another game. Maybe your uncle could put a few words in the proper ears, too, to make him lose interest. But until then, you'd better stay in."

"But," protested Regina, torn between a sense of the ridiculous and a growing feeling of trepidation, "what's to prevent him from . . . bursting in here and carrying me off like a Sabine woman?"

"Well, I wouldn't know about them, I never heard of that family," Belinda pondered. "But there's things even he can't do. You can't just burst into someone's house and carry them out, you know, miss." And here she looked at Regina curiously. "Didn't you know that? You might be able to do that in the country, but not here."

Regina assured her that that wasn't the case in the country either and, sighing, removed her gloves. She would stay in. She didn't believe Belinda's warnings implicitly, but after her experience of the night before, she realized that she knew very little of the morals and tendencies of these that dwelt in the city. She felt uneasy enough about the situation to remain in the house, although, she thought, I shall feel like a proper fool if uncle comes home and tells me that it was all a hum.

"Belinda," she ventured, "this is an incredible situation, is it not?"

"It's the way of things, miss," Belinda said knowingly. "It's the way of it."

III

St. John woke to the gentle sloshing sounds of pouring water. He opened his eyes to find himself in his own sun-filled room, his valet moving silently as he prepared his bath. He yawned and stretched and sank back against his pillow. He accepted the drink that his valet handed him and, propped up on one elbow, drank the potion down rapidly. "Hilliard," he asked, gasping, "what was that foul mess?"

"The recipe you gave me, m'lord," his valet answered calmly. "The one His Lordship said was all the thing this month."

"Well, it won't be my thing again," St. John said, rising. "Although it does clear the head, the shock of it isn't worth it."

He bathed and, wrapping himself in the wide towel Hilliard offered, sat by the window and allowed himself to be shaved. It was a sunny, satisfactory morning, he thought as Hilliard labored over him, save for the remembrances of the night before which slowly began to filter back to him. He had not liked the duke's sly presumptions about his reputation. And, he thought, he had not liked awakening alone. With Annabelle safely invested to James, he had gone around later in the evening to a promising young creature at Madame Felice's establishment, but he had found her to be too humorless and too dedicated a handmaiden. She had made him feel as though he were a chore, a difficult project to be gotten through meticulously, with all the proper moves in all the proper places, as though she had memorized the rituals. No, he thought, she was not a candidate for installation in Annabelle's former residence. But, he thought with a small feeling of optimism as he allowed Hilliard to pull on his boots, the search might provide entertainment. And he would continue the search after the business of his day was completed.

"To a turn, Your Lordship," Hilliard commented approvingly as St. John inspected himself in a pier mirror. His boots gleamed, his breeches clung tightly, without a wrinkle, his black coat fitted snugly. "Yes," St. John agreed, and pocketing the several invitations and letters that Hilliard handed him, he strolled down the stairs to breakfast.

It was well after noon when St. John faced the world. He called for his high-wheeled phaeton and the chestnuts, and drove carefully through the streets to his first obligatory call. He had promised himself another look at Melissa Wellsley, the current rage. He had only stood up with her twice at Almack's, but he had approved of her manner and, while he did not fall into raptures about her face and form as many of his contemporaries did, he had to admit that the entire effect she presented was charming. And she was reputed to have an income exceeding that of any other of the young women who had made their bows this season. She was considered the catch of the season, and he felt he owed it to himself to check her again, to see if there was any possibility of her catching his interest.

Once inside the morning room to which he had been ushered, he passed the time in making polite conversation with Lady Wellsley, amusing himself with the effusive way she agreed with his comments, the eagerness she showed to be pleasant to him. But he understood that all the while, she was weighing him, measuring him, estimating what she had heard about his income, his history, and his family ties. Despite half of it, he knew, she would be bound to consider him one of the most eligible partis to grace her drawing room.

As to the income, he thought as she burbled excuses as to her daughter's tardiness (which he knew was because she had been sent to change into something devastating to receive him in), she could find no fault. As to his title, she must find that exemplary, she had only two barons and an earl on the string at the moment. His ancestry, he knew, she would find impeccable. But if she were a wise woman, he felt, she might hesitate about his more recent ancestors, and his own behavior.

His father had been a compulsive gambler, blithely spending both his wife's portion and that which was left of the dwindling estate that he could legally touch, in any fashion that might provide a gamesman's interest. After his wife had died (gossips said that it was from boredom), he had gone on solely for the purpose of spending every last penny he could before the grave overtook him. The rumor was, after the Marquis had himself expired, that the estate was shot to pieces and the new Marquis would come into his estate to find it a paper one, all back debts and penury. But within a few years, when St. John had finally decided to grace Society with his presence, there wasn't a banker in the whole of London who wouldn't have given him unlimited credit. The mystery of how the young man had repaired his fortunes lingered, but fortune it was, so the issue was dropped. The young Marquis had been welcomed to the ton, with open arms.

Other segments of society had welcomed him thusly, too, and if Lady Wellsley chose to be very exacting, she might have had a qualm about this prospective suitor for her daughter's hand. It was well known that St. John was in the petticoat line, that his doings among these graceless females exceeded that which could be called normal in a man of his position. There were tales of mistresses, and wild parties and license. But his behavior in the drawing room was impeccable, even if his behavior in other rooms was wide open to speculation.

But when Melissa entered the room in a froth of pink lace and giggles, and St. John swept a bow and kissed her hand, Lady Wellsley subsided gracefully and took a position far from the pair. "So she approves," St. John thought with amusement, "reputation and all."

As they chatted about the weather and various doings about the town, St. John viewed the girl before him with speculation. She was very attractive, he thought critically, but no, not beautiful. Her black hair was coaxed into enchanting ringlets, her face was lightly dusted with powder to increase the contrast between white complexion and dark hair. Her nose was, he thought, a trifle too snub, her dark eyes a bit too off-center. No, he thought, no beauty, but well enough for her style. Of her figure, he reserved comment. For now, he thought, she was well enough, but a slight plumpness clung to her outline, and he was almost sure that in a few years she would balloon as alarmingly as her so charming mother had. And since he was looking for a female for the long term as a wife, he was not sure that she could fill the bill. But he was willing to reserve judgment. So long as he continued his interest, he knew, Lord and Lady Wellsley would keep her available.

"La, My Lord," she lisped, flushing becomingly, "surely there must have been another lady at the affair who caught your eye as well?"

"But none who caught and kept it," he promised.

He tired quickly of the light banter and, sweeping another bow, he took his leave of the two Wellsley ladies, leaving them to speculate about his attentions as he took himself off into the outer day.

He waved the phaeton away with his groom, and strolled to his club, where he had an excellent lunch. It was when he prepared to leave that he caught sight of James, who was frantically signaling to him from across the room.

"Sinjin," James began when he had beckoned the Marquis to another room, "there is a slight, very slight problem."

"What's this?" Sinjin smiled. "Has marriage impaired your style, James? Did the fair Annabelle find you lacking address, or something else?"

"No, Sinjin, listen," James whispered in a low voice. "It's just that . . . don't fly up, dear boy, but I haven't as yet found . . . suitable quarters for the gal . . . she's still in your digs. I'm sorry," James went on, looking at St. John's clouding face, "but there hasn't been time to transfer her yet. I haven't had time to arrange for my own place yet. I was out of the country for a spell, you know," he apologized, sensing his friend's annoyance, "and, I gave up my other place when I married, y'know, so I wondered if it were possible, if you could. . . ."

"James," said St. John coldly, drawing himself up so that he seemed to dwarf the anxious man at his side, "there are some things that go beyond friendship. I presented you with the female. I will not board her any longer. If you want her, you will have to find your own place for her. I want that house vacated, sir, on the instant, if not sooner. It is," he said noting the red-faced James, "a matter of honor with me."

"Oh certainly," James stammered. "No question about that . . . I was going to see to it. . . ."

"What was it you were going to ask me, old friend?" St. John smiled.

"Ah . . . nothing," James protested. "Just about a piece of gossip, but no matter, I haven't the time now." And he left the marquis standing there, smiling hugely to himself.

The afternoon went by pleasantly for the Marquis. He dropped in on a few friends, he chatted with a few acquaintances, he made plans for the evening. Late in the afternoon, he felt the need for some amusing conversation and so he payed a call on Lady Amelia Burden. She received him in her sitting room, without chaperone, but he knew that in her case, this somewhat daring action would not be misconstrued.

Lady Amelia had attained an age and position in society that enabled her to set rules unto herself. She was not ancient, by any means, in fact she was a few years younger than St. John himself. The fact that she was distant cousin of his would not, in itself, have allowed her the freedom she took in her relationship with him. But her position did. There had never been a hint of gossip about Lady Amelia, and thought St. John looking at her, doubtless there never would be.

She was tall and angular, but on the whole, her face and figure would not have been displeasing to St. John if it were not, he felt, for her one imperfection. It was unfortunate, he mused, as he invariably did when seeing her, that her fine brown eyes should be the seat of the trouble. For Lady Amelia had, since early childhood, been afflicted with a peculiar physical characteristic where one eye was perfect, brown and deep and intelligent, while the other was wont to wander slightly out to the side when she was weary, so that at those times she seemed to be looking out beyond one's left shoulder.

Still her fortune and position and calm, quietly amusing outlook on life had netted her several eligible proposals even in her first season. After all, the jest had run among several highly placed gentlemen: with her charm and fortune, she may look as high or as low as she likes, whenever she likes. And in the dark, they reasoned, one would not notice where she looks. But she had refused them all, and had remained unattached throughout eight seasons, and the Social World, although puzzled, had accepted that she would remain so.

St. John had felt an affinity for her from the first, when the eager little ten-year-old had grasped his hand one day and dragged him away from a stultifying family gathering to show him her pony and comment with startling candor on all the assembled relatives. He had kept in touch with her ever since, standing up with her at dances, paying courtesy calls that became less courtesy and more friendship as the years went by. If St. John had ever bothered to think about it, he would have admitted that she was his one real woman friend. For the question of dalliance had never arisen in his mind. He knew that he could never be attracted to a female with any physical defect, and had, over the years, developed an easy, sexless amiability with her.

This afternoon, he complimented her on her rosy appearance, and she rang for tea for her visitor. She sat herself carefully on his left side, so that if her troublesome eye wandered it would not face him, for she had known for a long time how very much her occasional peculiarity discomfitted him. She thought he felt it made her uncomfortable. Although, truth to tell, he was the only man she had ever known who seemed, no matter how he tried to conceal it, disturbed by it. But then, he was the only man whose opinion had ever really mattered to her. Amelia felt that it was only because he watched her so closely that he noticed, and she was pleased by both his attention and the sensitivity of his nature. She admired him the more for his deep concern for her over what was to others, a triviality.

"Sinjin," she smiled, "I've heard how very particular your attentions have become with regard to the new Incomparable. Am I to welcome a new cousin to our family soon then?"

"Only if you decide to cast off your veil, my dear," St. John grinned, "and take some fortunate fellow's imprecations to heart, for I have no immediate intention of adding to our illustrious family at the moment."

"On this side of the blanket, you mean, my dear," she said, relaxing.

"Very wicked, Amelia," St. John laughed. "If only everyone knew what a dreadful Miss you are."

"Why, you know, Sinjin, and still you put up with my shocking behavior."

"Ah, but that is because I like to be shocked," he

said. "Now tell me some shocking things, you minx, or I shall think I've paid a call on some very proper young woman, and that would not suit me at all."

They sat and chatted for a half hour or more, till the shadows began to color the room and St. John realized, in the dimming light, how quickly the time had passed. Truly, he thought, she could entertain him, always knowing what sly comment would amuse him, always gauging his mood perfectly, always bringing up the bits of gossip, the little anecdotes that would please him. Ah, he had often thought, if only the Lord had gifted her with a perfect face, he might have been able to make a match of it with her. But as it was, there were still times, even after all these years, when a chance glance at her unguarded face when she was weary brought a little chill to his heart. No, it would not do. It was a pity, he often thought, for in all other aspects she would suit. But he could not bear any physical deficiency in his marchioness. That lady, whoever she might eventually be, should have to be as perfect in the eyes of Society as she would be in his own. And that would have to be absolute perfection. So, although Amelia might only have a slight impairment, to him it would always loom as large as any insurmountable obstacle. Still, he thought, I shall always have her as a friend.

As he rose to leave, she placed a hand tentatively upon his sleeve.

"Sinjin," she said quietly with unaccustomed sobriety, "your sister has asked if I would accompany her down to Fairleigh one of these days. She is having a difficult time with this confinement, and thinks a spell of country air would help her condition. But she implores me to accompany her. She says she will perish from the sulks by herself."

"I would have thought she would have succumbed to them ages ago," St. John laughed. "What is this to be . . . her fifth? She and Gordon seem determined to populate the world by themselves." He laughed, thinking of his silly, vain little sister now fast becoming the most prolific female in the country. "But why the long face, Amelia? If you think you will be bored to tears, simply refuse her, tell her that there is some ball or other you cannot in any conscience miss."

"Ah, but I don't mind. I think I could use a change of scene as well, but she is determined to rusticate at Fairleigh. Her childhood home, she says, comforts her in time of stress."

"And so?" asked St. John.

"But it is your home, Sinjin, and I should not want you to think that I am imposing upon your hospitality without consulting you first."

"Amelia," he laughed, "there is room in that old pile for a dozen of you. Go and rusticate by all means, but be sure to return to me with all your faculties intact, for I do need your wit to ease the way. When shall you be going?" he asked as he went to the door.

"Not for several weeks," she said. "For she does not suffer so that she wishes to miss the Prince's gala next week, or the Castelreighs' party, or the——"

"Dear Mary," the Marquis laughed. "She must certainly be ill, then, for a healthy female surely would contrive some excuse to avoid those crushes."

Raising her hand to his lips, the Marquis took leave of his cousin and sauntered off into the deepening twilight. But Lady Amelia did not immediately turn from the window where she watched him stroll off. Rather she stood quietly, and watched quietly, for many moments after his tall figure had gone out of her sight.

St. John walked for a long time, far longer than was usual for him. He seemed to be strolling aimlessly through the darkening streets. He watched the lamplighters set about their tasks, and only when he was sure that all the fashionable carriages had returned home, only when he was convinced that all the members of his elite fraternity were safely home preparing the evening's pleasures, did he turn his steps and walk with determination. For now he did not want anyone to discover his direction.

He did not mind his contemporaries seeing him entering into low houses of assignation, or houses that contained festivities that loftier members of the Beau Monde

would have been aghast at. He would have braved all
their stares if they had discovered him attending a cock
fight or an exotic exhibition, of the sort that Madame
Felice was famed for. But his destination this evening
was one that he wished no other man of his station to
determine. Quietly and quickly, he melted into the evening's darkness.

IV

The Marquis was in a rage. He stood on the top step of
the house and confronted the little ginger-haired maid.
The air of imperturbability which he so carefully cultivated was gone, his fists were clenched, and in a moment, he felt, he would have to shove the girl aside if he
must, to gain entry to the house.

"I said," he swore through gritted teeth, "that your
master is expecting me. He is always expecting me.
Now move aside, my girl, and let me pass."

"Well, I dunno," the girl said with maddening slow-
ness, assessing the elegant gentleman that stood on the
doorstep as urgently and impatiently as if he were being
buffeted by cruel winds and biting cold, although it was
only a cool, fair night outside. "You're still not saying
what yer business is, or if you come from that handsome
coach out there."

"Devil take it," hissed the Marquis. "It's because of
that coach that you must let me in. Now do you open
the door, or do I do it myself?" he threatened.

This seemed to confirm the girl's worst fears, and she
made as if to close the door on him. As he reached out
one hand to stay her, he caught sight of a grim-faced,
middle-aged woman behind her.

"Mrs. Teas," he called out in relief. "Tell this fool to
give me admittance, at once!"

"Oh, sir!" gasped the older woman, and clutching the
maid by the shoulder, she spun her aside.

"Oh sir," she said, shutting the door behind the Marquis. "Excuse the girl, please do. She's new here, and doesn't know a thing. It won't happen again, I assure you. Belinda, get downstairs. I'll have a talk with you by and by, my girl, I will. Sir," she panted, having quickly escorted the Marquis to a study to the right of the door, "please sit down. Please to wait. The Master's just returned hardly an hour before. But I know he'll want to see you. He's just finishing up his dinner. Please to wait here, sir."

"Tell him not to hurry," St. John said, his temper cooling. "I'll wait here for him," and he took a large leather chair near a neat desk. "But mind you, Mrs. Teas, if the chit's such a fool as I think she is, kindly do not inform her of my name."

"Oh never, sir," gasped Mrs. Teas, red-faced. "That I'd never do, sir," she swore, and she walked quickly from the room.

"Aye," thought St. John savagely, that she had better never do. He sat back in the chair and crossed his elegantly booted legs. Here, in this small dark study, with its innocent looking shelves of books, deep turkey-red carpeting, and flickering lamplight, he was at the same moment both fulfilled and at his most vulnerable. Of all the places on the face of this earth, the marquis thought, this was the one place he must never be discovered.

When he had come down the street and seen, at the last moment, the coach waiting by the curb, with its easily discernible crest, he had known a moment of pure terror. But by then it was too late to retreat. He must brave it out, for if he had turned and left, he would have called more attention to himself. He had kept his face turned from the glow of the lamplight, and raised the doorknocker, hoping that the shadows concealed his face. And thinking that if perhaps the mission of the occupant of that coach was the same as his, there would be sufficient reason for the tale to go no further if he had been recognized. Two men entangled in the same endeavor would not cry attention at each other. But when

the maid had refused him admittance, he had known
that he could not turn and leave. He had to enter this
house, where he had always been welcome, never refused admittance, not for the past nine years and more.

Nine years, the Marquis thought. It had been nine
years since he had first entered this room. Since he had
been a desperate young man, encumbered with a worth-
less legacy, bequeathed a mountain of duns' notes, three
expensive entailed estates, and no future save that which
his name and few hoarded guineas could provide. He
could have sold himself on the marriage market, but
something within him rebelled at that. He could have
tried gaming to restore the estate to what it had been
before his father had gamed it away, but he had seen
too much of the result of that route in his own house.
He had heard, then, through the loose talk among his
young friends, that there were certain men of business. . . . Men of trade. Socially unacceptable men who
dirtied their hands with commerce but who were amass-
ing large fortunes. And who were always on the lookout
for fashionable patrons to cast their lots in with for
social advancement, for themselves or for their families.
Or for influence, should the need ever arise for that.

The trail he followed had led eventually to this room,
to George Berryman, a stolid man from a merchant
family, but a man who was reputed to have a touch of
gold. He had eyed the young Marquis and, sighing heavily, had asked finally the inevitable question. "And what
shall you bring to this enterprise, My Lord?"

"My money, such as there is left of it," the Marquis
had answered, "my connections, such as I can utilize,
and my influence, such as I will make if this venture
succeeds. But, never my name. No never, that I cannot
give you."

That, the merchant had understood. Obviously, this
was a proud youngster who had got it into his head that
it would be social suicide if it were known that he was
engaged so deeply in commerce. But he assessed the
grave young man and concluded that this was also a
bright one, and, by his own standards, an honest one.

And, perhaps this young Noble could, in a circumlocutory way, provide that information, that entree, that access, which he needed in some phases of his business. And so the bargain was struck. St. John Basil St. Charles, Marquis of Bessacarr, whose blood was documented from Norman times forward, became the silent partner of George Berryman, whose blood, though no less rich, was derived from as mixed a pedigree as any mongrel roaming the London streets.

Over the years, St. John had taken a secretive but active part in the business. He had told George Berryman of the plans and maneuvers of the members of Society that he personally knew. Which families were badly dipped, which noble names would discreetly but anxiously be willing to sell off which holdings. Which way the war seemed to be going, the words taken from the top, where George Berryman would never have been able to hear them. All of which gave the pair both the information and access to the goal they wanted. They traded in property mines in the north, holdings in the islands, shipping shares, war supplies.

There were other business dealings whose nature could not bear too close a scrutiny—certain dealings in a certain trade off the Ivory Coast, certain imports from across the not-completely-war-locked channel, business matters best left in the dark where they could grow full and rich, like mushrooms in a damp cellar. But profitable. The pair had profitted. And all that was required now, as always, was trust, and secrecy.

Nine years, St. John thought, which has given me time to regain all that my father had lost, and more than he ever dreamed of.

Enough blunt to restore the estates, to live at the top of fashion, to marry off one small silly little sister in a manner to which she had never become accustomed. Enough money to let me make the world what I choose it to be. More than enough, really. But the prizes were too rich to give up the venture now that the original goal had been reached.

And no one would ever know that the riches had not

dropped into his lap by accident, in the way, St. John felt, a nobleman should acquire his fortune. A fortune acquired as impeccably and easily as his birth and lineage, that was the hallmark of a true gentleman, and he would fight savagely to keep both his fortune and his title impeccable in the eyes of Society.

"Your Lordship," George Berryman said, hurrying in through the door and closing it carefully behind him. "My pardons, please, for the treatment you received at the hands of the maid. She's a new girl, and no one had told her . . . well, your visit was unexpected, My Lord," he continued reproachfully.

"Indeed it was, Mr. Berryman," answered the Marquis as he watched the elder man settle down behind the desk. "But I sent notes and messages, and received no answer. You were to have returned a week ago, and when I did not hear from you, I decided to come and see for myself if there were any problem. You know," the Marquis went on, "that if something . . . should . . . if any evil should befall you, there is no one, I hope, who would have the knowledge that I must be informed."

"No, indeed, but you have made that your stipulation, Your Lordship. At any rate, rest easy, if I should have . . . some evil befall me, there is no way to connect us. I keep no such papers. It would only mean that you would have to find yourself a new partner."

"No," laughed the Marquis, his good humor restored, "you and I are truly wedded, Berryman. If I should be widowed, I should seek out no other partner. I have all that I want now. I continue only because it pleases me to do so now. Now, what of Amerberly's holdings?" he asked imperatively.

"That is what kept me so long," Berryman answered. "He did not want to sell, not really. He equivocated, he hesitated, but in the end, as you predicted, he capitulated."

"Ah!" said St. John, his eyes shining, his languid airs gone, his body alert. "Tell me all, tell me all, I have waited for this. How much?"

The early evening wore on as the two men talked and

pored over their papers. The elder finally handed St. John a bank draft. "There you are, Your Lordship, your full and anonymously donated share. It was a good day's work, for all that it took me two weeks to accomplish it. I must be getting older."

"Old and slyer," laughed St. John, noting the sum on the check with a smile before he put it in his pocket.

"Well then," said St. John, rising and stretching himself. "Well done."

"Your Lordship," said George Berryman in an altered voice, "before you go, there is another matter which I would like to discuss with you."

Something in the elder man's tone made St. John pause. It was not like Berryman to detain him for even a moment after the work of business was done.

"It is a little difficult," the older man admitted, and stared down at his desktop.

What the devil is this about? St. John frowned. For nine years, things have gone on smoothly, does he want a larger share now, for his old age? Which is fast approaching, St. John suddenly noted, seeing as if for the first time the new deep lines in his partner's face, the imperceptible droop to his jowls, the sparse white hair, the pallid complexion. B'God, St. John noticed, he is growing old.

"It is not business, Your Lordship," Berryman went on. "It is in the nature of a personal request."

Now this is new, the Marquis thought, for nothing of this nature has ever been discussed before. When he thought about it, the Marquis remembered that he knew far less of the personal life of his partner than his partner knew of his own. For St. John was Society's darling, and every scandal of his was well documented, while his partner, a bachelor, as he did know, lived his life in quiet seclusion.

Seeing that he had the Marquis's undivided attention, George Berryman went unhappily on. "I have never asked anything of you, in so far as your social influence goes, but now, I am forced to apply to you for a . . . favor."

By God, the Marquis thought, has some lady of fashion caught his eye? Has he a nephew he wants to promote in the Beau Monde? He is in for a disappointment if he expects my help there. But he is too sly an old fox for that.

"Do go on," St. John said calmly, noting the other man's uneasiness.

"Ah, did you happen to notice the carriage out on the street, My Lord?" Berryman said softly.

Suddenly tense, St. John nodded curtly.

"Who would not? It's Torquay's crest, it's hardly anonymous. I was going to ask you about it myself, but it slipped my mind when you gave me the good news about Amerberly. What does he here, Berryman? The same as I? Have you become a bigamist, with two partners?"

"Hardly, sir," Berryman frowned. "He has money enough for both of us, but it is this house that he watches."

"Has he got wind of my involvement?" St. John asked, his lips white.

"No, no," Berryman said. "Nothing at all like that. It is such a foolish thing that I am almost embarrassed to mention it, but I did not think . . . I. . . . Your Lordship, you know I am a man of power, but only in certain circles. And, I finally admit, because I feel it these days, I grow old. Still, here is a situation that neither my worldly wisdom, what there is of it, nor my money can handle. Simply put, then," he said, seeing his youthful partner's impatience, "it is an affair of the heart."

"What?" drawled St. John, much entertained. "Has His Grace taken a fancy to you then, Berryman? I knew his tastes were varied, but really, I am much surprised."

George Berryman only responded with a weak smile. "No, no. But I do not think it a joking matter. It seems that he has taken a violent fancy to a young woman here in my house. If, from what my servants tell me, he is running true to form, he has expectations . . . of abducting her. This, I cannot allow. But who would hear the word of a common merchant against a nobleman?

And he has done nothing, actually, except station his servants to watch the house. No, I cannot say a thing. But, Your Lordship, many years ago you promised me . . . your influence in certain matters. I call upon that influence now, if I may, on the basis of the long years of association we have had. I do not like to do so, but I see no alternative. Could you . . . speak with the Duke . . . perhaps defer his interests? Deflect his fascination with my poor house, put a word in his ear? I would be most grateful."

The words came easily enough to St. John. "Of course, Berryman, I shall do what I can, but for the moment, although I doubt that Torquay himself is sitting in the carriage, could you show me out a back entrance? For it would hardly do for his servants to spy me leaving here. Servants talk."

"And Your Lordship," hesitated Berryman as he showed the Marquis to the back-stair door, "one other thing. . . . As I do grow old, if ever things come to a pass . . . that is to say, may I tell the young woman that she may make application to you for . . . protection?"

"Protection?" answered the Marquis, raising an eyebrow. "I hardly think you mean precisely that . . . not my sort of protection, but," he went on, noting his aged partner's extreme unease, "yes, certainly, as I said, I will do what I can."

Once out again in the clear night, St. John walked a circuitous route to where he could safely call for a hackney cab.

The words were easy enough to say, but he had known even as he said them that there was little he could do for Berryman. How could he make an application to that wickedly smiling Torquay, without Torquay, who was never a fool, oh no, he might be everything else, but not a fool, inquiring as to how, and why, the Marquis was concerning himself with the affairs of a bourgois commoner? "But Sinjin," he could hear the Duke saying in his distinctive whisper, "how came you to hear of my plots against a merchant?" No, he could never give the Duke that hint, that insight into his private affairs, his association with Berryman. The Duke was too quick to pick up a scent for that.

No matter, St. John rationalized as he signaled to the hackney, for it is probably only that new ginger-haired maid that Torquay has spied. It is only a little serving girl he wishes to entertain himself with. And she looks the sort to be well pleased with a moonlight abduction, no matter what her prim master thinks, I know the sort. And, he thought, settling back against the cushions of the coach, "I did say, I would do what I could, and in truth, I can do nothing."

"Regina," said her uncle as he watched the girl pace the length of his study, "please do calm yourself. It isn't so very bad, my dear. So you will stay within the house for a few days longer. Then, I assure you, I have set certain wheels in motion that will put an end to the matter and you will be free again."

"You spoke to the man who came here tonight about it?" Regina asked, shocked.

"I'm sorry," her uncle said, locking away certain papers in his drawer. "But you know I cannot confide business matters to you. I hold many people's confidences, but yes, I did make application to someone whom I believe can ease the situation."

Regina stopped and looked at her uncle, who sat dejectedly at his desk. Oh really, she thought, it is not fair. He tries so hard to make it all up to me, and I am ungrateful and stubborn, and he is such a good old man.

"Uncle," she cried, rushing to his side, "forgive me, you are so weary from traveling all day, and here I besiege you further. I will stay in. I'll read . . . or do needlepoint, or some such thing. I'm well used to my own company. Don't concern yourself so. You look positively ill, are you all right?"

"All right as I can be," he assured her. "It's only that I am no longer young, my dear. There are times when I could wish that I had gotten to know you sooner . . . could have watched you grow. But there was always another bit of business to accomplish. When you are young you think you have all the time in the world."

"You are ill!" cried Regina, her green eyes wide. "I'll call Mrs. Teas, I'll call an apothecary. . . ."

"No, no," he laughed softly. "Don't get into a pet, my dear, it's only that I at last admit that I am old. Many years older than your own father was, Regina. And I must now contemplate the fact of it, now that I have you to consider. Regina," he said, rising and looking at her, noting that what he had considered a soft, pretty child was in reality a glowing young woman. "I will be taking certain other steps to insure your future. At the moment, my sole heir is my nephew, your cousin, Harry. But that is not right. I've made an appointment with my solicitor. I'll change a few things in your favor. No," he said, seeing her about to protest, "there is nothing wrong with a little foresight, my dear. In the meantime, I have some other business . . . yes, eternally business, to clear up in the west. I'll be gone for about a week, and then, after I see my solicitor, perhaps you and I can take ourselves off to some resort spa. I can enjoy the waters, and you can try to bewitch some young men."

He eyed her with worry, for in truth, he did not have any idea of what sort of young men she could consort with. Her birth placed her below the correct people he felt she would be temperamentally suited to, her education placed her above the earnest young men he associated with. But perhaps, he thought hopefully, we might make a match for her with some impoverished younger son, or some young man just out of the military, or even, he dared to think, someone of exceptional family whose empty pockets might make such a match acceptable.

As if she could read his thoughts, she smiled softly at him, and kissed his cheek.

"Dear Uncle," she said, "confess it, isn't business easier to manage than a stray young niece?"

"At any rate," he smiled back, "while I am gone, stay within the house. That matter out there will soon be cleared up. And Regina . . . if, should anything untoward occur to me . . . for I am not a young man . . . that is to say, if I should ever be in a position where I cannot help you should the need arise . . . do not tell any other soul, but you may make application to St. John Basil St. Charles, the Marquis of Bessacar. Simply seek him out and tell him who you are. No, I cannot answer any questions. Just remember that."

"It is graven on my heart," she said, and made a child's sign of crossing her heart and sealing her lips. "I promise you, Uncle." She smiled, kissing her fingertip. "Honor bound."

V

Regina sat huddled in a large chair in the corner of the room as her aunt swept up to Mrs. Teas. It seemed that her vision was blurry, her ears were fogged, her head ached dully. Things had happened too quickly for her naturally resilient personality to have time to assert itself.

One moment she had been sitting in her room, helping Belinda pin up a dress, a dress she was planning to wear to celebrate her uncle's return the next day. And the next moment, this small fierce little woman had entered the house to announce that she had already had word from her solicitors, although how she could have discovered the news so shortly after the terrified servant had delivered it to Regina herself, she would never know.

Aunt Harriet had introduced herself to Regina, and then taken stock of the house that was now hers, or rather her son's. But one look had shown Regina that whatever Cousin Harry had, his mother would control.

Uncle George had fallen as he had entered the inn where he was staying, and by the time the landlord had gotten him decently into bed, he had not had much time left. The only message he managed to whisper to the physician before his ravaged heart had given way as surely as his late brother's had, was one for Regina. "Tell her," he had gasped, "that I'm terribly sorry."

Regina had not gotten to know her uncle very well, so she could not in all honesty be said to be pining for him. Still, the tears she had shed at his graveside were genuine enough. He had looked so very much like her father. His death had so nearly duplicated his brother's. And, selfishly, she knew that the safe harbor to which he had spirited her was now vanished.

Her aunt did not grieve at all. She was a small fury of a woman, and as adept at business as her brother had been. Though, even standing erect with indignation, as she so often did, she only reached to Regina's shoulder, the small wiry body contained all the ambition in the world. All the ambition, Regina had observed, that her poor cousin Harry had not inherited.

Regina could feel some sympathy for Harry, she realized, but very little. In the weeks in which he had moved in to her uncle's house with his mother, she had been aware, through all the confusion, of his apologetic presence. He was a few years older than Regina herself, but he lacked her glowing color. He was a pallid, dark-haired young man. His pantaloons stretched unfashionably across a premature little paunch that bobbled when he coughed, as he so often did, to attract attention. If he would not try, Regina thought, watching him from the corner of her eye, so very hard to be in fashion, perhaps it would not be so noticeable. But the tight-fitting jackets he aspired to only accentuated his perennial slouch and rounded shoulders. And his conversational attempts were poor mumbles, as if he expected to be interrupted at any moment. And, in fairness, she thought, he always was.

"Harry," commanded his mother now, "do say something. I have just told Mrs. Teas that her services will be no longer required. That as we are no longer a household containing only a bachelor and his niece, we require a butler, not a housekeeper. We have enough females here. She has asked for references. Will you take yourself off and compose one?"

"Ah," the unhappy Harry ventured, "but as I did not . . . that is to say, never employed her . . . what should I write, Mama?"

"Whatever seems reasonable," his mother shouted.

"Perhaps," Regina put in, trying to come to Harry's aid, "Mrs. Teas herself can suggest some of the required wording."

"Very good," commended her aunt. "Just so. Go to it, Harry."

When Harry and Mrs. Teas had left, Aunt Harriet sat herself down opposite Regina.

"It's good," she said, shaking her gray curls for emphasis, "that you're coming out of your sulks. I don't mind telling you that when I discovered that I had inherited you as well as this house, I was shocked. George never said a word about your presence, but you might as well know that we were never close. You do know it, so what's said is said. We were both very busy people, and I consider myself no more at fault than he was. But, what's done's done, when all's said. Still, you're a well enough looking girl, though you have more of your mother in you than Berryman, to be sure. But you've a quick mind, and a healthy body, so all's not lost. What do you intend to do with yourself, Niece?"

The abruptness of the question put Regina off balance. In truth, for the past weeks she had been trying to determine the same thing for herself. She was in no better case now than she was when her father had died. She had little money, and less experience with the world. She had never gotten out to see much more of the grand city to which she had been taken. At first, it was because she had lain in hiding from the omnipresent coach which had waited outside. But soon after her uncle's death, it had disappeared as suddenly as it had arrived. But then, her confusion and mourning had confined her to the house. Now a month had passed, and she still had no clear idea of what was to become of herself.

Still, she was never silent for too long, and giving her aunt a long measuring look, she spoke:

"I have a few options, Aunt. I have been considering them. If I could prevail upon you to lend me some passage fare, I could rejoin my governess at the school she has established in Canterbury and establish myself there as a teacher. I could perhaps seek similar em-

ployment with some well-placed family here in the city.
I would not, Aunt, throw myself upon your charge for
too long."

"What about marriage?" snapped her aunt.

"I am dowerless, portionless, and familyless," Regina
smiled. "Not quite a catch, Aunt."

"Your looks would take care of that," her aunt spoke.
"If any of my girls had had your looks, I would have
danced all the way to the bank instead of having to pay
off such doweries. There's hope in that line, girl."

"I don't want to marry yet," Regina said calmly.

"Want to wait till you're ruined?" her aunt cried. "For
take my word, girl, that'll be your fate if you're not
careful. Too good looking to mope about waiting for a
prince to snap you up. You won't be able to support
yourself too well with a bastard at your knee, Regina.
Oh, don't look scandalized, I speak it as I see it. You're
a good looking gal. Even Harry, whom I confess I
thought never had a tendency toward such things, has
been goggling at you."

"Harry?" said Regina with incredulity.

"Yes," her aunt continued. "And I'm glad to see it,
too. He hasn't looked at anything but his neckcloth for
years. He's been looking at you, though. Here's a proposition, Regina. Take it as I say it, and I'll only say it
the once. You can go off to Canterbury, if you wish, I'll
advance you the money. But if you go and don't make a
go of it, don't come back. I don't want any soiled goods
dragging back here. Harry's too soft-hearted and that
wouldn't be what I want for him. Or you can try to get a
position here in the city, only with your looks, all the
positions offered to you will be ones you won't want to
take, if you get my meaning. But if you're sensible,
you'll hear me out. Harry needs a wife. We've got
money enough to make up for your poverty. At least,
we already know your family. And you'll bring good
blood into the line. And brains. Which, my girl, you well
know isn't Harry's strong point. Now I'm not forcing
you, or threatening you, but I'm making a good clear
business proposition to you. Think about it. But not for
too long, I don't want him setting his heart on some-

thing he can't get. It'll make it harder for him in future
if he does. There's your choices, girl, and fair ones they
are, too. Think about it."

And nodding with satisfaction, her aunt walked off to
find the cook to terrorize.

"Well," thought Regina angrily, "I do hope the climate in Canterbury suits me, for it looks like I'll be
there for some time."

But when Regina announced her decision to her aunt
a week later, the week which she had felt would give
her time to send the letter to Canterbury announcing
her imminent arrival, her aunt had told her not to be so
hasty, to let things hang fire for a spell. Then, all at
once, Regina realized that Harry had been attempting
to woo her. She had not understood what all the desultory, incoherent attempts at conversation had been, but
when on the heels of her aunt's startling decision to
allow her to stay for a while longer, Harry proffered an
invitation to the theater to her, she had understood.

She had not had the heart to turn down his shyly
muttered invitation, and so, on this fine frosty evening,
she found herself dressing in one of the lovely gowns
her uncle had purchased for her.

"No mourning clothes," her aunt had warned her in
the beginning, "for I don't believe in them. George
himself wouldn't have expected it, and a fine sight I'll
be in all my bright colors, when my own niece is dressed
like a crow."

It will be only the one evening, Regina thought, guilt-
ily, and at least he won't feel like such a complete
failure, and oh, I do want to get out of this house for a
spell.

Belinda fussed over her hair for what seemed like
hours, patting in little curls, brushing out the long cas-
cading curl that swept over one shoulder. The little
maid wore a small, secretive smile.

"Belinda," Regina laughed, "Cousin Harry is not the
Prince Regent. Why do you go to all this extraordinary
effort?"

"Because, miss," Belinda grinned, "who's to say? It
might be an extraordinary evening."

"I'm off to Canterbury within the week, Belinda," Regina said. "As well you know it, for you will have to get a new position when I leave."

"That's as may be," Belinda grinned.

"Well leave off," Regina said, rising, "for I'm all finished, and now I'll have to wait an hour for Harry to get his neckcloth right and my aunt to have her hair papers taken out."

Belinda, smiling largely, tittered out of the room. Regina stared after her with deep distrust. She had never felt an affinity with the girl, and this new behavior she was showing was unsettling. As the moments passed, Regina sat quietly, thinking about her forthcoming trip, hoping that she was suited for the new life she was going to attempt to make for herself. While the tuition of small girls might not seem very exciting, she thought, there might be compensations.

Belinda poked her head in the door.

"Oh miss," she smiled, "there's someone to see you, and I've taken the liberty of showing him to the study."

"To see me?" Regina asked, and seeing Belinda's affirmative nod, realized that it might be another of her uncle's business aquaintances. Several of them had paid courtesy calls to her that first week. And since she could not think of another living soul who would seek her out here, Regina went down the stairs reasoning that it was some aquaintance of her uncle's who perhaps had been out of town when the tragedy had occurred. Only, she hesitated at the door to the study, what will he think of me not wearing black? And she gazed down at the sweeping green gown that she wore.

Ah well, she thought, as Aunt says, what is done, is done and said. And with Belinda hovering behind her, she entered the study.

It was dimly lit, and in the first moment her eyes had to accustom themselves to the shadowy light thrown by the sole burning lamp. She could hear Belinda giggle as she closed the door behind her. What is the matter with the girl, she thought with annoyance, leaving me alone here with a guest?

But a moment later, when she could see who stood

before her, smiling beatifically at her, she could only draw in her breath with a gasp.

She recognized him instantly, for he had never been too far from her thoughts, and acknowledging the recognition, he bowed. He looked, she thought inconsequentially, as disturbingly beautiful as he had that night at the Opera.

His pale hair reflected the dim glow of the lamp, his large innocent blue eyes smiled at her. The nose, she thought, is too long and thin and straight for a cherub, the face too lean, the mouth too curling. But there is such an air of disarming innocence. He wore dark evening dress, and she could see that the tapered coat that covered the slight frame did not conceal the long muscles of his shoulders, nor did the close-fitting breeches obscure the tight strength of his legs. When he spoke, it was in the same hoarsely sweet voice that had haunted her dreams all these past weeks.

"I see," he said softly, "that age has not withered you. I'm sorry I couldn't come sooner."

Her back stiffened, "But custom will stale me, sir. I take leave to tell you to get out."

He looked at her with great interest. "Wit too? I am most fortunate. But I shall not 'get out,' Regina, at least not yet, when it has taken me so very long to get in."

"How?" she began, but he cut her off with a wave of one long pale hand. "Very simple stuff, Regina," he said caressingly. "Nothing to even gloat about. A few coins, a few kisses on the right lips, and any door will open to you."

She shook her head, sending the curl of hair tossing back against her shoulder. "Why have you gone to all this trouble, sir? Following me, watching the house, and now, coming here? I made it quite clear the last time we met, when you insulted me, that I want nothing to do with you."

"It was no trouble at all, and not at all an insult," he said, smiling with some inner joy. "And what you want, Regina, has very little to do with it. I saw you, and lost my poor heart. I was enraptured," he said, placing one hand over his breast. "Is that what you want to hear? No matter. It's true. You are very lovely. And being inaccessible made you even lovelier, if possible. I offer you that much-used organ, Regina. Be mine," he crooned.

"Well, you certainly are mad." Regina smiled with relief, thinking it was only that he was a little deranged, or a buffoon. "But now that you have made your remarkable offer, I tell you that I am untouched by it, and want nothing to do with you. Now sir," she went on, disturbed by the ceaseless smile, "I'm sure that there are many women who would be most honored by your confession. Unfortunately," she shrugged, "I am not one of them. You find before you a female most singularly untouched by gentler emotions. So pray take yourself elsewhere, before I have to call my cousin for assistance in convincing you of my sincerity."

"Harry?" purred the Duke. "Oh hardly Harry. Can you imagine him laying hands upon a duke of the realm? Really, Regina, you are not giving me any credit at all, are you?" She noticed that now he had stopped smiling and was looking at her steadily. "It's very simple, my dear. Very unfair, if you will, but nonetheless, simple. I am not a good man. I am at the present, as a matter of record, rejoicing in one of the most evil reputations in all of England. But don't pity me, Regina, for I swear it is well deserved. But I am very wealthy, and I am a duke, a duke of all things. And you are a commoner. Moreover, much to my joy, you are a commoner with no connections at all. No resources. No protector. You are my natural meat, Regina. My natural prey. I want you. Not, perhaps, in a spiritual fashion, rather in a very mortal fashion. For I, too, am a creature most singularly untouched by the gentler emotions. It is not gentle emotions that I spoke of, though. But I do want you, and what I want, I eventually have. Do you understand? You will profit by the experience, I think. You most certainly will be much richer for it. So be a good, sensible girl, and come along with me now. My carriage," he said, sweeping a bow, "awaits."

"You are mad," she gasped, her eyes widening, "I am not a broom, or a tiepin, or . . . a snuffbox . . . a thing that you can see in a shop window and want, and take. I am not an object for your pleasure," she went on. "I am a living, breathing person. No one can just take me."

"You're making it all very difficult, but exhilarating," he said. "And you know very little. I can most certainly take you, Regina, any time I choose, even right here."

She backed against the door.

"But I think I won't," he mused, "because I do like leisure and comfort. And if you were a tiepin or a snuffbox, I wouldn't want you quite so much. And the fact that you insist on being recognized as a thinking person, with certain rights, makes you all the most stimulating," he said, now smiling radiantly.

"You are like some creature out of a bad dream," Regina cried. "For all that I speak sense to you, you smile and smile, and continue as if I had said nothing. You seem to be untouched by reality. This is my uncle . . . my aunt's house. I have a staff of servants here, my cousin and aunt are at this very moment waiting for me. Soon they will look for me. And you stand here and smile and tell me that you want me, that I am to come with you . . . surely you are playing some elaborate joke. . . ."

"You think," he said, considering, his head tilted to one side, "that the houseful of servants and aunts and cousins make a large difference?"

She heard her aunt's strident voice in the hall, and shored up by the shrill sounds, held her head high. "Yes, and now, Your Grace, if you would leave. . . ."

He had heard the sounds as well, and seemed to be listening closely to the progress of the noises.

"Yes," he said, and smiled again. He walked close to her, so close that she could scent the faint aroma of Bay rum and wine and tobacco on his person. The large wide blue eyes, now unsmiling, looked down into hers, and with a quick grace, he reached and drew her to him. His lips gently, she thought with surprise, very tenderly covered hers.

In that first instant, her shock gave way to surprise at the tenderness, at the small thrill that involuntarily raced through herself at the touch of those warm soft gentle lips upon hers. He held her as gently as she had ever been held, although her confused mind remembered that she had never been thus held. Still, he pressed his body to hers, and she felt him communicate an urgency of desire to her. In that first moment, she swayed against him, responding to the startling effect his presence had upon her, but before she could recover herself, indeed at the very moment she felt her resolve returning and her body tensed to push him away, instead, he cast her roughly away from him and said in a loud harsh voice, "No good, Regina, no good, I will not take you back."

She turned, startled, to see her aunt framed in the now open door, looking at her aghast, and her cousin, staring at her with shock.

"I'm terribly sorry," said the Duke, sweeping a bow to her aunt, "to discompose you good people. Allow me to introduce myself. Jason Thomas, Duke of Torquay," he went on, seeming very cold and contained. "Forgive me for this unseemly intrusion. But Regina had sent me a note of urgent import, and I came here posthaste. But," he said, his blue eyes cold and narrowed, "I found only that I was to receive the same message I have received before. I do apologize for entering your house unannounced, but she had said it was a matter of some secrecy. I beg your pardon, and will take leave of you now."

He walked to the door and hesitated for a moment, looking down into Regina's dazed eyes. "I'm sorry," he said in a clearly carrying stage whisper, "but it is over, Regina. I will not take you back. Your cousin looks like a good enough chap. Take care not to damage your future any further, my girl. For I will not acknowledge the child."

And with one more courtly bow and a set cold expression, he left.

She packed her things quietly but quickly, as her aunt insisted. She tried to shut out the sounds of abuse from her aunt, but still some of the words drifted through. ". . . Butter wouldn't melt in your mouth . . . sweet and quiet . . . battening on our largesse . . . throwing out lures to my son, and with a bastard already well on its way. . . ." She had to carry her own traveling case to the door. Belinda was nowhere to be seen. Regina felt she had already gone, counting the coins she had earned.

She wore a cloak, and was glad of the hood which concealed her face, for she did not want her aunt to see her tears as she said again, yet again, "I know you will never believe me, but it was not so. It is not so." Harry only stood and stared at her as though she were from some foreign land.

When the door slammed shut behind her, she lifted the case and descended the steps. At the bottom of them, when she reached the street, she felt someone take the grip from her frozen fingers, felt a hand propel her toward the street, and was roughly pushed into the carriage. She sank back against the cushions and saw him sitting across from her, smiling, smiling happily in the darkened coach.

"You see, Regina," he said in that curiously confidential whisper that she had shivered in remembrance of, "you see how very simple it was?"

VI

"I do not understand, I cannot understand," she said slowly, addressing him, looking toward the dim blur of his face in the shadowy interior of the carriage. They traveled unhurriedly on through the streets of town, the well-sprung coach swaying only slightly, and she had gotten a little time to collect her wits; so she went on in a low voice, almost reflectively, "You know, there are times, usually times of stress, when one is haunted by bad dreams."

"My governess was of the opinion that they were brought on by a bad conscience, or a surfeit of sweets ingested before bedtime," he said conversationally, relaxing against the plump cushions.

"No," she shook her head, "no, that is not what I'm trying to say. In these troubled dreams, there is often a figure . . . or an object, something that would be quite benign, actually harmless in a waking state. But in these dreams, this object is invested with all sorts of sinister, dreadful terror. One does not know what sort of harm it betokens, but one knows it would be ruinous to oneself, and so throughout the dream, one runs from it. But, even in crowds of people, even alone in a locked room, somehow, by the magic of dreams, it comes through, it confronts . . . you can never escape it."

"An object?" he said with amusement.

"Anything, I suppose it is different for each dreamer . . . anything from a table to an owl to a mouse, but the terror comes from the fact that you know it is malevolent, and you do not understand why it constantly pursues you, or what harm it means, and why you cannot escape it."

"But I am neither a table nor a mouse, Regina, and I mean you no harm. But yes, your analogy holds in one respect, you cannot escape me," he mused in a gentle voice.

"And if," she went on, lost in her train of thought, "you have not already been fortunate enough to waken, shivering in terror at your close call with danger, and if you go on dreaming, there are times when you turn and face the pursuer. But no matter what you do, it is unswervable. If you hack at it, the pieces rise to chase you; if you set it afire, it follows you in flames; it is indestructable, it is relentless. But it all is only a dream; through it all, some part of you knows that it is only a dream, for no living creature could be that deficient of reason, that implacable. A living creature could be reasoned with," she said, staring hard at him.

"Why, what interesting dreams you have, Regina. You must tell me more about them some time," he yawned.

"Why?" she asked, fighting back the tears, for somehow she knew that tears would be her undoing, that tears would disable her.

"Why?" he smiled again. "Perhaps eventually even constant lovemaking becomes fatiguing. We must talk at some time."

"You know what I have asked," she said, sitting up as straight as she could in the shifting vehicle. "Why have you done all this? What joy is there in this? You do not even know me. You cannot care for me."

"What a strange child you are," he laughed, and rising gracefully, he swung himself over to sit beside her. He settled back again, his pale head resting against the squabs, took one of her cold hands in his, and idly traced a pattern on the palm of it with one long finger.

"Of course," he said soothingly, in his normal clandestine whisper, "I do not care for you. Why should I? I care for very few people, Regina. In point of fact, I care for none. But the joy in it? Ah, then, there's a different story. I don't care to repeat myself, but you do undervalue your attractions. You are very lovely. Very new. Very desirable. I wanted you when I saw you. So I set out to get you. There is joy in getting what you desire, Regina. And as for other joys . . . you will come to understand them, too. I shall see to that."

"No," she cried, trying to snatch her hand away, but he only held it the tighter, in a surprisingly strong grip.

"No," she continued, but more quietly, trying to keep her voice even. "I will not find joy with you, Your Grace. There is no joy for a prisoner, for an object, for a creature that is fashioned to serve someone else's desires. It was not for this that I was born, and educated, and live."

"How well you speak," he commented, placing a light congratulatory kiss upon her wrist. "It will be such a diversion, after all these years of hearing nothing but giggles and sighs and ladylike sobs of mournful protest. You speak almost as well as a man. It will be a novelty to make love to a woman who seems to have a man's mind. Perhaps it will be the best of all possible things. But as for your protests, Regina, I hesitate to contradict such an enlightened mind, but you do not know of what you speak in that case. You are ignorant of all the things that I am master of. You are, since you do seem to enjoy analogous reasonings, rather like a newly hatched chick who asks the hawk what possible joy he finds in soaring. You will understand," he said, moving quietly close to her.

She could feel the warm dry heat that seemed to emanate from him and, forcing herself to look directly at him, not to shrink back, as she felt he expected her to, she said, "But there are creatures who were not born to fly, who were never intended to do so."

"Oh, but you forget our tender parting kiss that your aunt interrupted, Regina, I think you, at least, were intended to soar," he chuckled.

"Can't you understand," she cried, raising her voice for the first time, "that this is so wrong, so ridiculous for me? I do not want to be your mistress, or your diversion, or your desire, or anything to you. I only want to be let alone. I want to live my own life."

"And a good life it will be," he said, reaching out to smooth back a lock of her hair. "Why you shall have fine clothes, and a lovely place to live, and jewels, yes especially emeralds to go with your eyes, and congenial company. And when it ends, a tidy income to see you on to whatever your own desires will be."

"None of which I want," she raged, brushing his hand away. "If I cared for you, still I would not want those things. But I will not be forced into a life of servitude, a life which is supported by selling myself. I would sooner cut off an arm or a limb to sell, than sell my entire self for what you consider luxuries."

He looked at her with a growing puzzlement, his wide blue eyes suddenly deeper, a curious expression in them.

"I did not expect any of this," he said looking into her face closely, "when I planned this. You speak to me as if we were equals. Where are your womanly graces, Regina? Why do you not cry, or threaten, or rage, or bargain with me? Why do you not say, 'Not emeralds, sir, if you please, diamonds.' Or, 'Oh pity, sir,' or, 'Think of me poor mum, sir, who'll support her while I'm gone?' or even, 'What of my reputation, Your Grace,

however shall I marry now?' But no, you don't say a
word that I expect."

For a moment, Regina was taken aback. For it was
true. Why hadn't she struggled or screeched, she wondered with sudden shock? She had entered the coach as
timidly as a mouse and had sat and prosed on to him as
though they were on their way to an afternoon tea.
Perhaps it was because she knew herself guilty for
attending the Opera that night in the first place, and
could not find it in her heart to blame him for his
original wrong conclusion about her. But he had done a
dreadful, immoral unthinkable thing and she should be
roundly denouncing him and shrilling at him now. But
perhaps she hadn't because after all those conflicting
dreams of him, she thought of him as someone she could
sit and talk and reason with as though she had known
him forever. But that was foolish, for nothing he had
done since that first meeting had given her an ounce of
reason to trust him. Before she could order her whirling
thoughts, he moved closer and all thoughts vanished as
she realized how very near he was to her in the darkened coach.

"Why," he laughed, "here we are, in the midst of a
daring infamously vile abduction, and you sit there and
discourse at me, you reason and explain as if we were in
a schoolroom. Has it not occurred to you that you are in
the fell company of a vile seducer, a man without conscience, a man who has spent the better part of his busy
day daydreaming about the indignities he will soon visit
upon your person? No, you simply sit there and discuss
the situation with me, as if we were kindred spirits. As
if we were old companions met to thrash out philosophi-
cal questions about good and evil. Oh you are a delight!"
he crowed, and reached out for her.

But she put out two hands and held him off, saying
quickly, "But perhaps we *are* kindred spirits. For I was
not raised to have any more feminine graces than you
were."

He sat back and looked at her.

She pressed what she hoped was her advantage. "Only
think," she pleaded, "I may be just a commoner, of

mixed birth and shadowy antecedents, but I was not educated as were the other women of your world. I do not know their guiles or ambitions. I have been reared with different expectations. I was raised to think of myself always with honor, with dignity. Only for one moment put yourself in my position. Would you sell all your principles for a jewel? For a comfortable set of rooms? For a sum of money? Your Grace, only answer me one question please, only one, and then I will . . . then I can speak no more. You have been trained to give. You have been used to taking. But could you ever . . . sell yourself? And if you could not, can you try to understand why I cannot?"

She felt him almost physically recoil at her words. Then he began to laugh. A different laugh than that which she had heard before. A rich, full laugh. When the laughter subsided, he straightened and seemed to stare off into space. Then he turned again to her.

"Well done, oh well done, Regina," he breathed, a new and excited look on his face. "You have somehow managed to awaken the one last little remnant of that forgotten childhood quality in me—Honor. I did not think that any of it remained. And a certain sporting instinct. No, I should not say gallantry, I'm sure I never had that, but a certain sporting instinct, yes. You are an original. That face, that lovely hair," he mused, "the clean sweet scent of you . . . I do still want you very much, Regina. Perhaps now more than ever. It's pity you weren't born a titled lady. I swear I'd even propose on the spot if you were. But," he said half to himself, "delayed pleasure is often the best. Yes," he seemed to decide suddenly, "yes, it will be most amusing. Regina," he breathed, "I shall make a bargain with you. But one I am sure of winning. Still, it is a sporting gesture."

"A bargain?" she whispered, fearful of another of his swings of mood, yet hopeful for the first time.

"Yes, a bargain," he smiled, the same smile of inner satisfaction that she so frequently noted on his face. "I shall let you go. Go free, and completely on your own. I shall set you down in the midst of town alone. Completely free, as you asked. You have certain handicaps. No home to return to. No finances. You see, I did my research well. No family. Quite a dreadful situation for a young woman to find herself in, isn't it? But still, you have certain advantages as well. You have beauty and wit and a quick mind. But your greatest handicap will be that you are overburdened with a sense of honor. You will not sell yourself, you say. At least not to me."

As she began to speak, he silenced her with a wave of his hand. "Yes, I accept that you will not sell yourself to any other. After all, I have some pride in my external appearance. After all, there are some things that both my mistresses and my mirror do tell me. I am not yet aged. Or fat, or gouty. And although I cannot say why, I am yet unafflicted with the pox. Though not from want of opportunity. Has that thought been troubling you? Let me reassure you, this poor croaking voice of mine is a family characteristic, no foul disease yet taints my body. I shall not infect you with my embrace. Which is more, little innocent, than can be said for most of the men in my position these days. As for what foul breath taints my mind? That, no doctor could diagnose. I have gone beyond libertine, yet not—although that is open to argument—completely degenerate. At least," he laughed ruefully, "I have not yet lusted after exotic animals, or my fellow man, or formed a passion for any breastless children. You do not understand completely? All to the better. At least I know that you do not find me loathsome . . . physically, that much I do know, whatever you do think of my poor warped mentality.

"So. I shall set you free and you shall be as a little green-eyed fox in the forests of London. I shall keep my hounds on your traces. I shall know every moment of how you fare. Wealth has given me access to Argus eyes. Here, in the center of town, I shall loose you. What a fine game!"

"I may leave now?" she asked quietly. He raised himself and went to the window of the coach to signal to an unseen outrider and whisper some instructions. Settling back again, he went on, with laughter in his voice, his face showing bliss.

"Oh yes," he said, "but . . . oh, come now, don't look so crestfallen, you knew that there would be a 'but,' didn't you? But then, you must find a proper place for yourself. A safe harbor. A moral," he emphasized, "and safe harbor. If I find that within a certain period of time you have done so, I shall wish you joy, and keep only these tender moments safely locked away in my memory. But if you have not, I shall come for you again. And this time, Regina, you may play Sherharazade with a thousand tales of morality and honor and truth, it will not avail you. You will have failed the test. You will be mine to do with as I wish."

"How long a time?" she asked.

"Oh ho," he grinned. "Since I am the rulemaker, the inventor of the game, and the scorekeeper, that is my concern. Your concern is to prove to me that we are indeed equals. Or rather, since you have attacked me on the subject, that you are superior to me, if not in birth, then in that elusive thing—Honor. That you can forge a decent place for yourself in this world without using all those 'feminine' graces that you claim to be unaware of. That you can, homeless, friendless, moneyless, keep yourself from starvation with 'honor.' Give me a living definition of the word, Regina. For I swear, I have never seen it in a creature as lovely as yourself. It is a bargain? The game is to go on?" he asked.

She nodded, and they rode in silence for a small space of time. Then the carriage slowly came to a halt.

"Good," he said, looking out the window. "Not a back slum, not a place filled with terrors, simply the heart of town. You may go, Regina, and begin the game. But first," he added, as she rose to go to the door, "we must seal the bargain."

He pulled her down to his side, with the unusual strength she had noted before, and raising himself so that he looked down into her bewildered eyes, he spoke so softly, she had to strain to hear him.

"All bargains should be sealed with a kiss, Regina, haven't you heard of that cliché?"

He brought his lips down to her again, and though she tried to remain passive, she again felt the curious

response that came involuntarily to her. When he raised
his head, he smiled so tenderly that she felt confused
again. "Ah, how I despair of letting you go so soon,
even if it will only be for a little while," he sighed.

"But still, a bargain is struck, and the game is begun,
little fox. When I return, there will be time enough for
both of us. And I have the uneasy feeling that you will
take up a great deal of my time in the future. Still," he
said, letting her go, "the game is on . . . go then,
Regina." And he swung open the carriage door and
stepped out.

He handed her down, and she paused on the deserted
street and looked at him.

"Do go, go," he said kindly, "or I shall change my
mind. But remember," he called after her retreating
back, "I shall be watching. Make it a fair game. A good
game."

The Duke sat lost in thought as the carriage conveyed
him home. He had already given certain instructions to
the outrider, and he knew that there were other plans
to be made and arranged for when he reached his house.
Many diverse plans and counterplans. But for now he
sat back, the usually pleasantly amused face set in unfamiliar harsh lines. He was remembering, and he did
not care to do that.

The evening had not turned out the way he had planned
it. That was a novelty. For many years now, he had not
been surprised by the results of any of his machinations.
He had a quick mind, and was a good judge of character, and seldom found himself engaged in anything that
he had not prefigured in his mind. This evening, even
now, he had thought he was to have begun the girl's
education. Even now, he sighed, he had supposed that
he would have been slowly stripping off her gown, slowly
preparing her for the hours that he had reserved for her
company in his arms. But somehow, she had turned him
around, she had made him doubt himself, she had convinced him momentarily of her sincerity, she had somehow engineered the idea of the incredible game he had
invented.

He had not wanted to force her. He had never had to force any woman. The thought appalled him. He had always chosen women for both their beauty and their availability. There was, of course, always that initial coy show of reluctance; he expected it. It was all part of the game. But every initial protest he had ever encountered had always resulted in speedy, joyful participation. But she had gazed at him with those incredibly innocent eyes and spoken in that well-bred careful little voice and he had found that, amazingly, he wanted her good opinion. And though he would have sworn she was no better than any other female he had ever desired, he had hesitated to force the issue. How could he have believed her, he wondered, a chance-met female nonentity who had gone on the prowl for a protector at the Opera? But she had refused him. That was irrevocable fact.

"I am still in control, though," he brooded. "And the game will be a brief one. And the ending will make it all worthwhile," he reassured himself. "It will be great sport," he tried to tell himself. But still he was uneasy. Had she bested him? Was he still in control?

He did not care for uncertainty. He had planned his life to avoid it at all costs. He was not a good gambler. He lived a life free of risks. Or at least any of the risks that he cared about. His body, his reputation, were not things he especially valued in any sense. His inner person was the only untouchable thing he cared for. And he had made sure that that small unexamined part of himself was never threatened in any of the ways he threatened his person.

It had always been so. Even as a boy, when he scaled the tallest trees, took up any outrageous dares that the other boys flung at him, he never worried about the possibility of physical harm. And having no trepidation, and a naturally agile body, he had never come to harm. He had been forced to prove his physical superiority, for even then, his delicate, almost pretty face had marked him as prey to older boys. But once having confronted him, no other boy had ever dared him again. The slight frame concealed a wiry, hard body, and when he fought, he fought full out, with no fear of damage or even death. Even the much older and stronger of his peers quickly learned that he was in earnest when he threatened them. He was never bullied or taunted about his appearance more than once.

He had also learned early on how to conceal his heart. How to conceal it so well that he soon forgot about its existence altogether. His father, a nobleman many years older than his wife, had been a settled bachelor when the young girl whose beauty captivated him entered upon his life. After the birth of his first and only child, his wife had informed him that conception of another child would surely take her life. Confused and torn between desire and suspicion, the elderly Duke had taken refuge in his estates till a lingering disease forced him into seclusion. He had not even lived to see his son's fifth birthday.

But his youthful wife had no use for seclusion. She dreaded even one waking moment solely in her own company. She was as beautiful a woman as her son was as a boy. Pale and fair-haired, she too had an air of deceptive fragility. But her many lovers soon learned that she had an indefatigible strength. And a bottomless void to fill with compliments, and attentions and flattery. Even when she tiptoed into the nursery on rare occassions to see how her son was growing, she would whisper to him, "Jason, love. Do you like Mama's gown? Is her hair pretty?" And no comment of his that did not center upon her was attended to.

When the young Duke was let out of lessons early one afternoon in his tenth year, he had run away from his protesting governess and raced unthinking into his mama's gilded rooms to tell her of his progress in his studies. Paused in the doorway, he had seen for the first time how very much she required personal attention, and also how exactly a man and a woman could find uses for each other. The governess had held his head for an hour until he could retch no more. But he never mentioned the matter to his lovely mama again, and she had never asked him if he thought she was pretty in the head groom's arms, or if he had admired the paleness of her face against the head groom's dark groin. She had avoided him after that. And he had been sent willingly away to school.

She avoided him further, in his sixteenth year, when he had begun to show the promise of a radiant manhood even more spectacular than her blooming womanhood had been, when she discovered that the rash that had plagued her for years was, in fact, the French pox. Then she had taken herself off to foreign quacks, and spas and resorts, forcing herself to drink the foul concoctions, be immersed in evil-smelling baths, and have strange scented unguents rubbed into her skin, to alleviate the spread of the disease. In her son's eighteenth year she had dosed herself, and had drunk one bottle of laudanum and was halfway through the second when the sleep she sought had finally mercifully come.

The young Duke of Torquay had learned, from an early age onward, the uses of strength, the necessity for keeping one's own counsel, the importance of lacking affections, the frivolous nature of beautiful women, and the importance of living a life that held no surprises. There was only one lesson more that he felt the need of learning.

In his nineteenth year, when he took himself and his assorted servants off on a grand tour, he had made certain inquiries. One soft June night, in Paris, he had found himself in the ornately gilded, perfumed boudoir of a famous courtesan. She was not the first he had visited, nor was she, even then, nearly the first woman he had known. His astonishingly good looks and pleasing manners had already given him entree into many such rooms, redolent of perfumes, rooms so reminescent of his departed Mama's. And rooms that even his Mama wouldn't have dared to enter.

The woman had proven her worth, proven the reliability of her growing reputation, and an hour later, when she had turned to look up into the sweet face of the boy who lay propped up on one elbow, toying with a strand of her dampened hair, she had cooed, "You are satisfied, *mon Brave?* It was all you expected?" And had been shocked when he had merely smiled and, in that hoarse voice that had intrigued her so, had replied in his perfect French, "No, *ma cherie*, no, not at all."

"But this I cannot understand," she had cried, shocked. "Where have I failed? Where have I offended?" He had merely laughed and shaken his head.

"No, you misunderstand," he had said, staring at her intently. "What you do, you do very well. There may well be none better. But that is not what I came for."

"Well," she had said, much affronted, "if your taste runs to young boys, you have certainly come to the wrong place."

"No," he had laughed, "it is not that. Listen *cherie*, I came for something else, something very simple, that you have not given me. I have a small proposition to make to you," he had begun.

"No, no, no," she had cried violently. "If it is pain you want, you must go elsewhere."

"Listen," he had said seriously, "this is my request. You are famous for what you do, and, as I said, you do it very well indeed. But be honest, my little French *amie*," (and here she smiled, for this little cockerel, with his spare white body, to call her lavish configurations "little" was very amusing, but pleasant), "all that you have done tonight, you have done for me. And it was well done. But, to be honest, *cherie*, I have done nothing for you but enrich your purse and continue your fame. You did all the work, my friend, I have only responded to your excellence. And that is what I have always done. And, with your clients, my dear, what you have always done. Tonight, however, I seek more. I want you to show me, to tell me, to instruct me, as to what I can do for you. How I can make those little sighs and groans reality, how I can please you."

She had stared at him in incomprehension.

"Try to think," he had said, a half smile playing about his lips, "of what you like your own lover to do for you ... your pander, or your lady friend, I do not care to know. But only think of your own pleasure, and instruct me in the mysteries of your own body. That is what I require. I will pay well for this knowledge. And if you are a good teacher, I will learn quickly."

The novelty of his request caught her interest, it was the first time—and she had long past forgotten all her first times—she had been offered such a challenge. And he was good looking enough, she thought, to make such a venture amusing.

At first, it had been a novelty for her, almost embarrassed as she patiently instructed him. When she finally showed him, almost as if he were a physician, where the ultimate seat of all her pleasures resided, she had felt a little foolish. But he had been such an eager, pleasant child about it. He had eventually laughed. "After all that, this? This little hidden part? This valiant little imitation is the answer?" And she had, as the long night went on, showed him all, all she knew, till near dawn, exhausted, she understood that there was nothing left to explain to him. He knew her body and her responses now almost better than she did.

Resting her head against his chest, she had whispered, "You have certainly learned quickly. But why did you wish to learn such things?"

"Because," he had said, planting a kiss upon her dampened brow, "I did not know. Because, it is only good tactics to know your enemies' weaknesses, and because," and here he whispered so low that she was never quite sure that she had heard him correctly, "because such knowledge is power."

She had bade him farewell in the morning, and because he had given her a night that she was not to forget for many years, she had implored him, "Only seek out clean girls, *mon Brave*, do not infect yourself, take care of yourself." And he had answered quietly, "I always take care of myself, I lead a charmed life."

Armed with all his various knowledges, he had gone on to lead a daring life. He had gone from excess to excess, and had never swerved from whatever course his talents led him surely to. He had never cared for any opinion but his own. Except perhaps, for the once, on the one occasion of the short-lived marriage he had undertaken. When he had achieved the age of twenty-seven, he had for the first time acted the way a gentleman of title and possessions was expected to. As he had decided that it would be well to ensure the succession, and provide an heir to the fortunes he enjoyed, he had offered for the leading debutante of the season.

She was a pretty enough little thing, he had felt, a bit giddy and light of mind, but during the two times he had conversed and danced with her, her airy little laugh and fine-boned face had pleased him. And her fortune and birth were of the highest available that season.

He had quickly discovered, during the brief months they had together, that there was no commonality of interests between them at all. If her perception was not nearly so lively as her flighty demeanor had led him to expect it might be, he had at least held out some hope that there might eventually be some common ground that they might find so that the union might not be as unendurable as he was fast finding it to be. But all his arts could not move her to a natural, easy communication with him. She seemed, instead, to fear him, avoid him, and merely endure his company.

With all his wide experience, he still could find no way to wrest any real pleasure from the rigid little body she so dutifully presented him with each night. Nor could he, despite his unusual spell of fidelity and concentration, bring her to any enjoyment of the art he had mastered so long ago.

The last night he had tried, he had slipped into her bedroom as usual, after she had dismissed her servants, and quietly approached the wide bed where she lay, wreathed in white lace. As he had gently drawn the covers back, she had, for the first time, smiled as she greeted him. He had responded to that one gesture of friendship with ardor, but she had pushed him away and pouted. "Jason, my dear, that isn't really necessary any longer."

He had drawn away and asked, with a teasing note in his voice, "Why, have you found another diversion for these hours?"

"No," she laughed with genuine joy, "but we really don't have to . . . do that dreadful business any longer. I am with child already, you see." He stood back from her. "Dreadful?" he had asked with genuine surprise.

"Well," she had smiled, "but not when I understood that you must if you were to have an heir, then I could see that the thing was inevitable. But now that you have accomplished it, what would be the sense of it? I'm not one of your fancy pieces, Jason. There's no pleasure in such degrading things for me. Oh yes, I do know about all those . . . females, and I do understand why you must seek them out . . . now, more than ever, I suppose I do understand. But pray understand that I do not mind, so long as you are circumspect about it. And you needn't bother with me now that you are to have the heir you desired."

He stood looking at her for a long moment, and then with that strange half smile he so often wore, the one which frightened her so, he had said, "Needn't bother with you, my dear?" and had come closer to her. She shrieked and drew up her covers. "Jason!" she had gasped, "you forget, I am your wife! I am to bear your child. Do not attempt that vile business again! It has served its purpose. I am not to be disturbed in my mind, if the child is to be born aright!"

He had not disturbed her again. He had turned and left. He returned to her only when the child, a frail little girl that bore the stamp of her own face, had been born. He had stayed with her all during the time the child-bed fever had raged, and when it had taken her insubstantial body completely, he had stayed for her interment. Then, leaving the sickly child in the care of excellent wetnurses and staff, he had left again. And gone on to live his life as he had begun to live it before the mad notion of marriage had ever crossed his mind. He had gone on to excess, and the pursuit of self-satisfaction, and never again had cared for any other being's opinion but his own. And this philosophy, he felt, in its own way, had given him whatever happiness he felt he had the right to expect in the world he had made.

But this night, as he rode back to his house, he was disturbed. He had set out to accomplish one thing, he had begun another. He had named the game, but he had not really wanted to play it. He found himself, as he had said, now both scorekeeper and judge, inventor of the rules and keeper of the tally. But still, he had not planned it.

He'd been so sure that he was right. That the wayward chit with the glorious face and seductive eyes, newly on the town with no title, or family, or bonds, would have leaped at the chance to be his newest paramour. He had sworn he had seen the desire in her first glance at him. And he had been certain of it in her rush of response to that first kiss. That is what had armed him to go on to the lengths he had. She should have come to him willingly, with laughter at his daring and anticipation of her adventure with him. Perhaps it was just some new game she played to pique his interest and raise her fee. He would welcome a new game. He was, in truth, very weary of the old ones. But possibly, just possibly, she was in earnest. She had cast that stranger, doubt, into his mind. And so he had gambled.

He had acted impetuously. He did not like to gamble, for in gambling there was always the possibility of losing. He would not lose. He could not, he thought fiercely, lose. This, then, was the final honor left, the final one he admitted to. He would not lose.

VII

St. John Basil St. Charles relaxed against the cushions of his carriage and felt at peace, for once, with his world. The hour was late, the wind outside was wickedly cutting, but here, snugged in his well-sprung conveyance, he was at ease, comforted, drained of tensions and desires. He was sated with wine, with food, with pleasure, and only awaited his bed.

Maria Dunstable, a passable dancer, late of the Opera, had been, he reflected, a very good choice. She had made herself at home almost at once in Annabelle's old quarters, making quick work of stowing her clothes, displaying her various mementos, permeating the rooms with her own individual blend of perfumes. She was quick-witted, adaptable, and still young enough to be amusing, while experienced enough to be adept. They had not yet reached the point in their relationship where she wheedled for more liberties or felt secure enough to run up more expenses. How long she would last in her new situation, St. John felt, depended entirely upon her own actions; for the moment, he was well pleased.

He allowed himself the luxury of a most undignified gaping yawn and a long stretch of his limbs; still, he thought, it would be good to sleep now in his own, undemanding bed. The gray light outside the carriage showed that another cold dawn was fast approaching. St. John alighted from his carriage and walked slowly to his front door, pausing for a moment to scent the air. Snow, he thought, was soon in coming. For a moment, he thought he saw a small shadow detach itself from the darkness near the alleyway leading to the back of his home, but then he shrugged and paid it no further attention. On such a chill night, there would be little likelihood of footpads, and certainly none who would dare frequent this fashionable street.

A drowsy footman opened the door for him, but no sooner had he flung off his cape when he was surprised to see his man, Hilliard, enter the hallway, dressed as if it were broad daylight, and waiting for him.

"Surely you have mistaken the hour, Hilliard," St. John drawled. "It lacks five in the morning, not five in the afternoon."

"I understand, My Lord," Hilliard replied. "But there was a message for you, My Lord, that I felt might not wait until a retarded hour."

St. John gave him a quick sharp look. Hilliard was no fool; only a matter of importance would receive such unusual treatment.

"What is it, then?" he asked, suddenly feeling the languor dissipating and an uneasy feeling of alarm coming over him.

"A young person came here this evening, sir," Hilliard said impassively, "who looked quite the lady. However, she would neither give her name nor state her business.

She would only give me a message she said was to be hand-delivered only to Your Lordship. And she asked if she might wait for your arrival, even though I explained that it might well be late, or even this day when you finally arrived. Nonetheless, she was adamant, and insisted upon waiting."

St. John put out his hand to receive the small slip of paper Hilliard offered. He scanned it quickly, and it made him draw in his breath in a short gasp. For the message contained only two words scrawled upon it. It read only "George Berryman."

St. John stiffened. He shot a quick look at Hilliard. How much did the man know of his private affairs, how much did he surmise, to understand that these two simple words would indeed be of paramount interest to him? For George Berryman, St. John knew, was dead. Dead and buried these many weeks. Mrs. Teas had given him the hurried news when he last had visited the house, and he had bowed and, stating his condolences, had slipped away, as he had always intended to, never to return. That phase of his life, although entertaining, profitable, and much relished, was over with now. Over with the instant that George Berryman had drawn his last breath. But now, who wished to revive the matter?

Was it an attempt at blackmail? Or was there some unfinished business about which George Berryman himself had given directions that the Marquis of Bessacar should be sought out after his death? That would be unforgivable, and dangerous to his standing. St. John stood still, his eyes still bent upon the little note in his hand. He brought his hand to a fist over it, and then inquired, with deceptive calm, "And where is the young person now, Hilliard?" For he thought, it was not without the realm of possibility that Hilliard had some notion as to what his actions these past years were, they had lived in such close proximity. But still, he trusted the servant, and had known him for too many years to think that this was a ploy on the man's part.

"She waits outside, My Lord," Hilliard answered, and seeing the swift surprise in his master's eyes, continued, "As she had neither a maid nor a companion with her, and as I did not recognize her, I thought it best that I not allow her entry into your home, My Lord. And since she insisted upon waiting, I gave her leave to wait in the alleyway. If she is still there, she will have been waiting for some several hours, sir. Shall I fetch her? Or do you wish to let the matter pass? I did not presume to attempt to foresee your answer."

The Marquis relaxed. No, Hilliard was not part of this. He was too shrewd to wade into the murky waters of blackmail. This woman was obviously no confederate of his. He had signaled that to the Marquis by not allowing her inside the house. And he certainly would not have forced a confederate of his to wait in the street for all those hours on such a bitter night. By his decision to allow the creature to stand in the cold night, he had both signaled his innocence of the affair to his master and washed his hands of the situation, even though he had certainly known of its importance to the Marquis.

"I am intrigued, Hilliard, at the mysterious aspects of the affair," St. John said, pretending to stifle a small yawn. "So disregard the lateness of the hour. Lay a fire in the study and permit the woman to enter."

St. John was comfortably ensconced in a chair by the fire, a dressing gown drawn over his clothes, a brandy in his hand, when Hilliard announced the young woman. "The person to see you, My Lord," Hilliard sniffed, doing the best that he could at an introduction and having no name to go by.

St. John heard his man very well, and heard the door quietly close, and by the rustle of a dress, knew that the woman was within the room, but he played for time and ascendancy in the matter by continuing to stare into the fire for several moments, his back to visitor. When he felt that enough moments had ticked by, he said, without bothering to turn his head, "State your business, please. The hour is late, and I have only admitted you because your note was so cryptic. Begin, and tell me all that you would not tell my man."

A slight pause followed, and then he heard a soft, well-bred voice say, in a hesitant tone, "I am sorry to disturb you at this hour. But indeed, I did come earlier,

but you were not yet arrived home. I . . . I do not
know you, Your Grace, and neither do I understand
why I was told to seek you out . . . but my late uncle,
George Berryman, told me shortly before his death that
if I should ever need . . . advice, you would stand as
my . . . advisor."

At the word "uncle," St. John turned around quickly,
with a frown, to finally see who this visitor was. She
stood partially in the shadows, but what he could see
took his breath away for the second time that night. He
gestured to her impatiently. "Come close to the fire," he
commanded. She moved forward slowly.

It was strange, he thought, that he should recognize
her almost at once, although he had only seen her the
once, and so fleetingly. Although she was no longer
dressed with the elegant care that she had been that
night at the Opera, indeed, she seemed almost somber
in the dark cape she clutched to herself, her worn traveling case standing by her side, there was no mistaking
the high cheekbones, the small tilted nose, the dazzlingly
white skin, and most of all, the luminous dazzling green
eyes.

He rose and quickly ushered her to a chair near the
fire. Her hand, he noted, was cold as a dead woman's.
He poured her a glass of brandy and told her to drink it
quickly, standing over her as she did so.

"George Berryman, your uncle?" he breathed, watching her closely as she coughed against the unusual taste
of the drink. "Drink it, drink it," he commanded. "You're
chill as stone."

"I would not have had you wait outside on such a
night if I had but known, but my staff has explicit
instructions, and you refused to give your name."

"I understand," she said quietly, still sitting upright.
"You need not concern yourself. My actions were . . .
unusual. But if I might explain, you will see that I had
no other course open to me."

He drew a chair up beside her, and watched her,
fascinated by those expressive green eyes, and well
caught by the implicit drama of the situation. George
Berryman's niece? He could hardly credit it. She was a

magnificently lovely creature, with the airs and manner of a lady of Society. He felt a familiar racing of his pulses. "Take your time," he said in a comforting tone, "and tell me what the matter is about."

She hesitated once again, and then looked into the gray eyes opposite her. He was a formidable looking man, she thought, and faintly familiar looking as well, with his high Indian cheekbones, those changeable, heavily lashed gray eyes, and the perfectly sculptured, almost classical mouth. But when the mouth tightened, and the eyes turned to a cold steel hue, she felt he might be very intimidating. Still, there was a naggingly familiar cast to his features . . . although, she felt, she surely would have remembered such a fine looking man if she had seen him before. But she had expected him to be older, at least her uncle's age. She was chilled through her entire body. How many hours had she waited in the dark and wind-filled alley, shifting from foot to foot to keep her blood moving? But she had not known where else she could have gone. After she had stumbled away from the Duke, she had wandered the streets for a time, until the frightening moments when a group of young fashionably dressed men had accosted her, demanding her price, her rate schedule. She had fled them, and finding herself alone, had been forced to decide upon a course of action, any course of action.

She did not doubt that the Duke was serious at whatever strange game he had begun. He frightened her with his implacable surety, his nightmare power, and his mad conviction that this was a fair "game." She had no home to return to, no funds to see her through to Canterbury, not even enough funds or knowledge to secure a respectable lodging for the night. She was, as the Duke had said, singularly weaponless in this great city. But then, she had remembered what her uncle had said, she had remembered the name of the Marquis of Bessacar, and as much as she had hated to force herself upon the goodwill of a stranger, still she had reasoned, her uncle would not have directed her so without a good reason.

Taking all her courage, she had inquired as to his

whereabouts from street vendors she had seen, and while some had chased her away with lewd comments about her state, for she had quickly realized that without an escort she was as much as advertising herself upon the streets at this hour, finally a flower vendor had taken pity upon her and given her the direction of his house. After she had delivered her message to his man, she had no choice but to hastily scribble her uncle's name upon the paper and wait for his return.

Now, with the unfamiliar liquor warming her veins and giving her false courage, and the fire comfortably thawing her, she drew in a breath and began to explain the situation to the handsome, concerned gentleman who sat quietly, giving her his undivided attention.

He interrupted her story only the once, when she first mentioned the Duke. "Torquay!" he breathed, and then, when she paused, he said quickly, "Go on, go on."

When she had finished the tale, which was, she realized herself, almost fantastical in its brief telling, she sat back at last and closed her eyes wearily. Would he believe her? Indeed, she scarcely believed it herself. Somehow, the lateness of the hour, her own weariness, and the otherworldly quality of her situation made her for the first time feel volitionless, without concern, at last, for her own fate.

He sat silently for a few moments. Then he looked at the exhausted but still lovely face before him.

"Does anyone know of your whereabouts now?" he asked.

"No one," she answered quietly, "for I never heard your name at all except from my uncle's lips."

"Mrs. Teas never mentioned me?" he persisted.

"Never," she said softly. "And my aunt dismissed her soon after my uncle's death."

"This game of the Duke's," he asked slowly, "do I understand that he expects you to find a suitable place for yourself, alone and unaided, or he will claim you?"

"I can scarcely blame you," she said, opening her brilliant eyes, "for doubting that part of my tale, for I myself cannot credit it . . . it seems so melodramatic, so much of a. . . ." She fumbled for words, but he leaned forward and clasped her chill hand in his two warm ones.

"No, no," he smiled. "Though it may surprise you, I assure you, it does not seem at all fanciful to me. You see, I know Torquay. . . . No," he said comfortingly, as she gave a sudden start, "not precisely as a friend. I do not approve of his activities, although, I know them well. He is a man without scruple, a man who lives only for his own pleasures, a man . . . whose name is by-word for license. And a man with an eye for beauty—and my dear, it is only natural that he should have been drawn to your loveliness."

She withdrew her hands from his and sat up straight. "I go too fast," he mused to himself, and standing, went on, "Have you no other living relatives, then?"

"None that I know. None that I can apply to. Father and I lived a quiet life. The life of a schoolmaster's family . . . but no, you are not to think that I require . . . you to settle my future for me . . . no. You see, I still do not understand why Uncle gave me your name, and why he felt I should apply to you. But I only do so as a temporary measure. I need . . . a place to retreat to . . . only for a few days. For, you see, as I explained, my governess has a school that she now runs, and I feel sure that she will welcome me, but I cannot see how I may reach her. If I could but . . . borrow, only borrow, some funds from you. Only the fare to Canterbury. Once there, I could secure a position at the school, and repay you. I seek no charity. Only a loan," she insisted, color flooding her face in embarrassment.

"Let us have no talk of obligation," he said in a warm voice. "You did right to seek me out. Your uncle . . . was in the position to do me a great favor many years ago, when I was only a boy. I did tell him that I would be glad to reciprocate at any time. Any favor that I do for you, I consider in payment to that debt I owe to your uncle, Miss . . . Berryman?"

"It is Regina Analise Berryman, Your Grace," she said. "Only I do not wish to presume upon you for more than . . . a loan."

"Nonsense," he said heartily, in the most avuncular

fashion he was capable of. "I owe your late uncle a deal more than that." He turned and was lost in thought for a moment. And then he turned back to her.

"And I would very much like to thwart the plans of my good friend Torquay, for my own reasons. See here, Miss Berryman. . . . Ah, that is so stiffly formal, may I call you Regina, as I am sure your uncle would have given me leave to?"

"Of course," she said.

"Very well then, Regina. Now I have a very good idea. London is not a good place for you at present. Torquay is right, he does have eyes and ears everywhere. And for you to bound off to the wilds of Canterbury with only a hope of finding your governess well established and able to help you, is folly. I am sure that is one of the first places Torquay will seek you if he cannot find you in London. And if you haven't secured a position for yourself. . . ." He let the sentence hang. "But, if you follow my directions, we can establish you well enough to confound Torquay and ensure your own happiness in future."

She looked at him with hope.

"Come with me, Regina, now," he said. "We will ride to one of my estates, Fairleigh. You will have, I'm afraid, to travel with me in a closed carriage, but simply by being here this night I'm afraid we have already overstepped the proprieties. No matter, no one but you and I will know of it. And Hilliard, but I have his discretion. Once at my home, you can compose yourself. You can send a message to your governess and wait, in security, for her reply. If she cannot accommodate you, I have, I assure you, sufficient influence to procure you another position."

"But no," she quickly said, sitting up suddenly. "Indeed, I cannot . . . just cast myself upon your goodwill. It is not even a question of proprieties, My Lord. I did not come here for your absolute protection. I cannot expect you to accept full responsibility for my present position. No, no, I am sure that is not what my uncle desired, and neither is it what I expected."

"Regina," smiled the Marquis, taking one of her cold

hands, "allow me, please, to determine the extent of my debt to your uncle. And also, you must allow me to pursue the course to which my own sense of honor surely leads me, or would you also redefine my own code?"

She looked at the handsome, gently smiling face so near to her own, and felt the lateness of the hour and the effects of her long wait in the cold. In all conscience, she was wary of allowing a stranger to take the matter of her future out of her own hands, and yet, what other course was open to her? And as he said, it was not as if he were a complete stranger, and he had his own private score to settle with the author of her difficulties. Still, she felt she should at least offer up some further demurrers to this elegant benefactor.

"But," she added, "surely if the Duke discovers that I have gone with you, he will account it as a failure on my part. He was specific, in that I was to establish myself . . . without resorting to . . . 'Feminine wiles.' " She lowered her eyes.

"I assure you, Regina," St. John smiled, "that I do not put myself out so for any other female, no matter how distraught or lovely. No, I do this for your uncle. It is a debt of honor. Now, rest awhile, while I prepare for the journey. It would be well for us to leave before full light so that we will be unmarked."

She smiled in assent, and when he left the room, rested her head back against the chair, feeling oddly content, and secure, as she had not for a long time.

The Marquis of Bessacarr confounded his household by rousing them at an ungodly hour before dawn and ordering his traveling carriage prepared.

And before the first weak struggles of the sun to pierce the leaden morning skies had begun, he, accompanied by a caped and hooded figure, entered the vehicle which had, uncharacteristically, been drawn up to the back entrance. No one was there to see the strange departure except for Hilliard, who oversaw the procedure with customary aplomb, no one, that is, except for Hilliard and the barely discernible figure of a small street boy, who stood seemingly engrossed in his task of sorting through the curbside litter. And who left, at a dead run, as soon as the carriage had turned the corner.

It was high afternoon when the dusty coach finally turned into the long drive at Fairleigh. A few snow-flakes were filtering down from the now solidly leaden skies. St. John sat back and smiled as he gazed at his companion. At his insistence, she now slept quietly in the other corner of the carriage, a warm blanket tightly secured around her. Lovely, he thought, even with those remarkable eyes now shuttered. The thick rich chestnut hair had spilled out a little from its tight confines and traced an alluring shadow about her cheek. Yes, he thought, all would go well.

She had surprised him on this journey. She was not of his class, or of the Quality, that he knew just from a quick précis on her antecedents. She arose from a family of merchants, from an admixture of the stolid bourgoisie. She had even hinted of having had great-grandparents who were such exotics as Armenians—or was it Arabians?—and one branch of heritage that was certainly of the Jewish merchant class. But, he thought, she was like a swan arising from a barnyard nest. For her face and figure clearly bore the evidence of the fine-boned grace so desirable in his own class. She had, before he had advised her to sleep, attempted to entertain him as they rode the long, tedious miles. Despite her fatigue she had been in turn amusing, informed, and gracious as she had sketched her history with candor and charm. And her conversation was filled with wit, and intelligence and thought, which, he chuckled, was certainly not expected, particularly in young females of his own class. She was an original. She seemed to think, he mused, that it was proper, even desirable, for a female to have the ease of conversation and scope of knowledge that a man might wish to possess. She had evidently been reared in a most peculiar fashion, by that bluestocking of a governess whose protection she so relied upon. But her beauty banished all thought of straight-lacedness from his mind.

But, he warned himself, any attempt at physical close-
ness or gallantry on his part seemed to put her off, and
caused her to withdraw. Ah well, he sighed, surely that
was a barrier he could overcome. In those first moments, in his study, he had thought wildly of his options. Nothing could have been more fortuitous than her
arriving on his doorstep. It presented a perfect opportunity of settling the score with Torquay. What better
revenge than to steal her right out from under his nose?

But, he had cursed under his breath, there was Maria
Dunstable, newly ensconced in Annabelle's old quarters.
And there was not sufficient time to give her her congé
and vacate the premises. Neither was there time to
secure new apartments for his latest find. No, not safely, not with Torquay sniffing about. Then the thought
had come to him that Fairleigh would do well for all his
purposes. All the fashionable of his acquaintance would
be in town for the height of the season. The countryside
would be deserted. The old mansion would be empty
save for a skeleton staff of servants. There he could
board Miss Berryman. There he could woo her. There
he could win her away from the mad idea of incarcerat-
ing herself amid a pack of brats in the countryside.
There he could win her heart. There, eventually, he
knew, he could bed her. And then, he could return with
her, in triumph, to town, to flaunt his prize beneath
Torquay's envious and defeated eyes. And she would,
he thought, watching the quiet rise and fall of her breast,
probably last longer with him than any of the other
mistresses he had supported. He actually liked her. She
was innocent, as well, that he would swear to. It added
an extra fillip to the game. Yes, he smiled, Torquay, it
is an excellent game.

It was only when the carriage drew up to the front
entrance of the imposing brick manor that he gently
touched her hand, to rouse her. She woke instantly and
stared about her, as if she did not recall her surroundings. But once her eyes alit upon his face, she smiled.
"Are we arrived?" she asked, in a voice thick with
sleep. He restrained himself from bestowing the kiss

upon her flushed face that he felt himself yearning toward.

"Yes," he smiled. "We are here, you are safe."

But a moment later his eyes widened in shock as he saw the door swing open, and recognized Amelia Burden's tall form in the doorway, a pleased and quizzical expression upon her face. "Damn," he groaned to himself, for he had forgotten her plans to rusticate here at Fairleigh with his breeding sister. Forgotten, that is, that they would actually carry out the unusual plan at the very height of the social season. He hesitated; it was too late to whip up the horses and make for another destination. Too late to turn away without an explanation. He turned to Regina.

"My dear," he said, forcing his voice to remain calm, "leave everything to me. If I say a few things that . . . stray a bit from the truth, remember that I wish to keep your presence here a secret from Torquay. Servants do gossip. So bear with me, and only concur with me, and all will be well."

She nodded fearfully, and springing down lightly from the carriage, he offered her his hand. "I shall carry it off," he vowed. "And it might even add to the piquance of the situation to carry it off this way."

"Ah, Amelia." He bowed as he came abreast of her. "Allow me to present the daughter of a dear friend, who must, for the moment, remain a trifle 'incognito,' so I must call her 'Lady Berry.' All will be made clear to you in time, I promise. Unfortunately, her abigail took ill upon the road, so I must prevail upon you to procure her another. Lady Berry, may I present an old and dear friend, Lady Burden? I am sure you two will find much in common."

"Lady Berry," acknowledged Amelia, giving St. John a curious look. "Pray come in, it is freezing outside. You have arrived at a fortunate hour, we were just about to sit down to luncheon."

"Oh, please," Regina answered, with an odd look in her sleep-misted eyes, "no, no formality, please, you must call me only 'Regina.' "

VIII

Regina was unusually silent through most of breakfast. She sat quietly at the table, sipping at her coffee and watching the morning rituals of Fairleigh revolve about her. St. John, as he had insisted that she call him, sat at the head of the table, lightly fencing verbally with Lady Burden. His sister, Lady Mary, seemed to be devoting most of her time to consuming the enormous amount of delicacies upon her plate. "I'm eating for two, you know," she had simpered, and then proceeded to turn her entire attention to the task before her. What seemed to Regina's dazzled eyes to be a battalion of servants, silently glided in and out of the room, bearing in, and then away, platters of ham, kidneys, lamb cutlets, eggs, toasts, and muffins, and pots of coffee and chocolate.

Even in her extreme fatigue the day before, she had not failed to be impressed by the gracious opulence of the house to which the Marquis had brought her. He had explained her exhaustion lightly, and she had been, after only a brief introduction to his constantly smiling sister and her quizzical companion Lady Burden, immediately shown to a comfortable and lavishly furnished room. A tray had been brought to her by a quiet servant girl, and before she had had time to feel regrets or faint alarms about her surroundings, she had been assisted in disrobing and, soon after, fallen deeply asleep.

But this morning, she felt all the reactions to her new situation that she had not had the presence of mind to experience the day before. The household seemed to run on smooth, silent wheels. No one of the servants that she had encountered engaged her in the sort of conversations that the staff of her uncle's house had done. They all, from the parlormaid to the housekeeper, merely seemed to accept her and treat her with a deference that she did not know quite how to handle. Therefore, she had assumed a protective air of calm acceptance which, she was not to know, only served to verify in their minds the fact that however unorthodox her arrival had been, surely she was quite the Lady of Quality.

But she longed to speak to the Marquis alone, if only for a few moments, to discover how quickly he could dispatch the message she had written, immediately upon wakening, to her dear Miss Bekins. The sooner, she felt, that she was out of this house, no matter how comfortable it was, the sooner she could resume her own identity, the happier she would be. For it was not in her nature to act out a part, and the part she was forced into at present, inhibited her every movement.

She glanced over to Lady Burden. She had been listening to the conversation, and much admired the older woman's quiet wry humor, and would dearly have liked to have spoken to her without the stiff affect she now assumed. Lady Burden, she thought, had great presence and an air of deep and abiding calm. Regina sighed a little more deeply than she would have wished to.

"But my dear Regina," Lady Burden said quickly, "we have been neglecting you. . . ." She hesitated, for after all, she wondered, what was a safe subject to bring up? St. John had told her some mare's nest of a tale last night, which his sister had swallowed whole. But Mary was an avid reader of popular romances, and hadn't two wits to rub together in the whole of her dear little frivolous head, Amelia knew, so that any tale St. John had spun, from the most gothic to the most outrageous, would have served to satisfy Mary's never too powerful powers of comprehension.

But really, Amelia had thought, St. John had done it almost too brown. Lady Berry (a name that Amelia, who knew most of the important names of her contemporaries, had never yet encountered) was supposedly a young girl fleeing from a wicked cousin, who was trustee to her fortune, and who was attempting to marry her off to a spotty and dissolute young man before she reached her majority? Her birthday, St. John had explained, which was to be an occasion that would occur within a few months, would free her from her trustee's clutches. St. John, an old friend of her deceased father, he had explained, was only accommodating Lady Berry until he could contact her maternal uncle, who would then succor her until her natal day dawned.

Really, Amelia thought, only years of training had kept her from giggling right to his face. In the first place, the child would certainly not turn twenty-one till at least another winter and summer had come and gone, and in the second, she had ceased to believe in wicked trustees and evil stepmothers the moment she had abandoned her nurses' knee. What sort of a coil has St. John gotten into now, she wondered. And the poor lovely child, it is obvious that she is a lady, if not the "Lady Berry" St. John has dubbed her, and also very apparent that she is deeply unhappy—with both this masquerade and whatever else has actually happened to her.

"No, no, really," Regina said hastily. "It is only that I regret my appetite is not equal to the variety of good things that I see before me. You know, the feeling that you had as a child when there wasn't room for one more morsel, and then the most delicious desert was brought out?" She laughed.

"But my dear," Mary quickly put in, "we haven't any dessert at all this morning. Is it what you've been accustomed to?" she asked hopefully. "For indeed, I haven't heard of it before. But you can, I'm sure, make do with some sweet rolls and jellies. If you wish a dessert, however, I'm sure we can have one for you tomorrow."

"No, dear little dunderhead," St. John laughed. "That isn't what Regina meant at all."

"Well," said Mary, carefully wiping up the last traces of her creamed cutlets with a small piece of bread and popping it into her mouth, "I'm sure it might be a good idea at that. At any rate," she sighed, smiling what she hoped was the proper maternal smile and delicately patting her burgeoning belly, "I must ask you all to excuse me now, for the doctor said I must have my rest after meals." And, pushing away her chair, she rose as majestically as she could and left the room, listing slightly from side to side as she did so.

St. John laughed as she retreated. "My sister is a dear little widgeon, Regina, you must learn to take her exactly as she comes to you."

Regina wasn't sure as to whether she would allow herself the impudence of the smile that had been hovering near her lips, or whether she should rise to the defense of the Marquis's sister. Again, she felt wretched, not knowing exactly what her position here was to be.

"And now," began St. John, rising, "I do have business to attend to today. I'm sure you can find something to do today, Regina, until I return."

"But," Regina cried, rising even as he did, "if I might, that is to say, do you have a few moments, My Lo— Sinjin? There are a few things that I fear cannot wait until you return."

Amelia busied herself by peering down, with great interest, into the dregs of her chocolate. St. John glanced at Amelia quickly, frowned, and then said lightly,

"To be sure. Come into the study, Regina, and I'll see what sort of problems you feel have arisen."

Regina, looking helplessly back at Amelia, swiftly followed St. John's exit. Once seated opposite him in the luxuriously appointed study, she began at once, stammering,

"Your Grace, I simply cannot, cannot do it. I don't know what sort of story you've told Lady Burden and your sister, but I, I am no good at dissembling at all. And I haven't the faintest idea of how to go about as 'Lady Berry,' a young woman of fashion. And as I am to spend time with Lady Burden, please, can there not be a way that you can take her into your confidence? Else, I am sure it would be to both our advantages if you would just . . . send me off to Canterbury on the instant. I know, I just know that I will make a cake of myself. I am not fashioned to be an actress. Oh, and yes, here is the letter to be posted to Miss Bekins." Withdrawing it from her skirts, she went on hurriedly, "Still, if it is a choice between acting a part until I have her answer and going immediately perhaps it would be better not to post it at all, but rather to post me—with haste." And she laughed shakily.

He stared at her for a moment. In the early winter light that shone weakly through windows, she looked very young, very dewy, very vulnerable. Her pallor suits her, he thought, but then anything would. Yes, he sighed, looking into the candid widened green eyes, she would make a blunder. Amelia is too sharp for her. Some compromise with the truth must be made.

"Very well," he said, smiling, "I will speak to Amelia, but we needn't bother with altering one detail of the story with my sister, I assure you. She delights in the tale I have told her, and pays so little mind to reality in any case that it would only confuse her to be told aught else at this point. But Regina, I cannot tell *all*, for my own reasons—you must trust me—to Amelia. Please bear with the few, very few discrepancies I must include in your story. All right?"

She nodded. He took the letter from her outstretched hand, tapped it a few times on his own hand, and then rose and went to the door. He found Amelia pretending to be engrossed in a rapidly cooling muffin.

"Come girl," he laughed. "You have no more interest in consuming that than you have in partaking of plum pudding, at the moment. Come with me, and all your curiosity will be satisfied."

Once inside the study, St. John stood with his back to the nicely crackling fire and began to tell Amelia the true story of Regina's appearance.

"Only remember," he prefaced, "that I take you into our confidence at Regina's insistence. She will be here for a spell, and I believe wishes to be friends with you, only not on a note of deception. But we both trust your unswerving honesty, my dear; it is most important."

Amelia, too interested to take offense at St. John's tone, readily agreed to absolute secrecy. St. John went on with the story, but, Regina noted sadly, although he told mostly the bare facts of the matter, still he left her exact name and patrimony a secret. He would only say that while she was not "Lady Berry," he could not divulge her true name or circumstances. Only that he did indeed owe her family a debt. He also said nothing of her attempt to gain a position teaching with Miss Bekins, rather only that she must remain in hiding from Torquay until "a certain family member" of hers could be located. Ah well, Regina thought, that much at least, I can keep my lips closed about, although why he found it necessary to dissemble about her family and plans for the future, she could not fathom. Still, she thought, half a loaf is indeed better than none.

"How enthralling!" Amelia said, her face animated. "In hiding from Jason! Delightful!"

"You, you know him?" Regina asked, aghast.

"Indeed, who does not?" Amelia answered. "And although, yes, I agree that he is most probably totally evil, and not at all the sort of fellow you should consort with, forgive me, Regina, but I do hold a warm spot in my heart for him."

"Wicked wench," St. John laughed. "Only you would say that, you know. Is there anyone you despise at all on the face of the earth?"

"Oh a great many, Sinjin, really, but not Jason, for you see, he is the only man of my acquaintance to have ever made a totally, neither financially nor matrimonially induced, but gratuitous, indecent proposition to me. It was wonderful for my vanity, although I do feel he offered just to cheer me up. He does have excellent taste in females, really."

St. John flushed. "Really, Amelia, I hardly know whether to credit you or not. If it would cheer you, I should have offered you just such an opportunity myself."

"Ah, but I should know for a certainty that you were offering out of goodwill alone, Sinjin, whereas Jason did it so beautifully that I shall never be sure of what his intentions really were."

St. John bowed with a cynical smile.

"Amelia, my dear, I leave you to care for our little fugitive, my only fears being that you will corrupt her more completely than ever the Black Duke could."

"Never mind, Regina," Amelia smiled. "For I am really a paragon of good taste, and for all my wicked tongue, I blush to say that I have never overstepped the bounds of propriety, no matter how much I may have longed to. Now that I am included in your confidence, I propose to entertain you without a shadow of hesitation. For Mary really does not need me at all, and I confess that until you arrived I was very angry with myself for consenting to accompany her here. It appears that all she requires is a stack of dreadful novels, a handy paper of sweets, and a large bed to doze in, without interruption from either her devoted husband or her assorted offspring. But with you here, we shall have a good time while Sinjin attempts to contact your relative. In fact, this very afternoon I shall take you on some calls to acquaint you with the local gentry."

"Is that wise?" Regina asked fearfully, her eyes involuntarily going to St. John's tall person lounging negligently by the fireplace.

"Of course," he reassured her. "After all, he does not know your direction, and even if he did discover it, even Torquay has the taste not to snatch you from Amelia's keeping. No, he will not presume to steal you away from here. Even he knows that a gentleman does not poach upon another gentleman's property."

Amelia shot him a curious look, but then, gathering herself and composing her features, she extended her hand to Regina.

"Come, Regina, let us leave this tiresome gentleman to his business for now. You must change clothes and accompany me, and I assure you, with the business I am about this afternoon, I shall be very grateful for your company."

St. John watched them leave, a calculating look coming into his eyes. Yes, he thought, it can be done, even under these circumstances. He stood lost in thought for a few moments, and then turned to leave the room. He paused only for a moment while, almost as an afterthought, he carefully fed the letter he was holding to the merrily crackling flames in the fireplace.

The days spun by so pleasantly that Regina had hardly the time or the inclination to wonder why her dear Miss Bekins was so tardy in answering her letter. Amelia was the most delightful of companions. She was witty and well informed, and while she was kindness itself in all her dealings with Regina, and all other members of the household, her tongue was never stinting in her candid, sometimes too perceptive comments about other members of the society in which she moved. She had been at first amazed, then genuinely delighted at the scope of Regina's knowledge which she had gleaned from books, but appalled at the depth of her lack of experience in society. She had quickly designated herself both friend and tutor to the younger girl. And Regina felt a real warmth and affection for her poised and immaculate new friend.

She still held the Marquis in great awe. And try as she might, she could not bring herself to act naturally in his presence. His cool good looks intimidated her, his amused and benignly tolerant attitude toward her made her feel like a veritable bumpkin, and his unexpected friendship still puzzled her. Yet she enjoyed their frequent *tête-à-têtes*, their customary strolls about the grounds when the weather was clement, and their quietly stimulating evenings, when the three would sit downstairs and play cards, or chess, or group around the piano and sing. Lady Mary, Regina soon found, partook of none of these activities, contenting herself with infrequent visits downstairs when any of the local gentry came to call, preferring to spend most of her time luxuriating in her increasingly evident state, at ease in her rooms, surrounded by sweet meats and novels.

In all, Regina would have been pleased with her sojourn at Fairleigh if it weren't for three nagging details that assailed her nightly, when at last she was alone in her room. The first was, of course, her governess's lack of response to her letter; the second was her never repressed sense of obligation toward the Marquis for his solicitousness and his protection; and the third was the observation that she had first doubted, and then later become more and more convinced of. For now she was sure of it—each time St. John came close to her, each time he allowed his lips to brush her hair whilst he whispered some strategy in cards at her, each time he asked her to accompany him for a short walk, she could feel Lady Amelia's reaction.

She had quickly noted her new friend's eyes constantly, if surreptitiously, tracked his movements in whatever room they were in. She could sense the way her companion's spirits would rise when he joined them, she could almost feel, with the ends of her skin, how Amelia's interest rose and fell according to his entrances and exits. No, she no longer had any doubt about Lady Burden's true feelings, nor, sadly enough, about St. John's lack of either interest in or understanding of them. But she liked her new friend too dearly to ever indicate that she had discovered what, she was sure, was supposedly a secret known only to Amelia's own heart.

For herself, no matter how solicitous or handsome the Marquis appeared to her admittedly inexperienced eye, she still felt a certain constraint with him, a lingering shyness in her manner. Although they talked together long into the nights, and played cards, and took long walks out about the grounds, she still considered him somewhat withdrawn; that formidable dignity she had at first noted in his manner was still there.

This evening, they sat in the downstairs study, Regina's favorite room, and played cards. Regina was a wretched player—St. John always laughed and told her she would never win until she learned to cover her delight when she was dealt a fair hand—so tonight, she watched as Amelia and St. John matched wits at the game.

"I shall never understand," Regina sighed as the game came to an end.

"What shall you never understand, my dear?" St. John laughed, as he folded up his hand and signaled Amelia's victory. "What possible subject do you find beyond your comprehension?"

"Your friends," Regina blurted, then, coloring, tried to amend her rash statement. "That is to say, the manners prevailing among them, that is. . . ."

"What Regina is struggling with," Amelia put in with

amusement, "is the shock of her meeting the Three
Graces this morning."

St. John threw back his head and laughed, with genuine amusement. "Did she meet them today? Oh, that is
a scene I would have given a pretty penny to see. Our
resident bluestocking coming up against the Squire's
fair litter."

Regina blushed at the laughter the other two gave
way to. It was true, however, that the morning had
brought about her introduction to the three daughters
of the local squire. They were pretty enough, in their
fashion, she supposed, to have been given the nickname
in the locality of "the Three Graces." But the hours that
she had spent in their company had been totally unnerv-
ing for her, it was as if she had been forced to spend the
morning in the company of Hottentots, so complete was
the lack of understanding between them.

The oldest of the girls was engaged to a minor baron-
et, much to her family's glee; the middle girl was due to
be presented this season, when an attack of measles in
the household had curtailed her plans; and the youngest
was looking forward to her own season in a year's time.
They had arrived, in a veritable snowstorm of ribboned
bonnets and lace and what Amelia had dubbed "fashionable folderols," by pony cart, accompanied by their silent, timid governess.

And, after being introduced to Regina, they had proceeded to fill the morning with an avalanche of small
talk. They could, to Regina's dumbstruck discovery,
talk for hours on end about bonnets, skirt lengths, and
slippers. They did, to Regina's slow and vaguely horrified comprehension, sweetly and thoroughly demolish
the reputation and pretensions of every female of their
aquaintance, up to and including each other's. For Miss
Betty was heard to softly mention that her sister's
affianced was so delighted with the wedding arrangements that he vowed he had put on two stone just from
sheer happiness. Miss Lottie had countered sweetly that
Miss Betty was so overjoyed herself at the thought of
the forthcoming event, that she had broken out in spots in
anticipation of her sister's forthcoming nuptuals. And

while Miss Betty's graceful hands hastily fluttered up to her face to verify her smooth complexion, Miss Kitty had silenced both her sisters by observing, with a charming lisp, that she had indeed noticed how haggard both her elders had become with the excitement of having measles in the household. "I vow," she had sweetly said, "that they both have lotht their lookth over the thircumthtanthes."

For Regina, the morning had been both educational and frightening. It accentuated the gap between herself and these young creatures of fashion. For while Amelia seemed quite able to keep up her end of the conversation, Regina had sat close-mouthed, unable to think of a blighting comment on one of their acquaintances, or a trenchant observation about the new fashions, either of which, she was sure, was the only acceptable contribution she could have made to the conversation. She had no way of knowing that her glowing good looks struck a terrible animosity in the hearts of the Three Graces, mitigated only by their desire to learn more about this mysterious visitor to Fairleigh. Already the most bizarre rumors as to her identity had begun to circulate in the vicinity. She had been guessed to be everything from an émigré countess from across the channel, to being that wicked St. John's new mistress.

When the three young ladies had become aware of the time that had passed, fruitlessly, for their twofold ambitions of discovering more about Lady Berry, or catching a glimpse of the headily handsome and eligible Master of the Household, they had taken their leave. But not before accomplishing the purported main reason for their visit.

"Now that all ith well in our houth," Miss Kitty had announced, "you mutht come to the ball that Father ith giving. It is thuppothed to mend our hearth for our abthenth from town thith theathon. And jutht everyone will be there. Even my thiththerth beau."

"You absolutely must come," the other two had insisted.

"Even though it may seem provincial to you," Miss

Betty had said to Regina, "it shall be quite the affair of the year for us."

St. John sat laughing at Amelia's wicked descriptions of the visit and her uncanny imitation of Miss Kitty's affected lisp, but his face became immobile when she mentioned the invitation to the ball.

"So you see, Sinjin," Amelia went on blithely, "we are to have a chance to show Regina some real country sport, after all, for I am sure she has never seen the likes of the ball that Squire Hadley is going to give."

"I have never attended a ball," Regina said hastily, noting St. John's suddenly cold demeanor, "for . . . there were not many of them in our locality," she finished lamely. "And I do think it would be wiser if I did not go, after all, Amelia."

"Regina is right," St. John said coldly, cutting across Amelia's protestations. "She would feel out of place there, and it would be better if she did not attend."

"Stuff!" cried Amelia beligerantly. "Sinjin, surely you and I could make her feel at ease, and it would be an opportunity she should not miss."

"Oh no," Regina said hastily. "For one thing, I haven't a ball gown, and for another . . . I don't wish to shock you, Amelia, but I cannot dance. Not one step. I," she went on, noting the horrified look on Amelia's face, "well, that is to say, neither my governess nor my father seemed to ever think that was important."

"Sinjin," Amelia protested, "surely you can practice with Regina. Within a day, I'm sure you can teach her enough to account herself creditably at the ball. And I can surely lend her a ball gown."

"No," St. John said with a guarded look upon his face. "Not that it wouldn't be a pleasure, Regina, but you seem to forget that Regina is, in effect, in hiding here. It would not do for her to attend a large ball. Surely her presence would be remarked upon, and just as surely, it would bring Torquay down upon us."

"But Sinjin," Amelia went on, puzzled, "you yourself said that even he would not 'dare to poach upon another gentleman's property.'"

"No," he said with suppressed anger, "but let it be,

Amelia. There is no reason to stir up the calm we have found here. There is no reason why some paltry local ball should precipitate events that might be disturbing to Regina. At any rate, she will soon be gone from here," he concluded mysteriously.

Amelia let the subject drop, but it was clear that she was displeased with the turn of events, and shortly after, suppressing what were surely huge mock yawns, she took herself off to bed.

Regina rose to follow, but St. John stayed her with a light touch upon her arm. He stood before her, an unreadable expression in his smoky eyes, and said finally, flicking back a stray wisp of her hair with his forefinger, "Understand, Regina, that I do what is best for you."

"About the ball? Oh, but that makes no difference to me at all, surely you must know that," Regina protested, a little nervous at the Marquis's closer proximity and closer scrutiny. "But what you said later . . . is it true? Have you received any answer to my letter? Is there any word from Miss Bekins? For although it has been pleasant here, I confess I yearn to be on my way to my new position . . . before I become too unused to working, before I begin to actually think myself 'Lady Berry.' "

He smiled. This was a theme she constantly enlarged upon in his presence, her desire to be "her own woman," to be less beholden to him and his "charity," as she termed it. He looked down at her, and again was drawn to the clear green eyes, again felt the desire to kiss that small indentation to the left of her lips, again controlled himself against the impulse to hold her to himself and run his hands along the surprisingly ample curves that shaped the slender body. But as he took a step nearer, he could feel her corresponding retreat.

"Not exactly," he sighed. "But soon, very soon, I have the feeling, Regina, you will be away from here, you will be safe and taken care of, and so pleased with your new life, that you will not regret in the least the lack of your attendance at some trumpery local ball."

She looked at him in some doubt, for how could he be so sure of something she had not a hint of happening?

"Do you mean," she asked quietly, "that you have some idea of a different position suitable for me if I do not hear from Miss Bekins?"

"Yes," he said, his gray eyes darkening. "Oh yes, a much more suitable position . . . and soon, I think."

"Then I am again very grateful to you, Sinjin," she said, and aware again of the strange new tension in his position, she sketched a curtsy and withdrew.

"Soon," he said to the empty room. "Yes, very soon."

For the time was ripening, he thought. He sat back in a chair and studied the fire. Soon, he would achieve a twofold aim. He would have her under his very real protection, and have Torquay in an unenviable position.

Torquay. He let his thoughts stray to the irritating subject. How very often that hoarse sweet voice had mocked him. How very often he had recoiled when he had heard their names coupled. It was true that he pursued much the same game as the Duke, but something in him rebelled at being dubbed the successor to the title of most debauched nobleman in town. And yet, the time he had gone around to Madame Sylvestre's establishment when he was in his cups and had found Torquay there, in a gilded doorway, with a bright-eyed, salaciously smiling slender young female at his right side and an overblown garishly painted ageing trollop snuggled protectively on his left side—the Duke's flushed face and glittering eye left no doubt as to his plans for the evening's entertainment, and when St. John had allowed a faint deogatory smirk to touch his lips, Torquay had turned and whispered in that obscenely honeyed voice, "What? Distaste, Sinjin? But wait a few years, my dear boy, and you will find yourself pursuing the same sport. Unless you care to join me now? I'm sure Aggie," and here he hugged the old bawd, "has room in her heart for both of us."

And St. John thought of his involuntary shudder as he turned away without a word.

He thought of the many times he had professed interest in a new female only to find that days later, she had become the property of the Duke. He remembered how often Torquay had sidled up to him when he was at the height of enjoyment at some of the more disreputable parties and had stripped him of all pleasure by a well-placed word, by an accented innuendo. He winced at the way the Duke, almost intuitively, always knew just how to disconcert him at any occasion. He thought of the immense fortune the Duke controlled and could not seem to dissipate. In all, he thought, if he were to be honest, he both envied and feared the man. Envied his possessions and the skill with which he led his dissolute life. For with all his excesses, he still had entree into all but the most conservative of fashionable circles. But he feared the reputation the Duke held, and the slow, sure way it was beginning to settle upon his own shoulders.

Damn the man, St. John thought. And I shall. For this is one time he has made a wager he shall lose. And I shall win.

IX

The clouds were scudding by overhead, but with no real mean intent, so Regina, having dressed warmly, ventured to take a long walk alone across the wide and various grounds of Fairleigh. She had felt an overwhelming need to be by herself, to walk until her feet numbed, to think, and to finally plan again her own future.

For no, it would not do, she thought, shaking her head as the skirts of her long coat brushed against the long grasses on the meadow track she paced, for her to let herself drift any longer. Things were becoming uncomfortable at the house, and there was a great deal to think about. Amelia was still angry this morning at St. John's command that Regina was not to attend the ball, and that there was to be no further discussion of the idea. Amelia had tried to cajole Regina into reasoning with the Marquis and impressing upon him what a snub it would be to the Squire if she did not attend, and further, that her noncompliance with the invitation would

surely spike more gossip about the mysterious lady at
Fairleigh than ever her attendance would. But Regina had
remained adamant. After all, she reasoned, she was here
only on St. John's charity, which was a thing that Amelia
did not know, and it would not do for her to impose.

But impose she had, she sighed, for here she had
already caused a breach between Lady Amelia and the
Marquis. This morning, at breakfast, they had hardly
spoken to each other, and the conversation, such as it
was, was carried solely by Lady Mary's meanderings
about "breakfasts she had known."

And then there was St. John's veiled comments about
her own future. Could it be that he had discovered that
Miss Bekins was indeed in bad financial straits and
could not employ her? Was he even now disturbing
himself as to what sort of position he could find her in
its place? And honestly, she mused, his attitude lately,
his increasingly familiar attitude, the easy endearments
that slipped from his lips, the unavoidable admiring
glances she had intercepted, these might all be part of
the affect of any eligible nobleman, but they disturbed
her and made her feel unsure of herself. For while she
liked him well enough, and trusted him completely, she
knew very well that there was no point in entertaining
any warmer thoughts about his intentions. For when all
was said and done . . . he was a titled nobleman of
great wealth. She was an impecunious commoner, with
no standing in any social world that she had yet encountered. And he was beloved to Amelia. While she was, in
truth, only an imposter, landed on him by her uncle.
No, she insisted to herself, it was time she moved on.
But to where?

She was brooding on possibilities she might consider,
ways in which she could win free without insulting his
honor or hospitality, when she became aware of the fact
that she was no longer alone in the wintry meadow. She
looked up from the path she had been staring down at
as she walked and saw a figure ahead of her, leaning
negligently against a half fallen stile.

Oddly enough, her first thought was not one of fear,
or horror, or panic, but rather one of amused annoy-

ance. Must he always, the thought came unbidden, be capable of such dramatic appearances? For as if the frozen day itself were in league with him, at the moment she discovered him, a weak ray of sunshine broke through and illuminated him, in all his casual splendor, making an unlikely halo around the fair wind-touseled hair.

He leaned back, at ease, clad in dun-colored skin-tight buckskins, a scarf knotted carelessly about his neck, his dark gold coat accenting the fair complexion, his mobile lips drawn back to reveal even white teeth, and his lucent blue eyes now lit with real enjoyment.

"What?" he said in his distinctive whisper, "the maiden spies the dragon and she does not give a piercing shriek? Or take to her heels? Or swoon, with considerable grace, to the floor? Come, Regina, you disappoint me. Rather than losing your head with terror, you are looking absurdly put out. Petulant, I might say. But the look suits you. As indeed, what does not? You have grown, if possible, even fairer, here in the wilds of the countryside. The winds have not been unkind to you. Your nose does not show a red tip, your eyes do not water—what an extraordinary beauty it is that even the cold enhances. This inclement weather has only brought a rosy glow to your alabaster cheek, only shined your eyes till they sparkle like the sea on a turbulent day."

She walked up to him, after that first moment of surprise, and said, almost before she was aware of it herself, "Can you not speak straight out? Must everything be couched in that sinister poetry you affect?"

He seemed, for one second, taken aback, and then he let out a genuine laugh, oddly pure in contrast to his hoarse voice. His eyes lit up to the shade of a summer's day.

"Oh, you are not afraid of me any more! Here's a new turn. You are so cosseted, so protected, so sure of yourself, that at last you are no longer afraid of me." His eyes grew grave and he added, "But you should be, Regina, indeed you should be."

She recognized that what he had said was true; no, she did not fear him here, and now. It was as if she had in some small, hidden part of herself been waiting for him to reappear. The thought of him had so often alternately both chilled and warmed her during the nights when she could not sleep, turning her stomach to ice but also changing her heartbeats to drumbeats. Somewhere here, in the reality of the dappled light of a cold country day, in a meadow, so close to her friends and protectors, she no longer feared him at all. Rather, she looked forward to their encounter.

"No, you are right. I don't fear you here. For what can you do to me here?"

He laughed luxuriously.

"Oh my dear," he said, "countless things, I assure you. I could signal to my henchman, who might be hiding in the brush, and toss you into my carriage, which might be secreted down the lane. For I have no honor, or very little, and I do not care for Sinjin's opinion at all, and whatever Sinjin might say about me would quickly be discounted in the circles we two are best known in. Or," he went on, after a quick glance under his long lashes at her face, "I might become impatient and toss you to the ground right here, and have my way with you. Only, you are right, it would be very cold, and very uncomfortable, and not at all in my usual style or the way I plan to end the matter. Still, no one would be concerned with your fate at all, 'Lady Berry,' once it became known that 'Lady Berry' is not quite the titled lady it has been hinted she is. In fact," he mused, "yours is a very false position, and it has given you a false sense of security. For I'm sure even Lady Burden and His Lordship's sister would be most put out if they discovered they had been entertaining a fraud—a common chit thrown out of her own family home for her indiscrete carryings-on with a hardened rake. Oh, I would weather it, it would be only, after all, another black mark on a long list. And Sinjin would be winked at, as he and I are cut from the same cloth. But the ladies . . . ah, I think they would be devastated, betrayed, and uncommonly angry at the little cheat they had taken to their bosoms. For they would not be angry at Sinjin, love, his sister dotes upon him, and

Amelia, well . . . she is not as unaffected by His Lordship as she would like to be thought to be. No, the onus would all be upon you, my love." And, seeing her arrested expression, he went on, "No, it is a cruel world, Regina, you ought to have thought of that yourself. You ought not to have been cozened into a false sense of security."

She stood silent, watching the sun play upon his hair.

"Yet, in a sense," he said softly, "but only in a sense, you are right. Here, and now, you have no real reason to be afraid of me. I did, after all, make a pact with you, and the game is not yet played out, although it draws to a close. But here, and now, yes, you are safe. But as for tomorrow?" He shrugged, and an ugly expression crossed his face. "And tomorrow might come very quickly, love. For although I know you are not yet Sinjin's mistress, he is, after all, living too close to his sister and her good friend at the moment. I wonder at how soon you two plan on consummating the event? You will not, you know."

But at this point a sense of such outrage gripped Regina that she scarcely saw the harsh look that had flitted across the usually pleasant face before her. A sense of outrage at her present situation, a sense of fury at the suggestions he was making, a sense of the preposterousness of the present confrontation. That this seemingly angelic man lounging against the stile before her should have forced her into the straits she found herself in, magnified by the humane and polite treatment she had received these past weeks, overwhelmed her sense of proportion. She spoke in fury, she railed against him:

"No! No, all you say is dirtied by your own false perceptions of the world around you. You are to be pitied, My Lord Duke, in that you see your world through eyes that cannot discern good from bad, through a philosophy that has nothing to do with the way real people live their real lives. You are like a man mad for a taste of wine. He does not see the scenery around him, he does not see the people going about their lives, he sees only opportunities to drink, his eye picks out only those

places, those establishments, those people, who can provide him with his need. You do not see with any clarity
at all, you are so drunk with the need for debauching,
for degradation of yourself and others."

"No," she went on, shaking her head, "I do not think
Lady Burden would despise me. No, I know Lady Mary
would not. And I don't think Sinjin would allow you to
merely . . . come along and destroy my life. I know he
would not. He and I . . . we have no plans for any such
arrangement that you speak of. I applied to him for help
because my late uncle instructed me to, should I ever
need help. And with no self-serving thought, he has
assisted me. You are certainly mad. And no," she said,
holding up her head, "no, I do not fear you so much as I
pity you from the bottom of my heart."

"You may well be right to," he mused, watching her
closely, "I do not argue that. But it is 'Sinjin' now, is it?
Ah well, he is more clever than I thought. So George
Berryman was incautious enough to mention the great
Marquis to you——"

"You knew my uncle?" Regina gasped.

"Yes, of course," smiled the Duke. "Who among us
who ventured into business did not? Only I did not deal
exclusively with him, as some others did. An honest
man, your uncle, according to his lights, that is, for
whoever deals overmuch in business cannot afford to be
too honest. As your father soon found out. Ah yes, I
know all about you, Regina Analise. I do not wager on
dark horses. I make it my business to know all the odds
in whatever game I choose to play."

"Why, for once, without dissimulation, why? Will you
tell me why you choose to play this particular game?"
Regina demanded, still raging at the slight figure before
her. Seeing his closed expression, she softened her voice
and almost pleaded with him, "Since there is so much
that you know about me, can you tell me something
about yourself? Some true thing?" she asked, watching
him, realizing that she knew nothing of the actual man
that hid beneath the blandly smiling, smooth exterior he
presented.

"Some true thing?" He laughed. "Oh my dear, there is no true thing about me at all. But come, sit here beside me and I will tell you all you wish to know about me. There has never breathed a man who would not be pleased to tell all about himself, ad nauseum, to a young and beautiful woman who looks at him as you now look at me. Come and sit with me, Regina love, and I will tell you stories about myself, Oh I will sing you songs of me till darkness falls, and beyond, if that is what you wish. We will talk as old friends, or as new friends, for however long you like. But remember, I am most certainly mad. And placating me, and talking with me, and trying to understand me, will not alter that. I will still keep you to our game. I will still oversee you to make sure you keep to all the rules. But yes," and he grinned, the expression, the sunlight, the wind-touseled hair making him seem suddenly younger, less threatening, more human than she had ever envisioned him.

She knew then as he waited, smiling, for her answer to his outstretched hand, that she could not turn and walk away from him, as every instinct cautioned her to. She could not, as a proper lady should, run trembling back to the warm security of Fairleigh. She must, she felt, confront him. Meet with him, so that she could reason with him, perhaps even appeal to him. Perhaps she could beguile him into betrayal of his true motives. For she could still not accept that he did all he did out of sheer perverse amusement. Certainly she could, she thought, know him. And all that she had been raised to believe told her that no creature she could know, could still remain an enemy to her. It was against all the sweet logic that Miss Bekins and her father had inculcated her with. Yes, she decided, she would speak with him.

She accepted his assistance, and perched herself up upon the stile beside him. And with the chill wind whipping around them, they talked.

Afterward, she could never reconstruct the conversation of that strange afternoon. They had stayed, talking, no she ammended, gossiping like two old cronies, while the sun sank slowly over the horizon. She had asked him questions, he had answered with wit and style. But although he spoke of himself, she could not learn anything about his motivations. He told her about his education, his travels. He regaled her with stories about the society he traveled in, till tears stood in her eyes and she gasped with laughter. He entertained her with anecdotes, he charmed her with rumors, he quoted poetry, and when she capped his verse with the next line, he capped her quotation once again. He showed her a glittering treasurehouse of a mind, but he showed her not one glimpse of the shadows within.

Every so often the oddity of the situation, the strangeness of their meeting was borne in upon her, and almost as if he could read her mind, he would lure her away from her thoughts with whimsy or humor. Ah, she thought, recovering from a wave of laughter he had submerged her in, how likeable he is! But then, suddenly, as if a cloud had passed over his mind as it had over the weakening sun, he spoke slowly to her, "You see then, Regina, that it will not be so terrible, after all, your fate to be with me."

She opened her eyes as if awakening from a dream, and looked at him. "No," she said, "this is so absurd, Your Grace, indeed you know it is. For we have spent the afternoon like friends. We have shared our thoughts, you cannot still be . . . serious about this ridiculous wager."

"Oh, but I am," he said seriously. "You see, you do not know me after all. How well you look in sunlight, Regina. Not many of my female acquaintances could say the same, but it suits you well, almost as well as candlelight. No," he said, taking his hand and turning her chin up, "perhaps even more than candlelight."

She pulled herself away from him and, trying to keep up a light note, said, "But it suits you too."

"Only because this afternoon is aware of the signal honor I have given it. I do not go abroad too much by day, see how the sun has tried so valiantly to flatter me, to convince me of its good offices? If it were better aquainted with me, if it knew it had my favor constantly, it would turn and slink behind a cloud. It is only those we hope to win that we put ourselves out for; those we have already added to our list of conquests, we can afford to ignore. When favor is won, it is foolish to go on courting, is it not? But shine as it will, it knows full well that this is not my time of day, I still prefer to be burnt by its sister moon, and bask in her cold silvery rays for my health's sake."

"Yes, surely," Regina said, "once we have won a friend, we do not go on 'courting' his friendship, because we know ourselves secure in it. Still, once we have a friend, we do not ignore him, rather we are at ease. There is comfort in not having always to be on one's best behavior."

"What lovely friends you must have, my dear," he said. "Perhaps if I too were poor and defenseless, and beautiful, I would have such friends. But then, I have found that it is very easy to befriend someone who has less than I. Someone who looks to me for favors. They are so easy to please. They are so willing to accommodate. They are so eager for friendship."

She recoiled from him. "No," she denied, "that is not friendship, that is patronage."

"Ah," he said, "you've put your little white finger on it. For I have found that when a man has wealth, influence, and position, he is hard put to tell the difference between friendship and patronage." He spread his hands in a gesture of dismay. "How is a man to know what is asked in friendship, and what is requested as patronage?"

"Friendship," Regina said, feeling foolishly like a governess explaining a moral lesson to a stubborn small charge, "is freely given, without expectation of recompense, of anything—except for the hopes of a return friendship."

"Then I think," he smiled, "that on the whole I prefer patronage. At least I can well afford that. It costs me really very little, whereas any freely given trust and concern would well bankrupt the little resources I have of those remarkable feelings. That could well cost me more than I care to lose. Don't look so outraged, my love, you will find that there are a great many men like me in this world. A great many who prefer those sorts

of well-defined relationships, such as employer and employee, debtor and benefactor, king and subject. For
example, my lovely little headmistress, do you honestly
think Sinjin offers you free use of his house, his resources, and, I am sure, his heart out of friendship?"

"No," she admitted, for even she could not claim to be
the Marquis's friend. "But," she said, "he offers me
comforts—not out of patronage, either, rather out of a
debt of honor to my family."

"Oh, Regina," sighed the Duke, his face strangely
gentle in the fading light, "you are such fool."

"You know," he said, more briskly, "that I will eventually hurt you, perhaps only a little physically, but I
certainly will hurt your pride, your sense of decency,
your image of yourself. I will show you a Regina Analise
that you never dreamed existed. I, likely, by the time I
am done, will have you despising yourself, as much as,
or more than you will come to despise me. For I will
show you what a traitorous body you are locked into. I
will pit the demands of that body against all the high
reasonings of that well-furnished mind. And I will win.
But with all that I will do," he went on, ignoring the
horror that had come into her eyes, "I will not break
your heart. No. Never that. For I will never ask you for
that. That I will leave to your own self. But you are too
generous with that poor organ, Regina. You are almost
promiscuous with it. And never doubt, it will be broken.
For you will give it where you should not. Take care
with it, Regina. I will have you, no matter what. But I
should rather have you intact, in all ways. I should
prefer it. But you are such a little fool."

She stood and shook out her skirts, tears welling in
her eyes. She did not understand him. She had spent
the whole of the afternoon with him, she had thought
she had come to some easy ground of acquaintance with
him, and now that evening had almost fallen, the slight,
elegant man beside her was as much of a stranger, as
much of a threat, as ever. She would not speak; she only
turned to return to the house.

He stayed her with one arm; the strength of it held
her still, she neither struggled after his first touch, nor

moved a pace to escape. He pulled her to him so that
they stood close enough to be mistaken for one figure in
the empty meadow. She felt the warmth and strength of
him held in check, and irrationally, was content to stand
there for those moments, so close as to almost touch, so
far as to only stare into each other's eyes. What she saw
flaring in his, and what she suddenly did not wish him
to discover in hers, forced her to drop her gaze to her
shoetops. Only then he stirred, and recollected himself,
and released her, only holding her lightly with a touch
upon her hand.

"I will see you at the Squire's ball," he said, looking
down into her lowered eyes.

"No," she said, "I shall not go."

"Oh, don't be foolish," he said. "Once again, we will
meet on neutral ground there. Even I do not seduce
women at a country squire's ball. Especially not when
mine host, the Squire himself, has plans for me becoming his son-in-law. You must come to see at least how
many 'friends' I do have. How well received I am in
society."

"The Marquis has said that I must not," she said,
childishly even to her own ears.

"Why not?" he asked.

"So that you would not discover me," she answered.

"Ah, but I have, so now you may come."

"I cannot dance," she said, despising herself for her
weak answer. "I have not the right gowns."

"All that is nothing," he laughed. "Surely you have
more spirit that that, Regina. You will not cower beneath the bed, while I caper at the ball?"

"No," she cried, her eyes flashing. "No, I shall be
there. But I swear, it is the last you will see of me. For
after that, I will be gone. Gone on to decide my own
future. As you stipulated. And then you can find some
other poor creature to torment for your pleasure. But
not me, I swear it." And she tore herself from him and
ran back to the comforting lights that began to appear
in the windows of house beyond them. She felt anger at
herself for her undignified haste to be away from him,
and for her complete capitulation in the matter of the

ball. Surely he must be laughing now, she thought dis-
gustedly, at the success at which he had manipulated
her response."

But the Duke of Torquay, leaning back against the
stile where she had left him, was not laughing. The look
in his wide blue eyes was rather the look of a dreamer,
but his tightly clenched fists surely did not signify a
pleasant dream.

"But where have you been?" Amelia greeted her.
"Sinjin and I were becoming worried. We thought you
were in your room, but as the darkness came we. . . ."

"We almost organized a search," Sinjin said, coming
toward her and taking her hands in his. "But you're
frozen! What were you doing out so late?" he demanded, almost in the tones of an angry father, Regina
thought.

"I was talking with the Duke of Torquay," Regina
said, with a shadow of a smile.

When they had bundled her off to the study and bade
Lady Mary to take dinner without them, both Amelia
and St. John turned their full attention to Regina. She
sat huddled in a large chair by the fire, fortified by St.
John's perennial cure for the chill, a glass of brandy,
feeling very much like a truant schoolgirl. Amelia's face
showed worry and concern, but St. John, standing by
the fire, seemed to her to be gripped by some inner
tension, so abrupt and cold was his manner.

"No," she explained again, "no, I did not think to run
back to you. Because," she said, appealing to St. John's
grim countenance, "I thought, I really thought, that if I
could speak with him . . . reason with him, I could
solve the whole of it."

"And did you?" St. John asked coldly.

"No," she sighed sadly. "For all we talked, for all I
said, for all he heard . . . he is unchanged. I cannot
understand". . . . She trailed off.

"Of course you cannot, that is the whole point. You
have no experience with such a creature," St. John said.
"And you were a fool to try to reason with him."

"That is much the same as he said," Regina murmured softly.

Amelia spoke. "And how did you leave it with him, Regina? Did he threaten you? Did he make any . . . advances?"

"We only spoke. And he said that he was looking forward to seeing me at the ball. When I told him I was not going, he taunted me for my cowardice. I'm afraid I lost my temper. I told him that I was not afraid, that I was going."

St. John made a muffled exclamation and Regina said hurriedly, "But you needn't worry about that. For I have thought the whole thing out, and I, of course, shall not go. For I shall not be here at all. It is time, it is past time," she said imploringly to St. John, "that I was gone from here. I have already stayed too long. This flight of mine has gone on too long."

"Yes," St. John agreed.

"Sinjin!" cried Amelia in shock. "How can you say so? How can you countenance Regina's leaving us when you have not yet heard from her relatives? It would be like casting her to the wolves."

"I said nothing about her leaving," he said. "She shall stay, and stay with the full accordance of all of us. But she shall no longer hide. No more futile flight. You will come with us, Regina, to the Squire's ball. You will come in full sight of Torquay, and he will be made to see that he cannot frighten you. And that he cannot have you."

But seeing Amelia's quick look toward him, he smiled. "Have you, that is to say, in any construction of the word."

"I don't want to go," Regina said stubbornly. "I don't desire to go. I don't wish to go. I only want to leave here."

"You are understandably overwrought," St. John said. "There is only one thing. For other reasons," he explained to Amelia, not looking at her, "it would be better if she remains . . . incognito. If she remains silent as to her visit here."

Amelia gave him a long look and rose from her chair.

"Of course," she said stiffly. "But now, perhaps these dramatics have taken away your appetites, but I assure you, they have only whetted mine. I will join Mary at dinner."

St. John stood looking into the outer distance until Regina said quietly, "I really do not want to go to this affair, you know. And I really don't understand why you insist on my staying here. And I don't understand why I am still to play the role of 'Lady Berry.' "

St. John came over to her and raised her from her chair.

"I know you do not, little one," he said caressingly, his expression softening. "But do you not trust me now? Did your uncle not give you to my care? Do you doubt me now? Have I ever done any wrong toward you?"

"No, to all those ungrateful things," Regina said, feeling ill at ease in his light grasp. "But I grow weary of this all, I am not fashioned for such . . . as Amelia put it, 'dramatics.' "

"No," he said, "you are not. And you will not have to continue in them for much longer. There is a new development, Regina. But no, now is not the time to speak of it." He traced a light caress on her cheek with his hand, and sighed. "No, not now. Now we must have dinner. Now we must make friends again. Now you must trust me. Do you, Regina?" he asked, looking deep into her puzzled eyes.

"Of course," she said. "I would not be here otherwise. It is as if you were . . . family to me now."

"But not father, I hope," he laughed, "nor brother. Preferably something at the same time much closer, and much farther." And with a laugh, he offered her his arm, and said, with mock solemnity, "To dinner then, Lady Berry."

X

"Make a curtsy to your father now, My Lady, and greet
him warmly, for he has come a long way just to see
you," the governess commanded, and obediently the
little sallow girl dipped and swayed, and executed a
neat little mockery of a curtsy. Only there is no mockery in her eyes, her father thought, with a curiously
unreasonable pang of discomfort somewhere in the re-
gion of his chest as he gravely regarded those clear blue
eyes, so uncannily like his, yet so completely alien to
his. For they gazed at him bereft of expression, vacant
and cold.

Not an auspicious meeting, he thought wryly, wondering again whatever had possessed him, why in the
world he had obeyed that vagrant impulse, as unnatural
and beguiling as a breath of spring air in his December
room; that maddening impulse to be quit of the Squire's
vast company. And to quit that admittedly deadening
company for a return to his ancestral home, for a return, as it were, to the scene of his capital crime in
begetting this unloved, and unlovingly begotten child.
Age, he reasoned sardonically, encroaching age, it must
have been. Only that would account for this absurd urge
to finally see what I have left this earth heir to, to see
what I have given my name and fortune to. And, he
admitted, a not unreasonable urge to free himself from
the saccharine entanglements the Squire's unlovely
daughters seemed to be inviting him to.

The ball being a fortnight away, the Squire and his
dependents had regretfully let him go from their guest
quarters, blaming the pre-gala commotion in the household for his unexpected departure and promising themselves a dead set at him the night of the ball.

"Oh, the carpenters make such a racket, I do apologize, Your Grace," the Squire's wife had lamented. "But,

indeed, we must have lovely lacy indoor trellises around the ballroom to bedeck with lovely blossoms for the illusion of spring, you know?"

"The housemaids' deuced commotion, all that bustling about, and scraping and polishing, can't blame you for quitting us, sets a fellow's teeth on edge, all that smell of beeswax and soap. But you know how women are about such folderol," the Squire had commiserated heartily.

But they had been more than anxious about his departure, even though he had assured them of his return the weekend of the ball. They had been desolate at his leaving.

Amazing, he had thought, as the Three Graces waved him farewell with real tears in their eyes, amazing how acceptable I still manage to be. Not in the highest circles, of course, but then the Squire's household is far from those exalted reaches. But still, he had wondered in real bafflement, they have heard all the tales of my adventures in that demimonde which is as unreal to them as their little lives are to me, and yet, they positively yearn for me to bestow my tainted name upon one of them. "Come away from the Dungheap for a moment, My Lord Duke," they call, "and join us in wedded bliss. But be sure to bring your fortune with you, and wipe your feet please, before you walk us down the aisle." A great deal more than my feet must be wiped clean, my dears, he had countered to the silent enticements, a great deal more; my entire past, I do believe, my dears.

And here, he thought with heavy irony, is the object I rode all the heavy miles for, spurred by that unreasonable whim. Here is a little squashed and sallow girl child, who, by the look of her, has never entertained a fancy, much less a whim. She has much the look of her mother, poor thing, the Duke thought, too much the look of her mother. But then he had seen the eyes, and noted that her complexion was as white as his, and even though black curls trembled about her forehead and the nose had the same foolish tendency to point upward as her mother's had, still there was none of the light or inconsequential in her aspect or her demeanor. No, he thought, allowing his lips to curl in their first true smile since he had arrived. The poor lady never played me false. If she found no comfort in my embrace, she sought no other's either. I cured her of that tendency, if indeed she ever possessed such a tendency. She died as chaste in spirit as she was born. But see what we created, that pure lady and her impure wedded husband. A creature neither foul nor fair, but leached of all life.

The Duke of Torquay stood in his library, which he had not visited for six years, or rather his father's library, for so he still regarded it, as all he had done with the room since he had inherited it was to have it cleaned thoroughly and furnished in shades of maroon and gold to take the curse of his father's gray scholarship from it. He gazed down upon his only begotten child. She stood, small and patient as a marionette, expressionless, before him, dressed properly and expensively in a little blue dress chosen to accentuate her eyes, her feet in small blue slippers, her black hair falling to her shoulders. The Duke, dressed in riding clothes of various shades of brown, stood before her, his fair hair touseled, his face wearing a mannerly smile. We make a delightful picture, he thought with amusement, quite an admirable still life.

"I don't expect transports of delight, my child," he said in his low hoarse tones. "After all, you have only my word for it that I am your father, and the word, in any case, is meaningless to you, as we have never met. But I bear gifts, you see, to ensure a warm welcome here. Allow me to present you with a token. One which the shop girl assured me would be the envy of all your acquaintances."

He made a protracted show of unwrapping the parcel on his desk, and finally, after what seemed like a mighty struggle with the tissue within, shrugged and beckoned her to his side.

"See what a weak fellow I am." He smiled. "I cannot seem to unearth the thing. But you are all of . . . six, is it?" She only nodded gravely in return. "Ah then, and a fine strapping big girl, perhaps you can take it out for me."

She reached into the box and, without fuss, peeled the tissue away from the gift. It was a large doll, an expensive, overly dressed French doll, all bubbling lace and sleek satin with a porcelain head, with pouting lips and high color and long lashes that opened and closed over eyes almost as blue as her own. She gazed at it seriously, and then handed it to the Duke.

"Here you are, sir," she said quietly.

"But it is for you, child," he protested.

"Oh," she said quietly. "Then thank you, sir," and she held the doll at her side at a distance like an alien thing and looked at him again, waiting for him to speak.

"Well then," he said with false heartiness, thinking mockingly that he sounded like one of those fatuous avuncular uncles he had known as a child, or like an overeager child molester he had once seen trying to entice slum brats playing near the square until a zealous merchant had seen him and chased him howling down the street. "And what pastime did my sudden arrival call you from today? What had you been doing before I came and summoned you?"

"Lessons, sir," she replied gravely. "Drawing."

"And were you enjoying yourself?" he asked.

"Yes, sir," she answered.

"Well, then," he said, "I don't want to disrupt your schedule overmuch. You may return and we will see each other later. At dinner, then?"

"Yes, sir," she replied, and executing her perfect curtsy, she turned stiffly and left.

"Miss Barrow," he called, and the retreating governess turned and reentered the library. "Miss Barrow," he said sweetly to the spare, gray woman, "is she always like this, then?"

"Like what, Your Grace?" the woman answered, puzzled.

"So very polite, so very proper. I realize, naturally, that she doesn't know me from Adam, but does she never show any animation?"

"Your Grace," the governess answered, unsure of his tone, "it is not that she does not know you. She has been trained to be a lady. She has been taught that which is right and fitting in one of her station in life. Do you find that extraordinary?" she asked with a hint of steel in her voice.

Ah, then she has heard of me, the Duke thought, amused. "No, Miss Barrow, I quite understand. It is only that when I was her age, I was more inclined to childish pursuits."

"She is to be a lady, Your Grace," Miss Barrow replied. "She has to put such things behind her."

I should like to light a fire behind her, the Duke thought, and you as well. "Thank you, Miss Barrow," he said, dismissing her. He turned and sat in the great maroon chair that had been his father's. The sunlight glinted in the long windows, and although the maroon carpets absorbed much of it, the gold shone, the gold spun in the air in the little dust flecks that arose as he sank into the chair. The gold glowed from the draperies and echoed round his flaxen hair, and yet it seemed to him that the room was yet gray, his gray father's gray room. And why should I care that the world is determined to bring her up as a replica of her mother? It is, after all, only a case of one artificial flower reproducing another, he reflected. Would it be better for her to be a replica of her father, he thought, scornfully? And why did I even venture here to begin with? She has lived six long years in comfort without me, and doubtless will survive sixty more very nicely in the same fashion. Why should I care here and now, when I did not then? What has addled my wits and brought about this uncharacteristic fever of fatherhood? He lay his sunset-gilded head back upon the chair and closed his eyes, extinguishing their blue flame. Premature senility, he sighed, or an excess of boredom, or enforced celibacy, too much Squire and too many hopeful daughters have driven me to this charade of concern. But not boredom, he thought, opening his eyes again. No, this new game I have embarked upon is everything but boring. And she, and all my subsequent machinations since that damned night at the Opera, every plotted moment up to this unplotted one, have been because of her. And the game grows beyond my control. And that disturbs me more than anything has since I was that poor sadly squashed child's age. And that which disturbs me the most is myself. For I feel the stirrings of something very much like humanity within, and we can't have that, can we, My Lord Black Duke? We can't tolerate that at all. For I think, he sighed to himself, that it will result in a kind of death, one crack in that frozen void and, like a rushing spring thaw, I will be washed away in those unleashed torrents. It does no good to undam that which has been safely secured for so long. And for what, he laughed, for one poor, untried, untitled, unworldly female who has too many scruples, and a head full of bookish morality, and who, moreover, has not had enough temptation put in her way of becoming a saint? Oh no, Miss Berryman, he thought merrily, you of the exquisite face, form, and morals, you do not qualify as yet for a mantle of sainthood. All saints must be tempted to the limit, and I have not yet begun. Not nearly, he anticipated, brightening. And, feeling much better, the Duke of Torquay rose and stretched and went out into the chill air to find a proud mount to carry him on a nostalgic tour around his broad acres.

The day telescoped to three, and with each advancing hour he found himself becoming more unsettled. He was not used to spending so much time in his own company. In town, each night would provide its own diversions, and he could always ensure that there was at least some entertainment or some other human being he could converse or have some sort of concourse with. But here in the country, he found himself quite alone. He could not bring himself to open one of his father's books, as if the very dust motes would release visions of his youth, his father, his mother. And when he rode out to visit with his neighbors to reacquaint himself with them, he noted their wary attitudes. Those with comely wives or young daughters either hid them away or displayed them to him like pearls on a jewelers' cushion. On the whole, he preferred those men who secreted their daughters, but their attitudes were ones of uneasy deference. So he rode, and wandered, and watched his own daughter. And though he longed to be away, to return to the only life he knew, to take up the game again, perversely, he could not leave. At least until he had made some provision for his own daughter. For she unsettled him the most.

The little Lady Lucinda could not be said to be unacquainted with him now, and yet she was as still and stilted with him as ever. But, he noted, she was much the same with all those who came within her sphere. She showed no real emotion with her governess, with the servants, or even with other young children, those of his tenants that he pointed out to her when he took her riding with him in the afternoons. She was as cold and uninvolved with them all as she was with him. Only with animals, with her pony, with the stable dogs and kitchen cat, did she allow herself to smile, even, on occasions when she thought no one noticed, to laugh. And it was only on those rare occasions, that he saw, unclouded, his clear paternity in her unguarded face. On the third night then, since time was drawing close for him, and the ball he anticipated with such mixed emotions was only a little more than a week away in time, he sat at his desk and carefully composed a provocative letter. This done, he sat back with a rare real smile upon his face. If she still lives, this will provoke her enough to return, he thought, even if she is on her death bed. And, summoning a footman, he made arrangements for his note's immediate delivery.

It is only a small thing, he chided himself, and on balance with my sins, will perhaps only extinguish a very small flame when I am consigned to my eventual eternal torment, but it might make a great difference to the child, and I owe her that much at least. Owe? he thought quizzically. There I am speaking like a Miss Berryman again. But looking around the sumptuously furnished room, picturing in his mind's eye his rolling lawns and wooded parklands, his marble halls, even his daughter's exquisitely furnished rooms, the word *owe* did seem a little foolish. She has everything already, he thought, but perhaps, in deference to the absent Miss Berryman, there is, yes, one thing else that I owe her, and since I surely cannot provide it personally, I shall have another supply it. Thus I pay one debt. One moral debt, though, Miss Berryman, does not make a habit, I warn you.

She arrived exactly two days later, and, staring at her, he could not believe so many years had passed.

"You needn't goggle, My Lord," she remarked acidly, taking off her gloves. "No, I am not risen from my grave."

"Not from your grave, my dear Pickett, but rather from a night's sleep, for I swear you have not changed a hair."

"I have changed several thousand, Your Grace, unless your advanced age has clouded your vision, for as you can plainly see, they are all quite snow-capped now, and when last we met, they were the hue of a raven's wing."

"And this," he crowed with delight, "from the lady who would knock me silly for only a little fib. Why Pickett, my eternal love, you were gray as a goose when I last saw you. And why the 'Your Grace,' when I swear the only title you ever acknowledged me by was 'rogue' or 'devil' or 'wretch.' "

"Not so," said the small wiry woman, lowering her strident voice. "For once I was wont to call you 'Jason,' before you reached your majority, My Lord."

"Oh come," he said, taking her hand and leading her into the room. 'Your Grace' and 'My Lord' are uneasy on your lips. Call me 'wretch,' then, or 'rogue,' though I'd prefer 'Jason,' but do not bury me and our past under such a heap of civility. I am glad you have come back, Pickett, I truly am. You bring back my youth."

"I should not think you would wish it brought back," she said, her bright gray eyes searching his face. "Or anyone who brought it back to you."

"No," he said soberly, "not my youth, then, but you, certainly, for we shared the one endurable part of it, didn't we? You were more than governess, Pickett, you were my one friend."

She stood and stared at him for a moment and what she saw displeased her, for she pursed her lips and then shook her head.

"And still am your friend, but where is this 'squashed child' you wrote of? For nothing except the visions of a sadly flattened little person would have dragged me from my hearth in my richly deserved retirement. No, that is not true either. The world is filled with flattened children. Your unfortunate daughter alone accounts for my presence, Jason. Although I think that now, as then, you tend to exaggerate. Still, I am here, as you see. But I warn you, only to observe. I promise nothing else, as yet. Where is the child?"

"You shall see her at dinner. Which you shall have, my love, as soon as you freshen up. It must have been a weary journey. But it is a miracle how you have not changed," he commented as he led her up the long staircase to her room. But then he noted that although the years had not seemed to touch her at first glance, her carriage being just as erect, her homely, wise little face just as shrewd, her voice just as distinct and piercing as his childhood memories had enshrined them, yet she walked a little more slowly, a few more wrinkles sat upon her forehead, and her movements were a little more stiff. And yet, he thought, when last she saw me, my only sin was selfishness, my only crime, a child's thoughtlessness, my only lack, a conscience.

"I suppose, basically," she said, "no one of us really changes. Have you, Jason?"

"No," he said lightly. "No, basically, I haven't."

"Rest easy," Lady Burden caroled from the threshold, sweeping off her cloak and handing it to her maid. "For the foul beast has left his lair."

"Shh!" St. John hissed irritably. "For I'm about to put the poor girl in my debt for, I'd estimate, at least ninety-seven years. Your bid, Lady Berry, but have a care, for you owe me a king's ranson already."

"No," Regina laughed, putting her cards face up on the table, "I know when I'm beaten. But what 'beast,' Amelia? And why do you look so jubilant?"

"Bidding with such cards in your hand, Regina? Oh, you'll never make a Captain Sharp with this sort of play. I thought I'd taught you better. Well," Lady Burden said, plumping herself inelegantly down on a couch, "I've just come from a spirited visit to the Squire's, and lo! it's a house filled with lamentation. It seems all the chaos there, owing to their preparation for the ball, quite chased their honored guest away. Torquay just up and left them in the lurch, giving them some sort of nonsense about looking in on his daughter at Grace Hall. Which is a rare bouncer, if ever I heard one, for everyone knows he hasn't clapped an eye on his offspring since she appeared in the world. And Grace Hall has seen nothing but his heels since that day. He promised to be back for the ball, but much faith they have in his promise, and they are exceedingly distraught at his escape."

"Why should they be lamenting his departure?" Regina wondered, for she thought all polite society reacted as St. John did when he heard the Duke's name, with a slight moue of distaste.

"Why? Heavens, girl," Amelia laughed. "What sort of ball will it be with just a trumpery Marquis and a lady or two in attendance? A proper duke got away. Or rather an improper one, but still, he got clean away."

"I should think," St. John said, rising and walking the length of the table in the card room, "that they would be relieved for their daughters' sake."

"Oh come, come, Sinjin," Amelia gurgled, "not everyone is as circumspect as you are. Why the Squire quite fancied having a noble son-in-law for himself, to say nothing of his wife's being quite giddy from such a close encounter with such a sizeable fortune. Even the maids are sighing, for he has such a heavenly countenance, my dear."

"To hide a satanic heart," St. John muttered.

"Why, you sound quite priggish, my dear," Amelia countered, gaily, but keeping her eyes steadily on the Marquis's pacing figure.

"Can you have forgotten," St. John said earnestly, "what Torquay's machinations have caused Regina? Can you possibly have simply obliterated her flight from your mind? You seem to stand Torquay's defender. Why don't you just drop him a note and tell him to come around and pick Regina up this evening? You might pack for her while you are at it."

Lady Amelia flushed and sat quietly for a moment. Then she rose and straightened her skirt. "No," she said thoughtfully, "I had not forgotten. And I do know his reputation. But you do not have to suggest that I am acting as his pander either, Sinjun."

"Amelia!" St. John wheeled angrily upon her. "You go too far."

"No," Amelia said quietly, "I don't think so. You have said that Jason has designs upon Regina. I don't find that unusual, for Regina is an unusually lovely girl, who, as you have said, at the moment does not enjoy the protection of her family. I make no doubt that Jason is unscrupulous. But he is not, Sinjun, some unearthly demon from hell. He is, after all, only a spoiled, decadent Englishman, and Nobleman at that. He is not some muttering madman. He is still accepted in a wide circle of our acquaintance, and as yet, he has only badly frightened Regina with words. Or so you have told me. And as far as having a 'Satanic heart' goes, Sinjun, I am a full-grown woman, and although his reputation is bad, I know of gentlemen with much the same proclivities as his. You may detest him for your own reasons, but do not turn upon me as though I were some sort of heartless monster because I choose to make light of the situation, Sinjun. I swear I deserve better than that from you."

St. John moved swiftly to her, and grasped her hands in his. He looked steadily at her, and she could not tell, for once, whether he was as usual staring fixedly at the bridge of her nose, or at last, looking deep into her poor besotted eyes.

"Amelia, forgive me. I did not mean it as it sounded. It is only that I detest the man, and it seems, cannot take anything about him in a light vein."

Regina sat at the card table and watched them. Somehow, she thought, the two of them, standing so closely together, seemed rightfully matched. Both tall and straight, gifted and landed and fortuned, they seemed a true pair. Not for the first time, she thought herself an uncomfortable intruder in their own special world.

"Why do you detest him so, Sinjun?" Amelia asked. "You are no prude, my dear. Many times I have heard you laugh at adventurers far more lost to reason than he is."

His eyes wavered and he released her hands. He strode back and seemed to stare at the leaded panes of the frosted windows.

"It is only that I know what sort of fellow he really is, and it irks me to see him go scot-free, when a fellow of lesser rank would be rotting in Newgate for the same crimes."

It sounded weak enough, even to his own ears. Worse, he thought with chagrin, it sounded unlike him. Sanctimonious, priggish, even puritanical. Amelia, who had her ear to the social ground, had picked up the false note immediately, he realized. She looked puzzled. As well she might be, he thought viciously, for he was as well. The whole situation was damnable. There sat that lovely girl. All white and soft and compliant. All rounded and swelling, naive and ripe for him, and they were just friends. For these past weeks, he had had to play at being some stupid mythical fellow. Brotherly, fatherlike, everything but loverlike. She was homeless and friendless, she liked and respected him. How easily he could have moved her that one necessary step further into his life, had he been able. With little whispers, soft breaths, slight embraces, light kisses, and lighter promises, she could have been his by now; in gratitude, in pleasure, in love. But he had been thwarted, chaperoned and hedged in by circumstance. Forced to be natural and easy with Amelia, distantly friendly with Regina, and wary, always, of Torquay. Torquay, again Torquay. Small wonder he detested the man.

How easily Torquay could carry off a female, how simple he made the process. He had only to widen his china eyes and stare at some female of the demimonde and she was his. He had only to slightly court some light lady of Society and she closed her doors to all others. And, what was maddening, the stench of his reputation only seemed to enhance his desirability. And always, always, where he encountered St. John, there would be those light words, that little aside, that knowing smile, as if to say, "See, this is how it is with me. With you as well. You are no better, only, dear boy, far less successful." He seemed to amuse himself at St. John's expense, that was intolerable. And now, in this damnable affair with Regina, he saw himself in the role he played through her eyes: earnest, prim, and dull. While the absent Duke, by comparison, was all fire, all impulse. He did not want Amelia feeding any subterranean illusions Regina might have about Torquay. He did not want to lose her to Torquay, as he had lost others. Not this time. Not this woman. It was not fair. She had fallen, as if by fate, into his hands. And there he would see she would stay.

"At any rate," he managed to smile, "it's not important now, is it? If he is gone, then Regina's road will be all the clearer, and her freedom achieved sooner, as well. Come, let's forget the fellow, we all make too much of him. Let's play at cards, and be friends again."

"Very well," Amelia laughed, but the laughter was brittle.

"You must teach me better, Sinjun," Regina said sadly, "before I owe you my very soul."

I will own that, and more, St. John promised her with a quick look, and soon, sooner now than I thought.

And Lady Amelia forced herself to look down quickly at her cards, and commanded her hands not to shake.

And Regina, looking up into his warm gray eyes smiling at her, thought only of how fortunate she was in her friends, and how undeserving she was of their concern.

XI

"I vow," the Duke said, smiling down at the company from his observation post at the head of the table, "I do not know how any of you good ladies can manage to keep your eyes open during the day, after a succession of riotous evenings such as this."

"Unkind, Jason," Miss Pickett commented sharply as she spooned her soup, not missing a drop in the delicate rhythm she had established to clear the bowl.

Miss Barrow stiffened at the familiar tone the other lady had used, and straightened herself further in her chair. Little Lady Lucinda seemed unaware of the adults at the table, and merely edged a carrot in her bowl closer to a navy bean and appeared to admire her artwork.

They sat formally at the long damasked table, with footmen poised behind their chairs, alert to the immediate remove of each successfully accomplished course, and they sat for the most part silently, as they had for five successive evenings. Occasionally the Duke and Miss Pickett would rouse enough to involve themselves in what Miss Barrow regarded as highly improper banter, with Miss Pickett, she felt, too often forgetting her position, and His Grace never remembering his. But, she felt strongly, she did not wonder at his careless attitude toward his rank, and not even at half the tales she had heard of him, if that farouche, indelicate female opposite her had indeed been in sole charge of his early upbringing. For her part, she was determined to show by her impassive, but tangible disapproval, that his daughter's governess, at least, would spare this child such a slipshod education.

She had seen not only a slight, almost imperceptible although definite, to her hawklike vision, change in her charge's demeanor since the Duke's arrival. But a definite change, and not for the better, since Miss Pickett's appearance. That woman insisted on trying to draw Lady Lucinda into conversation at the most inappropriate times, with the most inappropriate questions. At an art lesson yesterday, for example, Miss Pickett had carelessly ambled, yes ambled, into the nursery and asked Lady Lucinda why she only put one blossom on her watercolor of a tree. And the child had answered, rightfully and dutifully, laying aside her brush, that it was to give the tree a proper modest balance with the rest of the landscape, and to avoid a vulgar blotch of colors. "Oh I don't know," Miss Pickett had replied. "My favorite trees in spring are those that are the most vulgar, the most positively garish in their display of color, aren't yours?" And when the child had tentatively, at first, and then with Miss Pickett's approval begun eagerly to overlay the tree with great conflicting stabs of color, horrendous blobs of color, Miss Pickett had almost cried out with delight, and Miss Lucinda, emboldened by the creature, forgot herself so much as to dissolve into giggles, all the while darting little sly looks at her outraged governess.

And that, coupled with the incident at the reading lesson, the contretemps on the nature walk, and the common display at the pianoforte, had put Miss Barrow on guard, and made each successive evening at the great dinner table more uncomfortable. And why she and her charge should be summoned to the dinner table with His Grace and that creature every night, instead of dining modestly in the nursery as usual, was a puzzlement. Miss Barrow glowered down at her rack of lamb with such force, that had it been a sensible thing, it would have cringed. She would wait them out. The Duke could not content himself with pastoral pleasures for long, she felt, and whatever freak of temper had sent him posting back to Grace Hall to disrupt his daughter's life would soon pass. She was only grateful that this shocking ex-governess was the only company he had summoned, and that he had not filled the Hall with the even more disreputable of his fell companions.

"Why don't you eat your potatoes, child?" Miss Pickett now asked, noting how Lady Lucinda was poking each parslied marble-shaped little orb into a corner of her plate.

"I don't care for them," Lady Lucinda replied carefully, and then with a glance at her governess, "at least not tonight, thank you m'am."

"I should think you'd prefer some nice fluffy potatoes," Miss Pickett decided, and was about to signal to a footman when Lady Lucinda hastily said, "Oh no, m'am, I'm not allowed them."

"Reasons of health?" Miss Pickett frowned.

"Reasons of manners, Miss Pickett," Miss Barrow stated ominously. "M'lady was prone to dauble in them. She would—and here all lectures were to no avail— continually play with them at table, making quite a revolting mess of her plate, so she has been forbidden them till she can make a more reasonable effort at the table."

"Play with them?" Miss Pickett smiled. "Why what on earth did you do with them, My Lady? Shy them at the butler? Lob them at the chandelier?" And Lady Lucinda gave a little gulping, half concealed giggle, but no further answer. "Well," continued Miss Pickett in ringing tones, "I can distinctly remember being more circumspect myself. I was fond of sculpting mountains in them, and your father, I recall, had a decided partiality for creating opposing continental armies, with a river of gravy separating the warring factions."

"Castles," Lady Lucinda replied unexpectedly, "and sometimes mountains, too."

"I do not find this amusing," Miss Barrow said dangerously. "I do not find the improper manners of a child a source of amusement, or a proper topic of discussion before her."

"But she is a child, Miss Barrow," her antagonist said unrelentingly, "and should on some small occasions be allowed to remember it."

"Your Grace," Miss Barrow said, quivering, half rising from her chair in affront, and appealing to the only voice of authority in the room. "I do not find this discussion proper in front of your daughter."

"I am seldom," the Duke smiled smoothly, putting down his fork, "called upon to arbitrate in matters of vegetables. But now that it is called to mind, I recall that yes, I did prefer those that were soft and smooth and rounded. But then," he added thoughtfully, "it is, of course, to be remembered that I would prefer any objects so pleasantly defined, even now."

"Your Grace!" Miss Barrow rose majestically. "I do not have to tolerate such topics of conversation and such vulgar innuendo."

"Of course you do not," he answered in bored tones.

"And you will do nothing to stop it?"

"No, nothing," the Duke answered, casting the outraged governess a level blue look.

"Then I shall have to leave."

"You must do as you see fit," he replied.

"I mean, of course," Miss Barrow announced, casting her last spear, "to leave your employ."

"That," the Duke said softly, his daughter's widened eyes upon him, "is what I assumed you meant."

"And now?" Miss Pickett said, her voice disturbing the quiet in the emptied room.

"And now," the Duke replied, carefully inspecting an apple that had been left in the bowl upon the table, "I am bereft of a governess for my poor child, and all due to your vicious tongue, Pickett." He shook his head slowly and regretfully. Miss Barrow had left with a gasp, Lady Lucinda had been sent to bed after a sweet and calm chat with Miss Pickett, and the Duke had waved away the footmen after they had cleared the remnants of the uneaten meal. The fire crackled quietly in the fireplace, and the candles guttered in their silver sockets.

"That you, of all people, should bring me to this, Pickett," the Duke sighed.

"Of course, it was wonderful how you engineered it, Jason," Miss Pickett said slowly. "And quite like the boy I knew. You knew, of course, what the sight of the stick that prig Barrow was converting that poor child into would do to me, and you knew my reckless tongue.

And, of course, you knew to a nicety, what her reaction would be, as you always seem to know what people's reactions will be."

"I am a knowing one," the Duke answered somberly, carving a small round disk from the apple. "Although 'nicety' is seldom a term applied to me."

"Of course, you did know how to entrap me, but wouldn't it have been simpler to simply dismiss her and ask me?"

"But simpler may not have been as effective, and there was the merest possibility that you might have refused," he replied reasonably.

"I would have," she said sadly. "I am too old, Jason."

"You, too old?" he said, his eyes widening. "Oh never, Pickett, you never were, you never will be."

And he remembered all the years before he had been sent away for his education, all the years when her vigilance had protected him, those early years when she would plan walks and tours and rambles, to keep him from the house when his mother was entertaining her "guests," her "gentlemen callers." All the years of her unceasing efforts in his behalf, her attempts to turn a slight, almost too beautiful and sensitive boy child into a responsible sturdy man. How she had introduced him to the groom, and the stablemen, and the boys who worked about the house, so that he could learn the art of fisti-cuffs, so that he could learn the world of men. Of how she had toughened herself, had cultivated her astrin-gent personality. She had hidden her concern for his bruises, both physical and mental, so that she would not smother him, cosset him, soften him, and all so that he could grow strong enough to face the realities she had so successfully hidden from him until that day he had escaped her notice and burst in upon his mother at her sport. "You too old Pickett?" he laughed. "When there is a need for you?"

"Too devious though, Jason," she sighed. "Oh I'll do it, of course, I'll raise her as best I'm able, but you did not used to be so devious."

"But it comes so naturally, I must have always been so, my dear, it just escaped your doting eye."

"Not quite so devious," she insisted, and then looking at him there, his legs stretched out, the apple and the knife held in his careful white fingers, his attention carefully focused on them, she blurted, "And all those other tales I have heard. Yes, I took care to try to hear about your exploits. Those tales, are they true?"

He did not look up from the apple, but only drawled in his fogged whisper, "Now which tales could you be referring to? There are so many. And rumor adds long tails to short ones. Ah well, for reasons of propriety, I cannot possibly go into them all. As well as for reasons of time, for although the night is yet young, it might take us till tomorrow to be done with them all. Suffice it then to say, yes, half of them, whatever ones you heard, are quite true."

"Half of them is too much, Jason," she said sternly.

"Send me early to bed, will you?" he smiled, looking at her now with that sweet smile that first won her when she had seen him all those years ago. There was such a melting power in that smile then, she thought, and even more now, no wonder he can go his way unchecked.

"Too much, Jason," she sorrowed. "I did not point you that direction."

"The bitch whelps true, Pickett," he said with a fleeting expression almost like a snarl. "I am my mother's child."

"And you court her end?" Pickett's voice rang out.

"Oh let be, my love. I live my life, I am well content, I harm no one but myself." He rose and walked the length of the table, stopping only to inspect the centerpiece with unseeing eyes. The silence grew in the room, and he absently shaped the candlewax with a stroking finger. "At least as yet," he whispered absently. "At least I think I have harmed no one else as yet. No, all were willing, all are willing to lead the merry Duke a merry dance for a pretty price. And if I prefer the dance, Pickett, what of it? I have been a wallflower. I have had connubial bliss. I am not suited to it, let me to my pleasures."

"And are they pleasures, Jason?" she asked, unrelenting.

"You put me to the blush, my love. At least I find them so. And others have assured me of it. At least," he qualified again, "as yet, they have."

"But not all?" she persisted. "Is there another person you are involved with now? You sound not as sure as a merry Duke should be. And this sudden visit to Grace Hall, this sudden concern for the child, is there a reason?"

For a moment in the dimness of the room, the years fled away for both of them, the old, anxious woman perched upon her chair watching the slim, fair impeccable man. For a moment, he hesitated, as if to talk again, without artifice, without concealment, to another being. But then a log cracked in the fire and the moment passed. He straightened.

"Another person?" he said quizzically. "Oh how full of tact you are my quaint Pickett. 'Another person,' so all the tales have reached you after all? But you hope that the 'person' is a female one, and a pure, honest, well-bred one at that, for somewhere in that reasonable breast lurks the unreasonable belief that your nursling will be saved by the love of a good woman."

She knew the moment had passed, and so she retorted, "Nonsense, arrant nonsense, Jason. The love of a good woman would roll off your back like water off a duck's. I make no doubt you've enjoyed the love of a good many women and some of them good women at that, but that would not change you in the least."

"So glad," he bowed, "to see you have not lost your senses, or have been spending your retirement wallowing through reams of bad romances."

"But," she said succinctly as she rose to leave, "the love *for* a good woman . . . ah that, my lad, would make all the difference in the world."

"As ever," he said half to her retreating back, half to the candle he had sculpted, "you have an acid tongue, and a way with words, my dear, a remarkable way with words."

* * *

The moonlight drenched the room, and he lay there, on the great bed, silently. As well try to sleep in the glare of noon, he thought, but he did not rise to drape the windows, for he could never bear to sleep in pitch dark, never bear to lock out the moonlight. There will be dark enough in the tomb, he thought, no need to simulate it now. But he could not sleep, and blamed the moonlight, until he realized that while every muscle in his body yearned for sleep, no part of his brain would have any part of it. So he lay there, wide-eyed, seeing the shapes of the room, the edges of the great canopy, above him, much, he thought as it must have looked to his parents the night he was conceived, and to his grandfather the night his father was conceived. And doubtless, he thought wryly, so had his late wife studied the canopy intently the night that poor little wretch was conceived, in fact he remembered her unblinking gaze quite well.

He had dismissed his valet early, and the only concession he had made to sleep was in having had his boots removed, for he lay there on the coverlet, fully clothed. It was as if he awaited his departure in the morning with such eagerness that he did not even wish to bother with the convention of undressing, preparing for sleep, rising and re-dressing, as if all of that was just an unnecessary delaying tactic. Not for the first time he wished he could be at a place just by the wishing of it, without the bother of everyday mechanics to convey him. This visit to my childhood, he thought wearily, has made me as a child again, with a child's fancies.

While his body lay tense, yet inert, his mind ranged far. At least the child has Pickett now, he thought, and Pickett has another crusade to enliven her. Not the sheltering of a boy from a licentious mama, but the sheltering of a girl from a profligate papa. What cycles dear Pickett has seen, he thought, laughing lightly in the semidark. And so I have resolved all here, he thought, knowing that he had done very little, knowing once again that he had again only arranged things to his own comfort.

Comfort, he thought lazily, ah that would be a good

thing. The thing of it is that I am unused to celibacy. In fact, I cannot sleep without my strange comforts. It is that, of course, and the damned moonlight that keeps me lying here, stark staring awake while the rest of the household snores the roofbeams off. Some round, light, laughing thing here in my bed with me would ensure eventual sleep. But no, I am the model papa, as stern and pure and self-denying as a picture upon the wall, and thank God I will be off in the morning and about my pleasures once again.

And when he thought of his present pleasures, and when the image of that pale, green-eyed face swung before him, and the image of that white neck, and the breath that caused the high breasts to rise and fall, and the remembrance of that light step, and the recollection of that breathless little nervous laugh she gave when he shocked her, came, he rose from the bed and roamed the room thinking that such thoughts did not serve him well when he lay sleepless in an empty sacrificial thankless bed. But not empty for long, he thought, for I will have her, and that is becoming more important to me with every empty night I spend. For somehow she had killed his desire for others. And, confused, he accepted his continence and, uncharacteristically, refused to analyze it. Unable to change it, he had decided it was a clever and conscience decision on his part. He applauded his decision not to settle for substitutes at this stage, deeming it rather like a man refusing to gorge on sweets before a gourmet dinner. He had no desire to take the edge off his appetite, he reasoned.

Ah those appetites, he thought, holding his head in his hands as he sat on the edge of the bed. Appetites for shapes and textures of pleasures that seemed both never-ending in their sequences and curiously less satisfying with each encounter. But there was this aura about her, he insisted to himself, that did not seem only to spring from his habit of embuing each new one with imagined attributes to whet his tastes. There was that in her which he would not have made up, that which he would not, left on his own, have imagined. That curious moral rectitude, that gallant and naive assumption that there was such a thing in her world as honor, as fair play. What had she said that curious night in the coach, she would not sell herself, would he?

What a shock that had been. It was as unexpected to him as roaming through a pleasant field of flowers and gathering one with a wasp inside. It's true he had gone too far. He knew that, but each time in the past when he had thought he'd gone too far, even he himself had thought so, Society had only clucked and shrugged and looked the other way. And what was the difference, he had thought, between this abduction and that other? That giggling little serving girl that he had accosted in the hall at a friend's house that cold winter's night. That . . . Emily, yes, Emily Ketchum, had been her name. The one with the provocative birthmark near her delightful lips. "Come live with me and be my love," he had breathed in her ear, half flown with good wine, as she had helped him on with his cloak. And she had simpered and a calculating look had come into her eye and she lain her little hands on his chest and pouted, "But how? Your Grace, oh the mistress would skin me, and my mother, oh she'd tan me if I up and went off with you." "Shall I abduct you then, my heart?" he had suggested, tasting her earlobe and liking the flavor. "Oh yes, sir!" she had assented quickly. And he had laughed, and laughingly brought the coach to the back door, and stifled with laughter, doubled with laughter, carried her giggling, wrapped in his cloak, out into the night. And she had fared well when he grew tired of her, in comfortable keeping even now to an acquaintance of his.

So why had this been different? She'd had no real prospects, no connections, no family. She was of common birth, with only that mushroom of an aunt and that simpleton cousin. He had expected her to turn to him, there in the coach, eyes sparkling, and accept his terms with pleasure. What better could she have done with herself? Why had she gone, so desirable, available, and unchaperoned to that blasted Opera, if she had not been looking for such an accommodation? And if she had lost courage then, had he not made it that much easier for her? She had responded to his kisses, he knew. She must know of his fortune, where was the impediment? What woman had he known in the last decade who would not settle for money and pleasure? But no, she had turned on him. She had repulsed him and had given him a stern little lecture on morality instead. Almost as if she were Pickett, transformed, young and lovely.

She disturbed him. She fit no pattern. He had not meant to speak to her again until the game was up, but had gone to meet her there then, in that freezing meadow, out of a desire to understand where the impediment lay. And she had been a delight. They had talked the afternoon away. There were times in that strange, cold afternoon when he had forgotten he was conversing with a woman, so far did her interests range, so quick was her clever tongue. And so each time, when he had refocused upon her appearance, her loveliness had come to him with breath-catching shock. And still she had prosed on about honor, and friendship, and morality, as if she were some sort of odd, seductive little deacon. Yet he swore her eyes had hinted at less pious delights. And almost she had him convinced of that impossible innocence when she had risen to go back. Back to St. John, and his protection. And what sort of innocence would lie undisturbed in St. John's house, in his very bed? Did she believe he would continue his exemplary behavior once beyond his sister's and Lady Burden's watchful eyes? That, indeed, would be innocence to boggle the mind.

He did not know why he disliked the Marquis with such violence. It was, after all, rare for him to dislike anyone with like intensity, for to dislike someone was to indulge in some form of passion, and he had thought that he had used up his passion in mere passion long since.

Perhaps it was because that strong, tall, socially impeccable young man nightly wallowed in his same sewer, and daily walked the road of righteousness, raising his eyebrows in distaste at tales of the Black Duke's misadventures. Perhaps, he admitted, it was that in St. John's eyes he saw reflected his own past, and his own sure future. Or perhaps, he thought, with the clarity that only solitary, exhausted late-night thought delivers, it was that St. John so often, as if by reason of some malevolent fate, had seen him at his worst, had seen him in situations that he himself shrank from remembering in the cold daylight.

That night, for example, that he only allowed himself to remember on nights such as these. The night when he had gone around to Madame Sylvestre's select establishment for an evening's diversion, and had discovered what his world's estimate of himself was. In recent years he did not care to patronize such establishments. He much preferred to have some light creature in his own keeping, some female who would, at least, pretend to look up at him with some semblance of recognition and delight when he opened the door. But at that time, for some reason he could not remember even now, he was by way of being a frequent customer there.

He had been greeted graciously and, taking his cloak, they had led him to a gilded room. Entering, he had found a lovely young woman within. She had taken his coat and prattled softly, laughed deliciously, and given him glimpses of the delights that lay in store for him. She had looked to be exquisite, a prime, healthy young creature, and after a few embraces he had been sure of a pleasant evening. But first he had had to order and partake of a quantity of wine, a thing he often had to do in such arrangements, to deaden a certain relentlessly critical portion of his mind, to free another segment of his brain to unhesitatingly appreciate such a treat.

But some time during the preliminary tangle, in the wine-soaked explorations and preparations, the door had opened and another female had come in. He had been, in that moment, amused at the proprietress's estimate of his needs. But then, even though fully fogged with wine, the appearance of the second female had stopped the play and he drew back with difficulty and gaped. She was not the sort of woman one expected to find at an establishment such as Madame Sylvestre's. She looked like Covent Garden gutter ware. Ageing, overblown, overpainted, not overly clean, with impossibly hennaed hair, she simpered and began to remover her tawdry finery.

"C'mon lovey," she had cajoled, reaching for him and revealing a gap-toothed smile. "It'll be lovely, it will. The two of us for the one of you. There's a lot I know."

At first, he had been amused, and for one mad moment had wondered at how it might be, a night of textures, an opportunity to explore textures and differences and shapes. But then, even in his castaway state, he had recoiled.

"Awww Aggie," the younger woman had laughed. "You've gone and lost your golden guinea. I told you to wait a bit, but you rushed in too soon. You see," she explained anxiously, unsure of his reaction as he sat staring, "Lord Barrymore, he's outside, and he payed Madame a sum, and he brought Aggie here and promised her even more to entertain you. He's wagered a sum, he said, with another gentleman. He wagered that you'd throw no female creature out of your bed, so long as she's willing. Ah, but look you, Aggie, he wants no part of you."

Nervously, the older woman backed away, holding her wrapper closed around her ample breasts. "You're not mad at poor old Aggie, now are you, sir?" she cringed, whining. "I only did it cause they told me as to how you'd like it. I'd like it fine," she said encouragingly. "And they all said as how you'd think it a rare jest and go along."

Of course, it has come to this, he remembered thinking as he rose to pour himself more wine with a shaking hand. It is, after all, only a natural progression. And in some strange fashion, he'd felt a small satisfaction at his own aghast reaction. Why should they not think it, haven't you worked diligently toward this? They believe there is nothing you are not capable of. Even attempting a poxy Billingsgate whore. And what shall you do now? What a comedy it would be for the blackest of them all to go raging out of here crying his discretion, his taste, his honor. All, everything, except this, then? You dare ask them to believe that? Then let them believe what they will, he swore, for no matter what the protest, they will.

"No Aggie," he had finally said when he could control his voice. "No, I'm not angry. And you shall have your golden guinea, for you may tell Lord Barrymore anything you like. But," he said smiling, holding up his hands in mock horror, "there's an extra coin in it for both of you if you swear not to tell a soul that I have imbibed so much this night that I truly fear I cannot please either one of you and am best off retiring like a monk to my own cell."

And after fending off their concerned attempts to reassure him as to his capabilities, he gave them both some silver and led them to the door, an arm about each of them. And then, there in the doorway he saw St. John, the lofty Marquis of Bessacarr, regarding him with loathing. And in the throes of his own strange exultant humiliation, his own soul wincing, he had whispered fiercely to the Marquis, "What? Distaste, Sinjun? But wait a few years, my dear boy, and you will find yourself pursuing the same sport. Unless you care to join me now? I'm sure Aggie has room in her heart for both of us."

And later, standing alone, his hands stretched out stiffly against the table to forbid them from trembling, and staring down at the bottle of wine he scarcely believed that he had drunk, so sober was he now, he had thought, yes soon, at this rate it would not be long. Soon there will undoubtedly come the day when I will no longer care. And all will be lost in the endless search for textures and pleasures.

All what? What was there left to lose, he thought now in fury. What was that last vestige he feared losing? That remnant he guarded as jealously as that green-eyed wench protected her virginity? Her favorite word, Honor?

Honor, he thought wearily, as dawn bleached the sky, no matter, soon she will come to me, on my terms, and without honor, and I will take her without honor, and whatever honor there will be in it, will be that I was right again. And there will be the end of it.

And knowing that sleep was gone, for he had often spent similar nights, being used to uneasiness in his own company, he rose and pulled on his boots, and dashed some water against his face, and swirled some in his mouth to take the taste of the bitter night away.

He opened the door that led out into the hall and soundlessly began to pad toward the stairs when he saw a small shape outlined against the tall windows at the head of the stairs. Knowing that he moved silently, he brushed against the wall to warn her so that he would not startle her too much.

"Really, Pickett," he said softly, "if you are going to wander at this ungodly hour, allow us to provide you with some chains to rattle so that your perambulations do not go to waste. The house needs a spectacular ghost to give it some pretensions."

"It is not an ungodly hour of the night," she countered. "It is, rather, an extremely godly hour of the morning. Old bones do not care for long rest, knowing that a longer one awaits. But you are up early, Jason. Are you so eager to attend matins?"

"No, my love," he smiled. "Have you forgotten? I am away today. I shall leave my house and my child in your capable hands. I trust you will keep them both free of small insects and large problems. Come, break bread with me, and I will give you my direction, and complete written authority to do as you wish."

"I would wish," she said, seeing in the increasing light the scars the long night had left beneath his eyes, "that you might give me the same license with your own person."

"Ah love," he said, bending and placing his hand along her cheek. "I do believe that when his Infernal Highness comes around at last to claim me, and lays his fiery collar about my neck, my own dear fierce Pickett will be there to challenge him, and swear, against the damnation of her own soul, that her poor misunderstood nursling has been wrongly accused, and stands innocent of all wrongdoing."

"I think you wrong yourself the most," she said sadly. "And look hourly for that gentleman to come and release you from yourself. And I do not think he could do half so good a job at torment as you have done."

"Torment?" He paused on the stair and threw his golden head back and roared with laughter. When he had recovered, he said merrily, "Pickett, you observe a gentleman in haste to be on the way to a gala ball, and on the way to collect on an important wager surely soon to be won, on the way to triumph, in fact."

She followed him silently down the long stairs, but in the hall she paused, and lay her hand upon his sleeve.

"When you were a boy," she said, watching him with troubled eyes, "we two had an important wager once. Do you remember? It was a picnic we were to go on, half a day's drive away. Oh, you were so excited, for we had your mama's permission to take a luncheon, we had an invitation to see some fine horses you had admired. We were to be allowed to be away until nightfall. For a week, you watched the skies, and noted the winds, and daily you wagered it would rain that day and cancel our trip. And I swore the sun would shine. And on that morning it poured rain, I believed it was the beginning of the flood. And you came to me, with tears in your eyes, and said, 'Pickett, at least congratulate me, for I've won.' Is it to be another such triumph?"

He stared down at her, his face gray as the uncertain light. "What matter?" he spoke softly. "It will be a wager won. And," he continued, "surely you do not begrudge me victory?"

And so I do, my lad, she thought silently as he gave her his arm to lead her in to breakfast. I begrudge you all such triumph, and all your bitter victories.

XII

The carriage moved almost silently through the night toward the broad entrance of the drive to Squire Hadley's manor house, but three of the occupants of the carriage were as silent as their conveyance. The only voice that chatted happily on was that of Lady Mary, who blissfully and without interruption prattled on about the forthcoming delights of the evening. The others sat quietly, each wrapped in their own silence of thought and speculation.

There had been a brief flurry of light chatter when they had all met in the hallway before they had left Fairleigh, Regina had been complimented fulsomely by both of the other ladies. She had been dressed with care, and Lady Burden's green satin ball gown had suited her unique coloring to perfection. Although she had been shocked, and then worried about the extremely low neck of the gown, low enough, she realized with some fear, to show the swelling rise of her breasts, her maid had assured her that contrary to her expectations, it would be considered a modest gown, and all the crack this season. When she had descended the stairs, she had seen that even the gown that the swollen Lady Mary wore had a more daring cut, and then her fears had been allayed completely by the slow and lingering smile that St. John had briefly worn when he had gazed upon her.

There was a brief roundelay of mutual compliments, Regina being quite careful to phrase her admiration for Lady Mary's quite inappropriately pink and white draped gown, and her very real esteem for Amelia's elegant amber velvet dress. St. John, she noticed, was looking so handsome in his severe black evening dress that she felt shy of turning a word of praise to him. Somehow, dressed as he was, she felt he was even more unapproachable than usual and his tightened expression as they entered the coach chased any lingering thought of easy conversation with him from her mind. Again, however, she mused, as she half listened to Mary's incessant chatter, she had caught the vestiges of a feeling of something she had forgotten, when she had first seen St. John this evening. But now her foremost worry was how she was to behave this evening.

Both St. John and Amelia had told her clearly that she had nothing to fear from the Duke. That she could, indeed, if she wished to, even speak with him as lightly as she wished. But that the best course of action would be to ignore him completely. But how, she wondered, wishing that she were not wearing long gloves so that she could comfortably nibble at a fingertip, could she ignore him? Or be sure that she would know how to act at a ball? For, under no circumstances did she wish to embarrass any one of her benefactors. But Amelia had only laughed, and heartlessly stated that there was no way in which she could disgrace herself at Squire Hadley's ball unless she became disguised and cavorted barefoot in the punchbowl, and even then, the Squire might think it all the rage to do so and join in her romp.

When she entered the large room to which they had been ushered when their wraps were removed, Regina was at first too dazzled by both the quantity of brightly burning candles and the panoply of dancers, to single out any individuals. Lord, she breathed to herself, as she half heard St. John introducing her to the largely beaming Squire and his breathless wife, there must be upward of a hundred people here! She had no way of knowing that what was to her an unimaginably elegant, brilliant, and crowded ball, was to her London-bred companions merely a dull, sparsely attended, inelegant local country dance.

Lady Mary was led to a comfortable chair among the dowagers, where, perceiving her interesting condition, she was immediately drawn into a—to her—delightful round of reminiscences of confinements and other homey discussions of mutual childbed experiences. St. John and Amelia stood watching the proceedings with Regina, until St. John, stifling a yawn, went off to fetch both ladies small glasses of ratafia.

"He does not seem to be here at all," Amelia said quietly to Regina, with just a trace of regret in her voice. "I suppose it was all a hum on his part, and after we were all expecting some ferocious confrontation. Ah, well," she went on, "he does have an odd sense of humor, at that."

Regina did not have to ask who "he" was, and scarcely trusting herself to do more than nod, she watched the dancers forming a country set. She had been so involved in searching the whirling room for the slight, familiar form that she had not noticed the stir that she herself had caused when she had entered. Her face, her form alone would have ensured a certain response in any male member of the company, but her mysterious reputation had preceded her, and mercifully, she was as yet unaware of the curiosity concerning herself. But when a tall young man detached himself from his fellows and bowed an introduction to Regina and Lady Burden, she gave a start as she heard herself being invited to join the dance now forming. But she didn't know how to dance, she thought with panic, and understood suddenly how a man who cannot swim feels when the water is closing over his head.

Amelia, smiling pleasantly, waited to hear Regina's response, but at the girl's stricken look suddenly remembered that it must have been true, that incredible claim that she could not dance, and with the quickness of mind and sure instinct for social grace that she was noted for, smiled sweetly and said, "Ah, but Mr. Birmingham, our dear visitor Lady Berry had the most unfortunate accident only this morning, oh nothing dire, but she did turn her ankle, and regretably cannot join us in the dance this evening. But, since you did journey all the way across the room for a dance, if you would not mind escorting Lady Berry to a seat, I will join you in her place."

Mr. Birmingham, repressing the keen disappointment he felt, bowed, and said, "But that would be beyond all goodness of your part, Lady Amelia," and, having deposited Regina in a comfortable chair on the sidelines next to the dowagers, chaperones, and mamas, gallantly escorted Amelia to the dancers.

Regina watched the dancers for a while, noticing that St. John had been snared by a burbling Miss Kitty, who was lisping and giggling and making play with her lashes in a manner that surprised even Regina. The ladies that Regina was seated among, after having murmured quiet introductions, eyed her suspiciously, and then turned back to Lady Mary, who was vying with the Squire's wife in detailing particularly dreadful parturitions.

After hearing the explicit details of a hopefully exaggerated difficult confinement on the part of one of the mamas, Regina began to feel uneasy. Watching Amelia whirl about with her third partner, and realizing that now that St. John had been captured by Miss Lottie, he would not soon make an escape, as Miss Kitty and even the betrothed Miss Betty were eyeing him as if he was to be their last supper, Regina began to feel increasingly the dreamlike aspect of her position.

She had bathed, and powdered, and dressed with care. She had come to this ball, but now felt as if there were a pane of glass separating her from all the others here. She could not speak with any authority about childbirth, and the only other young woman in her proximity was a poor young creature who was afflicted with a blighting galaxy of spots upon her face, and who glared with such ferocity at any young man whose mother had prompted him to approach her that he summarily retreated. No other young men approached Regina, and she felt that surely they all must think her of little consequence and less looks, or perhaps, in some supernatural way, had ascertained her deception.

She had no way of knowing that her beauty quite took their breath away, and coupled with the mysterious linkage she enjoyed with the powerful Marquis, they all felt she was far beyond their touch. Her refusal to dance had only fed the rapidly whispered rumors that she was of high social station and a complete snob, or a French émigré who could not yet master the language, and there were even some mean souls who whispered that she was part of a colossal joke the elegant Marquis was visiting upon his country hosts, and she was in actuality only an expensive bit of muslin brought down from London as a lark. Therefore, no girl of any reputation dared speak to her, and as no young man wished to be rejected by her, she was left quite alone.

The musicians played country dances, the young people formed sets, and Regina watched them lightly make their way through, what seemed to her, the impossible complicated forms of the dance. Slowly, her sure eye began to tell her what her experience could not. St. John and Amelia were certainly the best dressed, most elegant couple there. The other men seemed to her at once both too young and too old for fashionable attire, and their clothing seemed both too overly elaborate or too casual for the affair. The girls were often dressed in unsuitable colors, and their hair was dressed in styles which she intuitively knew were not correct. Occasionally a gentleman would glance in her direction and then either glance away or give her a calculating longer look. The women would either ignore her altogether or seek her out with a piercing look and then whisper some comment to their companions. Even while she admired the grace and precision of the dance, she was aware of their ill-concealed curiosity toward her.

After what seemed to Regina to be an interminable amount of time, she felt that she could bear the situation no longer. It is as if I didn't exist at all, she thought wildly, and beset by terrors brought on by her own trepidation, guilt at her false position in the Marquis's household, and fears of embarrassing her hosts, she, trying to keep a calm expression on her face, rose and went quietly toward the back of the rooms where she hoped to take refuge in the shadowy recesses of the window embrasures.

Once she had achieved the windows, she spied a small antechamber off the main room, where a large, curtained window stood slightly open to admit a few cool breezes to flicker the candles. Gratefully, she went swiftly to the window to stare out at the darkened, bare gardens.

It was with no real sense of shock, but rather with a

surprisingly pleasant feeling of expectation, that she heard the husky voice say from behind her, in velvety amused tones, "Come, this is no way to accept a challenge. Rather I expected to see you spinning about the room, causing me to fall into paroxysms of jealousy as I spied you dancing with delight, locked in Sinjin's arms."

"Ah, but I cannot dance," she replied, without looking around her. "Did not your extensive research tell you that?"

"No, really?" he said. "That I did not know. But wouldn't your gracious host have instructed you in the rudiments?"

"He did not think it necessary," she said primly. "My expectations are to teach young women in several regimens, dancing is not one of them."

"Dancing should certainly be one of them," he said, and placing one hand upon her waist, he swung her around toward him.

He outshone the candles tonight, she thought. Impeccable, his black evening clothes contrasting with his golden head, his eyes glinting like deep water in the refracted light. He seemed so full of life and vitality that, once again, her breath caught in her throat and all the clever, cutting things she had vowed she would say to him caught there and died on a sigh. He placed one warm strong hand on her waist and she felt the touch of him would crisp the sheer material of her gown through to her skin. He tightened his grip and caught her wavering protesting hand in his other. Then he began to pull her slightly toward himself.

She looked up into the laughing blue eyes and gasped, she had not expected such a frontal attack and was momentarily without words, only the color rushed to her cheeks.

"Oh no," he laughed with delight. "This is not rapine, my innocent. This is merely the prefiguring position for that lovely dance the Squire has so daringly allowed to be played. The Graces assured him it was all the style in London this year. And so it is. It is called a waltz, and it is very decadent, the dowagers insist, as it comes from the continent where all things decadent, save for your obedient servant, come from. But it is quite fashionable and the advantage of it is that a man may hold a woman in the same position he usually dreams of holding a woman in, except in full view and with the approval of all her protectors. So I must hold you thus if you wish to learn to dance it."

"But I do not wish to dance it," she protested, unnerved by his hand, which had swung her so dangerously close to him.

"But you must," he said quickly, "or else anyone spying us here, you in my arms, thus," he said, drawing her closer, "would think that we are lovers met in assignation, and since you haven't given out one little scream or protest, what would that young woman watching us, think?"

Regina was too thunderstruck to look about for the witness he spoke of, and, wanting to avoid any scandal, said quickly, "Then show me the dance, quickly, and let me go. You promised you would not attempt any . . . seduction here."

"And I am a man of my word," he said, beginning to move in the motions of the dance. "But if you think that this is how I begin seduction, I really must instruct you further in that art as well. But not here, certainly. Here I shall initiate you only to the wonders of the dance." And slowly, counting her steps for her, he eased her into the whirling grace of a waltz.

She found, to her surprise, that it was a simple thing for her, and, listening to the music, she soon discovered a certain delight in the dance. They spun and dipped and danced until she found a rare laughter about to bubble up in her throat. She had never danced, and it was a heady experience. When at last she heard the music end, she looked up to see him staring down at her with new interest.

Glancing over his shoulder, she saw that he had swept her into a different room, a smaller hall off the small antechamber she had originally fled to. Now that the music had ended, she made a small move to remove herself from his arms, and found herself, instead, drawn closer. And then closer still, and then discovered herself

being kissed again. She fought free and was about either to deliver him a resounding slap or to tear away
completely and run, but while these two excellent plans
revolved in her head, she heard him laugh merrily and
say, "But you don't even know how to kiss yet! Do you?
Most unsatisfactory. Sinjin has been very remiss."

His comment stunned her so that she turned to stare
back at him. The idea that one had to know how to kiss
had never occurred to her, and was the last thing she
had expected him to say. She instead only stared at
him, with a look of real puzzlement.

"You see," he said, "you still kiss exactly like a small
child thanking an elderly uncle for a birthday present.
That is not how grown-ups kiss, Regina. No," he said
gently, "not the thing at all. You see you cannot kiss
with your lips locked so tightly together, as if there
were some secret behind them that you must never
divulge. A kiss must tender up all secrets. You must
part your lips, thus," he said, placing a finger upon her
full lower lip. "As if you were, indeed, about to impart
some delightful secret at last to your lover, or as if you
were about to partake of some rare wine, to sip something of fine bouquet. You cannot taste, or drink or kiss
through sealed child's lips, Regina," he said, and seeing
her bemused expression, her waiting lips, he lowered
his head, and kissed her then, again.

But this time, she did not draw back, or fight free,
she only leaned forward, as if bewitched, into the long
sweet, entirely new experience he presented her with.
But when his hands began to leave her waist and travel
up slowly until they reached her breasts, she shuddered
suddenly, and broke free.

"No!" she cried, looking into his depthless eyes. "You
shall not. . . ."

"Oh I shall, Regina," he said quietly, strangely solemn. "But the point is, isn't it, that you shall? And you
begin to know it now?"

"*No!*" she said, confused. "Let me return. Let me
alone. You told me you would not——"

"I only said that I would not attempt to seduce you
here, and although I don't know exactly how extensive

your education has been along the lines which most
interest me, I assure you that it is exceedingly difficult
to complete a seduction of a young woman who is entirely dressed while she stands alongside of you in an
anteroom. Not that it cannot be done." He seemed to
speculate, with a laughing look in his eye. "But not done
well at all, no, most unsatisfactory." He nodded with
mock regret.

"I thought you were not here tonight," she went on,
avoiding his eye, aware that he still had both arms
locked about her waist, aware of his warmth and the
subtle pull of her own body toward that slight, insistent
frame that held her so close. "I truly felt that you were
not here tonight. I only left the others because I needed
to get away from the dancing. I did not . . . no, never
intended to see you here."

"But I am here now, Regina," he said. "And now
what do you intend to do?"

"She intends," came a cold voice from the doorway,
"to come in to dinner with me."

St. John, his face white with suppressed anger, stood
looking at them. Regina stared, with a guilty start, but
the Duke only smiled his immovable seraphic smile.

"Regina," St. John said tersely, "Amelia is looking for
you, go to her. I shall join you shortly. Go now!" he
commanded, as he stood and stared at the Duke. Regina
hesitated only a moment, until she saw that neither man
had any eyes for her now, rather they stood quietly
facing each other locked in some inner combat. She
turned and left quickly, welcoming the blinding glitter
of lights in the room she approached, even though they
swam suspiciously in her now dewed vision.

"But Sinjin," the Duke said slowly, relaxing and smiling up at the taller man, "I did tell you that I had set
my sights upon her, and you did decline my invitation to
compete for her. You said, I believe, for I do have an
excellent memory, 'I'll leave that field open for you.'
Now all I am doing is cultivating my field: a thing
which, to my complete amazement, judging from her
response to that simple caress you so rudely interrupted, you have not begun, and you are become an unex-

pected impediment. As well as taking an unexpected advantage. Sheltering her, clothing her, for all I know, and even introducing her as 'Lady Berry.' Not at all the thing, dear Sinjin. Very ungentlemanly behavior, passing off a poor penniless chit as nobility. Think of your hosts tonight. Why, half of them think she is your new mistress already, and the other half have been wagging their tongues about her all night. They would not be pleased to find out who she truly is. Unless, of course, I am altogether mistaken, and you have serious intentions, in which case, I offer you my felicitations, wish you joy, and will, of course, bow out completely. But in that case, my dear boy, is the announcement to be made tonight, or would you prefer that I remain mum until I return to town?" And he smiled warmly.

St. John stood still, his face very white, his fists clenched at his sides. All he could think of was how much he destested this man before him, and how little ammunition he had that he could battle with. Torquay's last words, however, had sent a shiver of pure terror through him, the soft words had held a volume of possible blackmail in them. He said then, in a placating tone he did not feel,

"Come now, Torquay, you know that I have no serious intentions toward the girl at all. And neither have I any long-term plans for her. It is only that you will allow that she has some freedom of choice in the matter herself. And if she seeks my company rather than yours, you can hardly be spoilsport enough to blame me for her preference?"

"Again, Sinjin," said the Duke softly, "I again understand what it is about you that so distresses me. So very little of what you say has any truth at all. I may be all sorts of a villain, but I do not try to dissemble at all. What I do, I do in plain sight of the world. While all that you do, you do in secret. I do believe, however," he said, cocking his head to the side, "that you half believe the lies that you tell, so that you tell yourself them at the same time you tell others and it all comes out so plausible both to yourself and to them. Oh, it's not a dueling matter," he went on, waving a hand at the Mar-

quis's newly aggressive stance. "I am quite adept at
pistols, even blades, as no doubt are you. But there's no
point in naming the killing ground, because although the
world will take a great deal from us, I doubt it would
ignore the slaying of one's peer. And I don't care for the
climate in Greece this time of the year, do you? No," he
said calmly, seeing the effect of his words on the Marquis, "it's . . . a matter of fact. Do you enter heavily
into trade? Ah, but then you do it in secret, on the sly,
and let the world believe that you have an independence
unsullied by the grubby touch of the shop and the ships
and the slave trade. Oh I know, I know, you needn't
stare so, there is little I don't know, my dear boy. While
my own poor fortune has roots that any fool can trace.

"I know, as well as you, that money is not in the habit
of breeding by itself in a vault, and that every well
eventually has a dry bottom. I too, have played the
merchant and the trader, in turn. But had you inquired,
you would have easily found that out. I make no secret
of it. And do you know, Sinjin, it is surprising, but most
people, even from the very best families, see only the
glitter of the gold, and give not one damn about which
mine it has been quarried from? But do not fear that I
will cry rope at you. If you wish it to remain a secret,
let it be. But know that I know.

"I, too, find fleshly pleasures exceed most others, but
I make no secret of my pastimes, while you slip and
slide and evade a path to all your mistresses. I have not
a damn for the world, and I flourish like a green bay
tree. As you do. I think that, yes, it is that which so
annoys me—your constant hypocrisy. That you are indeed to be my successor, I do not care. But that you are
forever presenting such a puritan face to the world, as
you do: that you pretend to be so repelled, so shocked,
so disgraced at my activities, while all the time you
emulate me—ah, that rankles. But that is not to the
point tonight.

"Now what is this nonsense about Miss Berryman—
pardon, 'Lady Berry'—preferring your company to mine?
The child sees you only as a sanctuary, not as a lover.
You've told her some nonsense about finding her a posi-

tion, haven't you? Don't bother to deny it, I have it from her own delightful lips that you have. It's rather like a mouse seeking sanctuary in a snake pit, isn't it? I know only too well what 'position' you have in mind. But incredible though it seems to me, she does not. One of the things I dislike the most, save you, my friend, is admitting an error in judgment, but it does seem that she has misjudged you as completely as I have erred in my estimation of her. But you see, Sinjin," the Duke went on, "it is only fair. I claimed her first. She is mine. And the only other moral justification I have, if you must have one, is that I have never lied about it. I have been extremely candid about my intentions. While you, with the same intentions, are spinning a web of lies so complicated . . . ah it does not bear discussion any further. Have done, Sinjin, turn her loose. I come to claim her now."

St. John stood quietly, his calm belying the murderous rage that he felt. Then he spoke scornfully.

"If I choose to try to protect my good name, you consider it a fault? If I choose to conduct myself with some sort of dignity so that my family and eventually my heirs do not find their names synonymous with disgrace and improvident to mention in polite society, you consider that a sin? Well, Torquay, you and I are indeed different sorts of creatures. But you are right to leave it for now, for it is a discussion that can have no end. To the matter of Miss Berryman, then. Suppose you ask her which of us she prefers? Which of us is the one she chooses? Would you accept her own decision? After all, we both encountered her at the same moment. So you cannot say she is your prior property."

The Duke looked at St. John with a considering eye. "But that is foolish, Sinjin," he said coolly, "for at the moment, she sees you, of course, in only a most avuncular fashion. You are only a kindly benefactor, and I a vile seducer. But I tell you, Sinjin," he thought and then, smiling radiantly, he went on, "if you were to make the same proposition to her that I have done, then yes. Oh, yes," he laughed, "in that case, with all the scales dropped from her eyes, with all the subterfuge pushed aside, if then you asked her for her decision, I would, yes, certainly abide by it. Are you willing, Sinjin, to come into the open? To finally put the matter to her coldly and clearly, without all these trappings? For that is a wager I will take you up on. It is, if you recall, exactly the one I offered to you when we both first saw her."

The Marquis wavered, seeing all his carefully constructed plans crumbling, but the Duke put in,

"Of course, if you do not tell her, you understand that I will. I grow tired of waiting. I desire her now. She is blossoming into a rare beauty. I like to talk to her. It's a novelty. Unless you hesitate because you feel sure that she could not prefer your protection. You are, of course, younger, and taller . . . but then I have *such* address, and such lovely blue eyes."

"No," St. John said, "then it will be as you say. I will have done with the charade. I will tell her. She will be given the decision to make. Will you abide by it?"

"Of course." The Duke smiled. "I love a good game, you know."

"But give me a day," St. John said. "I cannot tell her this night, for obvious reasons."

"Certainly." The Duke bowed impassively and, turning to leave the room, he looked back at the Marquis and, seeking exactly the right words, drawled, "I have looked forward to this day, Sinjin. It is so very pleasant to be proven right, to find that at last, you are willing to play upon my field, according to my rules, and in my exact mode. Why, at this rate, it will not be long until we are sharing exactly the same pleasures, and I should not mind at all, Sinjin. Remember, I have long told you that we are birds of a feather. Very black birds, though, I fear."

The Marquis felt an internal chill at the words, and stood, for a long moment, drawing in a shuddering breath, before he could face the rest of the company. It was now more important than ever that he defeat Torquay's plans, although in some small part of his mind, there rang a small, steady alarm bell.

The Duke strolled back to the ballroom and, finding

his host, joined him in desultory conversation, which mainly consisted of a documentation of the virtues of his three daughters, especially the two not yet betrothed.

Jason Thomas, Duke of Torquay, was at his best that night, smooth, urbane, delightfully conversant and clever. There was not a female that danced with him, of any age, who did not leave his hands feeling infinitely more desirable, and slightly, but delightfully scandalized, although he did no more or less than was strictly proper. There was not a youth who stood and spoke with him who did not walk away feeling singularly more sophisticated, nor an elder who did not shake his hand as he left, who did not think that surely the chap's reputation was exaggerated, for here was a man of rare good sense and opinion. He was at his peak; blithe, conversant, and deeply interested in every one who spoke with him.

No one in the room, no, no one in the world, could have guessed at the cold fear that gripped him, or the sick dread anticipation of failure, and some other emotion that he dared not name, which caused him to sit awake the unblinking hours in the Squire's finest guest room, while the whole house, save for the steadily working servants, slept peacefully through the last hours of the remaining night.

XIII

It was a strangely subdued party that sat in the breakfast room at Fairleigh on that dim winter's morning. Mary, pleading fatigue, had sent word that she would breakfast in her rooms after the excitement of the previous night. Amelia sat quietly sipping her chocolate and watching St. John's strangely tense face under her lashes. Regina seemed impervious to them both and, distracted, tried to bring her thoughts back from the unsteadying remembrances of the last evening.

She had seen the Duke again, but for the balance of

the night, his behavior had been impeccable. He had amused his companions, flattered his host and raised his hopes for the future of at least one of his daughters, danced with Amelia until her face glowed with pleasure, and said hardly one word when he had been formally introduced to 'Lady Berry.' Only at the end of the evening had he allowed his lips to linger over her hand for an extra heartbeat, and had whispered so softly, "The game is almost at an end, my dear, and it will be winner take all."

She had lain awake that night, her unruly thoughts returning again and again to that strange embrace, and wondering with dismay and near panic at the reactions that he had drawn forth from her traitorous lips. How could it be, she had agonized, that she could hold a man in such contempt for his manners and lifestyle, and yet, and yet, long for his kiss? It was against all the precepts that she had governed her life by. So now, while she felt secure and safe from him here, protected by her two new friends, she knew that she was not at all safe from him within the confines of her own mind. It is time, she thought again, for me to leave here. It is of utmost importance that I go far, far away. Although, she wondered, with an unsquelchable honesty, how can I go far from my own self?

Amelia left the table first, saying something about completing some correspondence she had to reply to. It was then that St. John rose and, looking over at Regina, said softly, "Regina, please I should like to speak with you now. About that position I mentioned to you yesterday."

She rose gladly, and made as if to walk to the study, when he smiled sadly, and said, "No, not here. I feel the need for some fresh air after last night's revels. I know you do not ride, so will you accompany me for a little stroll about the grounds? Dress warmly, there is a chill in the air."

Regina hurriedly put on a warm pellisse and, securing her hair, tied on a warm furred hat that Amelia had donated to her and was looking for St. John in the breakfast room, and then the study, when a glance out the window showed her that he waited, pacing slowly, on the drive in front of the house.

St. John paced as he waited for her to join him. He was thinking furiously, as he had all night. Too soon, he mourned, too soon. He had not had time to prepare her. He had played a slow and waiting game, considering that he had all the time in the world. And he well knew that she needed time. She still thought of him as a kindly brother, or a friendly companion. He had felt it unwise to rush her along too quickly, seeing how completely Torquay's complete physical interest had repulsed her.

But had it repulsed her? he wondered. Last night, seeing her in Torquay's arms, he had felt a rush of purely murderous rage. Seeing that grinning devil holding that lush body to his own, almost devouring her in his embrace, had sent the blood rushing to his head. It had been an obscenely complete embrace, it had filled him with envy.

But upon further reflection, he remembered that she had not been struggling, not been crying out in alarm, but rather seemed rapt in his kiss. Perhaps Torquay had read her character better than he had. He had thought her uncommonly bright, uncommonly sensitive and shy. And had sternly repressed all his desires to kiss that incredibly pouting lip, to stroke that lovely form, because he had considered her, in some ridiculous way, a lady. He laughed to himself. Perhaps Torquay was right again, perhaps I half believed her to be the Lady Berry' I myself invented. But Torquay had shown him the light. She was obviously no lady, not sprung from her origins, and he had mistakenly treated her as if she were his social equal.

Still, now his hand had been forced by his rival, and he must put all his persuasiveness to the test. She trusted him, there he had the advantage of the Duke. She knew him better, there was another point in his favor, for had they not spent so many idle hours together? And he was younger, he did not have the reputation yet that Torquay had. It can be done, he assured himself,

but he wished he did not have to be quite so precipitate.
But then, he sighed, Torquay did call the tune.

She joined him quickly, and they walked to the dor-
mant rose garden in back of the house. There, by a
wintery frozen ornamental fish pond, he paused, and,
looking about him to see if there was another being in
the vicinity, he bade her to stand with him. Here, he
thought, at least there is no one to overhear us. Although each word he spoke resulted in a little puff of
smoke on the frosty air.

"Regina," he said, giving her his full attention, looking down into the worried eyes, "it is now time for us to
speak about your future."

"You have heard from Miss Bekins?" she said hopefully, looking into his clear light gray eyes.

"No," he said, shaking his head, "not a word. But,
there is a future before you separate from that good
lady, Regina."

"Well, yes," she said doubtfully, "I do have an adequate education, Sinjin, but . . . no matter, if you have
found me a position among your circle, I am sure it will
be suitable. Please tell me about it."

"Regina," he said softly, "I fear you are not a very
realistic young woman, for all your education. The sort
of instructor that is required for young females in my
circle is a young woman who can teach manners, and
water colors, and etiquette, and . . . dance," he emphasized. "Very few of my acquaintances require a governess who will instruct their young daughters in Latin, or
Greek, or World History. It is not even a desirable
course of study for a young female. I think, to be honest, Regina, you must give up the thought of gover-
nessing."

"But then," Regina said desperately, "I have been
thinking, perhaps you know of an elderly lady who
requires a companion. . . ?"

"A companion," he said with regret, " to discuss balls
and routs, and the old days with? No, my dear, your
interests would suit you to become a companion to a
retired gentleman, or army officer, not a lady. For what
genteel old woman would wish to spend the long eve-

nings discussing the Roman Empire or politics? No, Regina, your upbringing has been so unorthodox, I fear, that it would be impossible to place you in such a position."

She looked at him with despair, her green eyes, he thought suddenly, the only touch of color in the drab, winter garden.

"Then I shall have to find a place for myself," she said stubbornly, lifting her chin. "And I shall not be a charge upon your hospitality any longer. No, no," she said, brushing away his protests, "even my uncle would not have expected you to take charge of me forever. And enough time has passed, I have battened on you long enough."

"You forget Torquay," he said cruelly.

"No," she said, "I do not. But I cannot make you responsible for my condition any longer. You owe me no further obligation, My Lord, your debt to my uncle has been paid. You have been a friend when I have needed one, but it has been but a stopover. I must travel onward now." She turned to go, but he held her arm.

"Regina," he said softly, "then forget my debt to your uncle, though I never can. Do you not know that I now have an interest in your fate which transcends that of mere obligation?"

She looked at him with amazement. He had been gallant to her in the past, but never outright in an loverlike fashion, but now his softened expression and warm look confused her.

"Oh, I know," he said ruefully, "that I have played mock-uncle to you, been the soul of discretion in your presence, but do you think I have not noticed your face, your figure, your smiles and fears with more than an uncle's interest? It was only that I did not wish to presume upon your distress. I did not want to add to your confusions. I am not, after all, a man such as Torquay. There is such a thing as consideration for the fact of your youth and ignorance. And what I have to say now may come as a surprise, but I cannot contain it any longer."

She looked at him with growing astonishment. They

had spent many long hours in each other's company, and though she had wondered at times at some of his gallantries, she had never thought, or allowed herself to think of him, in the role of a lover. Their conversations had always been remote, and erudite and unemotional. He was, she thought irrelevantly, an exceedingly imposing and handsome man, but for some reason, none of his grace or charm of manner had ever touched upon her heart. It was difficult for her to think of him in the manner in which he now seemed to wish to be thought of.

"I only speak now," he said, "because our time is so quickly running out. Soon my sister will return home for her confinement, Amelia must leave for her own establishment, and it would not do, you know, for you to remain behind here at Fairleigh with me, unchaperoned. There would then be talk that would be unpleasant for both your, and my own, reputation.

"Regina," he said urgently, taking both her hands in his, "you do not know me too well yet, but you do know that your uncle both knew and trusted me. Indeed, he trusted me with his most precious possession . . . yourself. And I mean to continue to take care of you, for your own sake—not out of any debt of honor any longer—and for my own sake. For you delight my heart, Regina. I can speak with you with ease and intelligence, and, although I don't wish to shock you, I find that I can even understand that . . . creature . . . Torquay's desire for you as a woman. For you are very beautiful Regina, surely you know that. But you may not know how very much I desire both your mind . . . and your . . . womanly qualities.

"I ask you to give me the right to continue to look after you, for both your own and my sake," he breathed, looking at her intently.

She found a breath to speak, shaking her head.

"But . . . but what about Amelia?"

"Amelia?" he said. "What about Amelia? She is an old friend, a very dear and old friend, what about her?"

"But," Regina protested, "I thought she . . . and you . . . that is to say. . . ."

"Oh, no," he laughed. "Nothing of the sort, we are only old friends."

Poor Amelia, thought Regina sadly, but seeing that Sinjin was waiting for her answer she said quickly, in a little low voice,

"But Sinjin, although I like you very well, I don't, I cannot, oh dear, I am grateful to you, but I hardly really know you at all. And I know that I do not love you, Sinjin, no, not at all in the way one is supposed to."

"That will come in time," he said smoothly. "At least do you admit the possibility of its someday occurring?" he asked, growing impatient with her reluctance.

"I suppose," she began, and found to her embarrassment that he was drawing her closer. "But Sinjin," she protested, drawing back a little in his arms, "I have no family, no fortune, no background, and you are——"

"I am only a man," he said, gazing at her. "And I want only a woman, not her background and history. I can protect you, Regina. I can give you comforts, security, and love. Can you not accept my offer, if only out of pity at first, and then allow other emotions to grow?"

Comfort, she thought, security, and love, and the flickering vision of that other mocking face with its offer of desire and entrapment rose before her. She looked into the strong face before her and thought, he is so good, indeed I don't deserve such a good man, only a monster could refuse such a good man, and allowed him to draw her close.

She remembered to part her lips, as Torquay had insisted, and, feeling his mouth upon hers, she relaxed against him. But she was surprised to find no answering thrill, no seduction of her senses, only a peculiar sense of herself standing outside of his arms, watching the kiss that was transpiring between the elegant tall young man and the woman close in his arms, the woman who saw another face before her closed eyes and heard other laughter in her ears.

He is such a good man, she thought desperately, clinging to him now, trying to blot out the other face, as the chill wind cut at her.

He held her to himself and kissed her deeply, a grow-

ing sense of need overpowering him. God, he thought,
she was a bewitching armful, if only he could take her
somewhere and go further, she was in such a yielding
mood. He fumbled with the buttons on her pelisse as he
held her, and insinuated his hand through the opening
he had created to stroke at one of her warm breasts.
She did not back away, and he cursed his luck at finding
her this acquiescent in this location. He held her close
and looked over her shoulder at the abandoned sum-
merhouse. Too exposed there, and someone might happen by. He knew he could not take her into the house
for any purpose, because Mary and Amelia were walking about in search of amusement. Lord, he thought, his
hand caressing her awakening breast, what luck to have
no place to carry her to now. He thought of the warm,
straw-filled stables, and his spirits rose.

"Regina," he whispered, his hand becoming bolder,
holding tightly, taking care to breath deeply into her
ear, "come with me now." She looked at him with surprise, she was having a hard time resolving the whirling
train of her thoughts. He stared down at her with an
avid expression, and she withdrew from him. He was
about to take her back in his arms, when a slight movement of a white curtain in one of the lower windows of
the house caught his attention. They had been observed.
He wanted to curse, but only sighed heavily. "Forgive
me," he said, releasing her, "I lost my head, but you
have made me very happy. I understand that you are
agreed?"

She turned from him and hastily buttoned her coat
securely. Her mind was in an upheaval. Why had she
felt nothing? Nothing but perhaps a sense of shock
when he had caressed her. When surely, she owed him
so much, and he was so very kind. But how could he be
so stiffly formal, and yet so ardent at the same time?
And all while he was asking her to be his wife? But no,
she thought, she was not a fool. He could give her
protection from all the cold winds of this world and he
could protect her both from the Duke and from herself.
She nodded.

"Good," he said briskly. "You understand, though,"

he continued, "that you are to say nothing? I cannot wait to have you to myself, to avoid this subterfuge, this . . . slipping about. But now, you understand, it is necessary."

She turned back to him, her eyes wide with amazement. "Say nothing?" she asked hesitantly.

He nodded. "We will simply tell them that your cousin found you a position in her house. You will leave, with appropriate farewells, in a hired coach, and then you can join me in London. I must go there at once," he went on, half to himself, his mind seething with plans, "to make arrangements . . . suitable house for you . . . near to my own, suitable clothes, all the arrangements. I will settle an adequate sum on you, Regina, although I know you will want to spend it more on books than on jewels and gowns. . . ." He paused, looking at her. She stood, stock-still, staring at him with an incredulous expression on her face. And then she began to laugh.

Her laughter rang out across the frozen landscape and brought tears to her misted eyes. "Oh, forgive me," she said, her voice curiously unsteady, caught between tears and laughter. "Oh, Sinjin, Torquay is right. I *am* a fool. A proper little fool."

He did not like the tone of her voice and, glancing quickly toward the house to see if any within had heard her peal of unseemly laughter, he asked her harshly, "Where is the joke, Regina?"

"It's a good one, I assure you," she said seriously. "Sinjin, would you believe," and she paused, realizing that for the first time she was speaking to him without that veneer of reserve and caution, speaking to him honestly and clearly, as she had spoken to Torquay, "that I thought, mind you, actually thought, that you were asking me to be your wife? Oh that is the cream of jests, isn't it? The mongrel Miss Berryman, or the infamous Lady Berry, whichever you prefer, thought that that show of passion and sentiment was a declaration of intentions? From a peer of the realm to a little beggarmaid. Oh my goodness," she said, wiping her eyes. "And then when you said I must say nothing, only then, mind you, only then did I understand. Why, you want me to be your mistress, Sinjin, just as Torquay does. Don't you?"

"Not just as Torquay does," he said tensely. "I really do admire you, Regina. I really do want only to be able to protect you. . . ."

"Only to protect me?" she asked quietly. "Not to make love to me?"

"That goes hand in hand with love, Regina," he said stiffly.

"Then where is the difference?" she asked.

"Torquay does not love you," he said solemnly. "He has never said so, has he? But I confess, I do. If the world . . . if my world, were different, I would marry you, Regina. But you would not understand. Could you bear to be rejected, out of hand, by all your friends, all your acquaintances, all your family, because of a misalliance? If it were true that we all only live for love and love alone, it would do. But in the harsh realities of this world, it would not do. And," he said, seeing her expression, "no, by no means is it only myself I am thinking of. How could I bear to see you rejected, refused entrees, refused invitations and snubbed in the street because my world thought you an adventuress? Because, be sure that Torquay would spread the story of your defection from your family, and the world would believe him. Your reputation would be in tatters, even my title could not protect you. But as my . . . secret companion, you could live in comfort, in security, wrapped about with consideration and love, your future assured. You have said that you do not love me, Regina, so your heart would not be involved. But use your head, and if you must use your heart, have some pity upon me. I could give you all that you have ever wanted, and you could give me the love I so desperately want of you."

She looked at him with a flash of something very close to hatred. But he was too intent upon his line of reasoning to see, and in a matter of seconds the look was gone, replaced by a closed, clear, calculating gaze.

"I know little of the life of mistresses, Sinjin," she said slowly. "Tell me, what becomes of a mistress when the . . . master grows tired of her?"

"I should never grow tired of you," he protested, but seeing her unblinking stare, he said quickly, "and as I said, there would be a sum paid. You would never be in need of anything for the rest of your life."

"And something else, Sinjin," she said, turning her footsteps to stroll back toward the house, keeping her hands tight together so that he would not see them shaking. "I know little of other . . . more important matters—in fact, I only learned how to kiss, I am told, the other day, but no matter—how can I be sure that my . . . lack of abilities in love would please you?"

He stopped her, with a hand on her shoulder. "I know you would please me, Regina," he said ardently. "Have I not given you proof of that just now? I would dearly love to teach you all you needed to know to please me."

She shook off his hand and strolled on. "But Sinjin," she said reasonably, "if I learn my lesson well, is there not the possibility of . . . children? I don't know certain aspects, but there are certain facts that are inescapable, even to me."

"Such possibilities can be avoided," he said, embarrassed by her tone. "There are ways."

"But not infallible ones?" she asked.

"Should such a thing occur," he said, feeling uncomfortable and eager to be away from her, to travel to London, to set the wheels of the arrangement in motion, "I am a gentleman. I would, of course, do the right thing, as regards money and care of the issue. But Regina," he said, "don't ruin this feeling we have for each other with such imaginings."

"But Sinjin," she said, pausing to look up at him with glittering eyes, "surely, the . . . issue, would not be a thing of my imaginings."

"I have told you," he said, unavoidably embarrassed, "that I will teach you many things. One of them will be a way to make such a possibility unlikely. But should the unlikely occur, I will continue to oversee your future, and the future of whatever else might result."

"But," she went on in a hard little voice, "how could you bear to contaminate your line . . . with mine? I am really such a mixed breed compared to you."

"I would do so gladly," he swore. "And if your world and mine weren't so dissimilar, I would do so legally. But what is a slip of paper to us, Regina? What is a five-minute ceremony to do with what I feel for you? I desire you, Regina, in every way a man can desire a woman."

"Except as a wife," she laughed. "But what about Amelia, and Lady Mary? What of their feelings when they discover the truth?"

"Why should they?" he asked. "Though you will all be in London, I assure you, your paths will not cross. You will live, as you did before, in different worlds. They will never know."

"But I should never see them again?" she insisted.

"Why should you?" he replied. "What are they to you?"

They walked in silence until they reached the door, and he halted.

"Go in, it is cold. I will go to London, I am impatient to go. I am eager to have you close to me, without deceit. Tell my sister and Lady Burden that some business has come up. I'll leave a similar message. You need only to say nothing. I will then send a note to you, purporting to be from—say, your new-found Cousin Sylvia, offering you a home and sanctuary until your majority is reached. Then all you need do is make your farewells, enter the carriage I will have waiting, and a new life will begin for us. I will send for you within a day. Think of nothing but our coming happiness."

She stood looking at him silently. He took her silence for acquiescence and, lifting her hand to his lips, he murmured, "You will not regret it." And, turning from her, he strode off.

Regina went into the house and walked quietly up to her room. She sank down upon a chair and buried her face in her hands. And stayed that way, unmoving, scarcely breathing, for a long time. The knock that finally came on the door was soft and hesitant. But after a moment, Regina rose and opened the door. Amelia stood there, unusually pale, with a small wavering smile on her usually composed face.

"May I come in, Regina?" she asked quietly.

Regina only nodded dumbly, and watched Amelia enter and find a small chair. She perched on the edge of it and looked up at Regina. Her gaze was fixed unwavering upon the younger girl.

"I don't mean to pry, I don't mean to interfere," she began, "but, no. That is not worthy of me. Of course, I mean to pry, else I would not be here. I confess. I did see you and St. John . . . out in the garden. Did he make you an offer, my dear?"

"An offer?" asked Regina, in a high, unnatural voice. "Ah yes, he did make me an offer. A most unexpected one."

Her worst fears confirmed, Amelia took a long breath and controlled herself.

"No, not unexpected to me. You see, I have noticed how he has looked at you, how he has deferred to you, how he has concerned himself about you." And Amelia, after one more shuddering sigh, sat silently. Both women stayed quiet for a few moments, Regina fighting for control of herself, Amelia finally allowing her last few vagrant hopes to die quietly.

"And," Amelia went on, as if there had been no lapse in the conversation, "what answer did you give him, Regina? I must know."

Regina stared at Amelia, and asked, cruelly, regretting the words the moment they were out, bald and curt, hanging in the air,

"What answer would you have given him, Amelia?"

"Ah," said Amelia, "then you do know? I was afraid of that. You have the habit of watching people, Regina. Not at all the thing, you know," she laughed unconvincingly. "I was afraid of that. But since you do know, then surely you know what my answer would have been."

"You would have said yes?" Regina asked in incredulity.

Amelia did not hear the note of horror in the other girl's voice, her emotions were riding too high now for her to pick up any nuance of speech. "You need not ask me that," she said unsteadily. "But I am a realist, Regina. And never, not really ever, did I really believe that he would ask me . . . no, not really. But your answer, Regina?"

"I gave him none," Regina said stiffly.

"But you must," Amelia said, now very agitated. "He has such a care for you. I have never seen him so truly concerned, so wholeheartedly involved. It would be a very good thing for him, it might be the making of him. For I do not delude myself as to his real character. Such a thing might be the very influence he needs to stabilize himself, to . . . allow himself to grow . . . to be complete."

"And do you think such a thing would be good for me too?" Regina asked, awestruck by Amelia's statement.

"Of course," Amelia said in excitement. "I am not a complete fool, Regina. I do not know who you are, or even what you are. But I do know that you are in some sort of difficulty, I do know that Jason is involved with you, I do know that Sinjin could not fail to make you happy. Ah Regina, you do not know him as I do. Beneath that veneer he affects, he is good. He is noble. Perhaps he has set his feet upon the wrong course for now, but all that can change. I would swear to it. Regina, please believe me, I do want the best for him. I so want the very best for him. And I feel that you could provide that. Whatever your history, you are young and very beautiful. But more than that, you are wise, and kind and loving. You could give him so much. So much that he needs. You must say 'yes,' Regina." Amelia stopped her discourse and searched for a handkerchief to stop the tears that had begun to flow. "Of all the women he has been involved with," she went on, muted by the cloth she held to her face, "only you have the soul and spirit he deserves."

Regina stood staring at Amelia, hating herself and St. John for what they had done to this usually careful and pleasantly composed woman. But still she could not accept what her ears had heard, still she could not understand Amelia's compliance with St. John's "offer."

"Amelia," she asked, curiously calm, "would you really accept the situation? Do you think it would be such a good thing . . . considering all the difficulties, not to mention the moral problems?"

But Amelia was almost beyond the limits of rational conversation. "Of course I do," she whispered, still clutching the handkerchief to her face. "I am trying to be honest, Regina. You know what I hope no other soul on earth knows, and I am trying to say the right thing for both you and St. John. But recollect, that I put his needs first. And I do believe he needs you. How can I in any honesty urge you to say anything but 'yes,' feeling as I do? It is what I would say. And as I love . . . as I have a care for him, I urge you to."

"Amelia," Regina asked, so softly she could scarcely hear the words herself, "would you say yes to being his . . . mistress?"

But Amelia had lost control, and did not understand Regina's question, or the purpose of it. She only sat weeping, flagellating herself for the despised tears, for the surge of sorrow she had felt when her fears, fears that she had harbored silently for almost a decade, had finally been confirmed. So she did not understand Regina's question, or the purpose behind it, and only took it as another symbol of her present debasement, an unaccountably cruel thrust by this friend and rival who had stolen all that she knew she could never have.

She rose and went quickly to the door, and answered through a sob, "His mistress, his slave, his footstool . . . yes to all, why do you do this to me, Regina?" And now weeping openly, she hurried out the door, thinking in her disarray, ah how shall I ever face Sinjin and his lady after this? How shall I greet Regina again, knowing that she knows all I have lost? How shall I be ever able to face the Marquis of Bessacarr and his new wife? And laughing a little madly, she thought as she reached her own room, What shall I wear to their wedding?

Regina shook her head, and shook it again, as if to clear it, like a dazed creature. Then she went slowly to the little inlaid wood desk in her room. She carefully extracted two sheets of paper and, without hesitation, began to write upon one. An hour later she looked down at the two notes, and the six others she had discarded. The one addressed to Amelia began;

"My Dear Lady Burden, I had never until this day understood the vast gulf that separates our two worlds. No, I had never understood that fact, that to all intents and purposes, we did live in different worlds. So I must ignore your advice, for though it might be applicable to a Young Woman of your world, it would not suit mine. My upbringing, perhaps, my petty moral sense, perhaps, but. . . ."

The letter to St. John was shorter, and more direct. It comprised only a few lines:

"Your Grace, A very wise man recently told me that there are some men who prefer relationships that are clear-cut, like that of employer and employee. I do not think I could be your employee. I do not think that either your or my spirit could grow in such a relationship. I am not such a person. Therefore, I would not be right for you either. I thank you for all past favors. I am afraid I cannot remain to be your Obedient Servant, Regina Analise Berryman."

And then, wearily, like a very old woman, she began to pack only those clothes that she had brought with her in the worn suitcase she had brought when first she arrived at Fairleigh.

XIV

St. John let himself into the small house quietly. It was still early in the morning by his standards, not even ten o'clock, and the ladies who dwelt in such large numbers upon this street were obviously still abed, since there was so little activity upon the pavements. How many years, he thought idly, as he opened the door, had he himself wakened, dressed, let himself out silently this early, to find the exterior world of this street so deserted at an hour when the rest of London was bustling with commerce. It was one of the pleasanter attributes of this discrete address, one of the primary reasons why the names of the actual owners of the houses was such a select roster of the peerage.

He felt curiously refreshed and alert for a man who had had so little sleep, who had ridden such a long way in the last afternoon and night. But after only a brief rest and a change of clothes, he had taken himself out on the streets at this ungodly hour to hasten the preparations he was making. He felt some small trepidation at the immediate task before him. Maria had only been installed here for a very little while and might be difficult to dislodge, but he could not suppress the small rush of joy he felt when he allowed himself to imagine her successor.

His reflections were rudely cut off when he entered the small hallway and heard a babble of voices. There was much laughter and giggling coming from the small sitting room to his left and, without a pause, he strode in the doorway, stopping the voices short. He looked at the assemblage before him with surprise. He had thought that Maria would still be in bed. Certainly, he had never known any of his mistresses to be early risers. But there, seated comfortably in the room, was Maria, in somewhat sloppy disarray, he thought fastidiously, her ample form carelessly wrapped in a feathered dressing gown, and her companions were two older, brilliantly dressed, highly made-up women.

One, a spectacularly raddled blonde with enormous black eyes, he immediately recognized as Lilli Clare, who was, if his memory served, the long-time consort of an elderly infirm Baron of his acquaintance. The other, a tiny curly-headed brunette, was Genevieve Crane, a giddy young woman whom he himself had enjoyed under his patronage a year or two ago. They looked up at him like guilty children, startled at his presence.

He had interrupted their poor version of morning tea, he imagined. He had blundered into one of their cozy chats. He had not thought of them as having a life apart from his nocturnal visits. But he shrugged and allowed himself to smile as he looked at them. After all, he thought with some charity, it was, for the time being, Maria's house, and she had no way of knowing that he was returned to town. It was not as if she were being unfaithful to their bargain; no male was present. And though he might deplore her choice of companions in his absence, it was really none of his business. As she would soon be none, either.

"Sinjin," she cried, gathering her gown together, "you did not tell me you were in town. It is too bad of you," she went on, giving her rapt companions furious looks and little waving motions of her hands.

Catching her eye, they rose promptly and, muttering little apologies, gathered up their belongings and left with admirable speed, leaving only a potpourri of assorted heady scents behind them.

"I had not planned to return so soon," he said casually, flinging off his cape, "but a certain change in plans has occurred."

She eyed him thoughtfully for a moment, and then, allowing her dressing gown to fall open more fully, walked toward him with the slow, seductive walk he had found so entrancing before and now watched only with amusement as he saw how her rather elongated breasts moved independently of each other as she paced toward him. Too much, he thought to himself, eyeing her rounded abdomen and the deeply defined bulge of her pubis. She wrapped two arms around his neck and sighed into his ear, "But *such* a pleasant surprise, St. John, such a pleasant surprise."

He took her arms away from his neck and stood back, looking at her sympathetically. All the mystery of her, he found, was gone. He could only feel a certain small sorrow for the confused looking woman who surely was running to a premature stoutness, and whose fading dark good looks would soon take her to other sorts of establishments, far from this fashionable street.

"I'm afraid," he said, "it is not too pleasant a surprise." He withdrew a check from his inner pocket and laid it in her hands. I'm afraid," he went on, "that my plans have changed in many ways, and that you will have to find a new abode. But you will see that I have been generous, and that you have profited from our acquaintance."

She looked, unbelieving, at the paper in her hands.

"But it's only been a few weeks," she shrilled. "You haven't even given me a chance! It's not fair. I've hardly even settled in. I haven't shown you all that I can do . . . there's lots more I can do," she continued, but he put up his hand.

"I'm afraid not," he said, and turned from her to look out the window.

"If it's the ladies who were here this morning," she said hurriedly, "well, you never told me I couldn't have in a few friends. We weren't talking about you really. We were just chatting. They are my neighbors, and all we do is chat. . . ."

"It's not that", he said in a bored voice. "It's only over, Maria. I ask that you remove yourself before the day is out."

"What have I done?" she wailed. "What will people think, you tossing me out so soon?"

"Say what you will about that," he said. "Blame it on my well-known capriciousness. But remove yourself from the premises, Maria. Our association is over."

But Maria Dunstable had been around the course too long not to know that her dismissal, so soon after her having acquired such a choice place, would look bad. And she was growing a little too old to be able to bounce back easily. She, too, had seen all the signs of her looks' decline. She, too, had seen the inevitable signs of where her path would soon lead her, and had been ecstatic at having attracted the interest of a fashionable parti like the Marquis. Her rage and disappointment got the better of her innate good sense, and she did what she knew was unforgiveable in a woman of her trade. She lost her temper.

"You poxy bastard!" she shrieked, losing all the soft-throaty cadence to her voice that she hoped she was famous for. "All right, I'll go, but it won't be a hardship. I'd rather sell it to a spotty grocer boy in the streets than put up with your fumbling grunting any more. I've had better. I've had ones who could make me feel something, too! Even poor Lilli's palsied old man can do it better! And even Genevieve's better off. She had you and she don't regret losing you! Not for a minute! I've had schoolboys who were——"

But he cut her off by turning and dealing her a hard slap across her face. White-faced, he gritted his teeth. "You will leave, Maria," he said coldly.

She looked at him, wide-eyed. She had slipped. He would never recommend her to his friends. He would call her a common doxy. She would never again have the comfort of her own apartment, she would have to work in a houseful of women, and then, as the other women became younger and more desireable, she would have to take to the streets. The enormity of her crime sank in slowly. She dropped to her knees and, throwing her arms around his boots, she wept, "Oh don't be angry. Oh God, I'm sorry. I didn't mean it. There was never no better than you, I swear it. I was only angry. Oh, forgive me."

Sinjin's lip curled in distaste. She was weeping uncontrollably into his legs. He forced himself to pat her head once. "I have forgotten it," he said grimly. "Now go and pack before I remember again."

When she had left the room and he could only hear her snuffling as she gathered her possessions together, he relaxed. He could see Regina here. He could see her sitting on the couch and smiling. He could hear her soft voice. Feel her lips. He thought of the evenings they could spend here, talking, playing at cards, discussing. . . . He caught himself up short and frowned. Daydreaming about a mistress who would talk and play cards with him? This was a flight of fancy, indeed! And yet, he remembered that there were those of his acquaintance whose mistresses served just such purposes. Men who maintained duel households, and seemed to treat their mistresses almost as they did their wives. There was, for example, poor foolish old Lord Reeves, whose weekly perambulations with his equally ancient mistress of many years was the cause of much amusement to all his acquaintances. For thirty years, as faithfully as a footman would wind an old clock, doddering

Lord Reeves would appear to take his now senile mistress for an hour-long stroll. A mistress until death did them part, St. John thought uncomfortably.

Yet he himself had never chosen his women for anything else but sensual pleasures. The Cyprians who enjoyed his patronage were always chosen only for their face, form, or reputation. Conversation was the one thing he never attempted with any of them. But, he mused, perhaps, just perhaps, if he were to set up another household, he would in time find himself in his dotage, making his unsteady way back to this little house every week, to visit with an equally infirm Regina. The thought caused his lips to curl in an unpleasant smile. He grew impatient, and tapped one booted foot as he waited for Maria to complete her packing so that he could then lock the door behind her. The door to his, and Regina's, new home.

When Maria had left, after giving him one long, last imploring glance, St. John let out his drawn-in breath. The fight had gone out of her. She had been docile and accepting of her fate at last. He noticed again, with distaste, as she had left, how sagging her body had been, how rumpled that face that he had found acceptable only a few weeks before. How entracing her somewhat humid lovemaking had been. But now he could only think of clear green eyes, of a long, slender, elegant female form. Of a soft, lemony perfume.

But, looking about the house before he locked up again, he felt a tremor of unease as he thought of the other women who lived on this street. Would Regina be willing to take tea with Lilli and Genevieve, or even Maria, if she were fortunate enough to find another wealthy protector? Would she take delight in comparing notes about their noble patrons, as surely Maria and her friends were doing? What would she discuss with them? Gowns? Their past? Their men? How could she even understand them? Who would her friends be? He shrugged off the unwelcome thoughts and left the house quickly. It was done. It had been an unsettling experience, that was all. But now, at least, the house was ready.

He had planned to go to visit Melissa Wellsley next, to let her know that he was back in town, to pursue that friendship a little further. Perhaps to the furthest. For now that he had Regina, he could contemplate marriage with a clearer eye. With Regina waiting for him each night on Curzon Street, he could easily tolerate a fashionable wife raising his family away, far away, at some country address such as Fairleigh. It was part of his plan and, he reasoned, a good one. It was, after all, time that he set about the business of ordering his own house, and providing himself with an heir. He would no longer have to search about for an amiable companion, as he felt sure that the liaison with Regina would never deteriorate to something as sordid and unpleasant as his recent scene with Maria. No, he would last with her for a long time, and take his ease, at last, with a delightful companion. One he could speak with as a lady. Make love to as a courtesan. He would teach her. It was all working out so smoothly.

But still, he did not, he mused, as he walked down the street, for some reason, feel like visiting with Melissa and her delightfully anxious mama as yet. It was not yet time to send Lady Wellsley into ecstacies. He laughed to himself, wondering if all men felt that way on the eve of a serious declaration. Did they all experience this . . . lack of enthusiasm at the prospect of holy matrimony? No matter, he reasoned, it would be easier done on a full stomach. He would take himself off to his club for luncheon first.

But luncheon did not sit well. And even the wine he sipped tasted slightly off. He was pushing the winestain from his glass into a series of little circular patterns on the snowy cloth when he became aware of someone settling down, heavily, into a chair beside him.

"Greetings, Sinjin," James slurred as he sat down abruptly.

St. John looked at his friend with some annoyance. James was red-faced, his eyes slightly unfocused, and his neckcloth in some slight disarray, that, along with the unavoidable fact that he had seated himself without even a polite by-your-leave, all confirmed the fact that his old friend was slightly disguised.

"At this hour?" drawled St. John, lifting an eyebrow. "Really, James, does one squalling infant reduce you to this? I confess you give me second thoughts about the delights of matrimony and patrimony, my friend."

"Never say you've finally been caught, old man?" James said in delight. "Who's the lucky lady? Do I know her?"

"No such lady as yet, not quite yet," St. John laughed. "But how do you come to such a state, James? The sun hasn't even begun to set and you are already in no state to be seen."

"Not so bad as that," James said with an attempt at bluster. "Just breached an extra bottle of wine. But I'm devilish glad to see you, Sinjin. Thought you'd rusticate forever. It's good to see you," he said, his round face shining. "I've been searching for you. It's been dull here in Town without you."

"Now, James," St. John said, smiling, "I've known you for too long to be too touched by your welcome. What is it you want of me, old friend? No, don't bother to protest, you are at your most charming, James, and always have been, when there is something you desire of me. Whether it was a pen wiper at school, or the name of some Cyprian when you were on the town, I do know that look in your eye."

"Put your finger on it," James muttered, looking around the almost deserted dining room, "That's it exactly."

"A pen wiper?" laughed St. John.

"Don't play coy, you dog," James whispered, sending out a heady breath of claret. "I need your advice . . . on a matter of some female."

"Really, James," St. John said in annoyance, "when will you begin to acquire your own amusements? It seems, no more than seems, to me that you are forever acquiring my cast-offs. And losing them as quickly as you acquire them. What became of Annabelle? I thought it was all settled with you."

"Drank, my boy," said James with ponderous import. "The woman drank constantly. Got sloppy about it. I had to give her a congé. But, Sinjin, you never told me about it," he said with an accusing whisper so redolent of wine that it drove all thoughts of dessert from the Marquis's mind.

"James," St. John said, drawing back from his friend's reddened face, "I only introduced you. I do not think it my obligation, or occupation to provide you with feminine companionship. Why don't you find your own divertisements?"

"Look at me," James said hopelessly, with wine-emboldened candor, spreading his plump hands wide. "Am I the sort to be able to dig up those dashing creatures you find with such ease? Don't know the first thing about how to go about it."

"Your money alone is enough, James," St. John said in a bored voice. "They are none of them in search of an Adonis. Merely an ample purse. Don't tell me you've been lying in wait for me to come back to find you another female?"

"But I have," protested James. "I've tried. But I don't want just any drab. The choice ones don't even seem to see me. And I won't settle for less. You've got a talent for it, my man. But look at me, I'm insignificant. Fattish, baldish, not tall or good looking. No, no, it don't matter how much blunt I've got. I don't attract the high fliers that you do. I count on you, my boy, to get me some worth for my money."

"James," St. John said with a flash of annoyance, "you're a married man now. Why don't you just disport yourself with your wife?"

James drew himself up to his full height, and a terrible look came into his eye.

"I won't have you insult my wife, Sinjin," he said so loudly that the few others in the room turned to look at him. "I won't have you saying such things about her."

St. John looked at his friend in alarm, and hastily put his hand upon his shoulder and said in a low voice,

"No. Don't fly into the boughs, James. I never thought to impugn the name of Lady Hoyland. Indeed, I did not. Whatever gave you such a thought?"

"Well," James said in a quietened voice, somewhat

mollified, "you suggested that I seek . . . that I visit my baser desires upon her. I can't have that, my man. No. I cannot countenance such talk. I know you're un-married St. John, and perhaps that explains it, but one doesn't think of one's wife in that fashion, no, one doesn't," he said, shaking his head ponderously.

The Marquis looked at his friend in amazement.

"What are you talking about, James?" he asked.

"I suppose," James began, with the somewhat heavy sentimentality that came easily to him in his condition, "that it's because you never knew your father. But I was fortunate to have mine for some years, Sinjin. And he gave me excellent advice. Fatherly advice. As a father should. Which is what you missed, I suppose. So I shall impart it to you. 'James,' he said to me, 'James, remember well when you marry, that your wife is a precious thing!' He told me that, Sinjin," James said mistily.

"Of course," Sinjin said, with a longing glance toward the door, "but I do have another engagement now, James, so if you will excuse me. . . ."

"No, no," James said insistently. "It's only right that I should tell you what my father told me, seeing as you had no father to tell you, Sinjin. You don't understand."

He dropped his voice to a conspiratorial whisper, and draped an arm over St. John's shoulder as he edged closer and breathed:

"Wives are not like other females, Sinjin. No female of our class is like those other women. They don't like it, you see. Can't blame them. They don't feel a thing, you know, except a notion to please their husbands. They hate the whole nasty business. You've got to be quick and neat about it. Got to get yourself nerved up for it, and have a drink and go right to it with no fooling about. And all along they'll just lie there and look up-ward, or aside at the bed curtains, and wait for you to be done with the whole nasty business. . . . Wait so patiently and with such fortitude for you to puff your way through the disgusting thing. They're not bred to it. They don't feel a thing. Aren't meant to. My father told me so, and he was right. If it's sport you want,

there are those other women . . . not a wife. You try
any of that sort of thing with a wife, and she'd die right
there, Sinjin. Just expire from shame and shock. Can
you imagine your mother or sister liking it? They don't
expect it . . . don't want it. Can't blame them. It's
base, Sinjin. Base."

"I see," St. John said, casting a pitying look at his
friend and disengaging his outflung arm. "But I really
do have to go now, James."

"Not before you give me a name," James insisted. "I
know it's base, but that sort of woman expects it. Likes
it. Got to give me a name. What about that Maria . . .
whatshername? You done with her, Sinjin? Or any other.
I'm . . . in need, Sinjin. But too much of a dull sort to
search out my own. They don't notice chaps like me,
with all my blunt. I don't do a thing for their reputations. Sinjin, please," he said, reddened now with both
wine and some internal struggle.

"Maria Dunstable," St. John said with asperity, eager
to be away. "Seek her out. I think she will greet you
with open arms, James, I really do."

"Sinjin," James went on, driven now by some other
forces and leaning his flushed face close to his friend,
"only tell me, because I can't ask her, you see, I simply
can't—I don't want a slut to laugh at me—but, does she
. . . does she . . . do the French?"

St. John hesitated. There was a new, sick feeling in
his stomach. He wished only to be away from James and
his drunken pleading.

"Does she do the French?" James insisted in a deep
whisper.

St. John thought briefly. "The French" that his friend
was shamefacedly whispering might be any one of a
dozen variations that he could think of off hand, variations that here and now he would rather not think of in
relation to James, but he thought, yes, Maria would be
glad to do any one of them for a new protector, she
would be desperate to.

"Yes," he said curtly, "yes and yes." And rising abruptly, seeing his friend beginning to speak, said only, "She
was at the Opera. You can ask after her whereabouts

there. Good-bye, James. Good luck," and turned from his friend coldly, to signify dismissal. James rose as well, and having the name he had sought, left hurriedly, muttering somewhat incoherent thanks.

St. John stood, curiously shaken, in a window embrasure and watched James make his unsteady way out to the street. The confrontation with his friend was really only a repetition of similar scenes that they had played out together on other occasions, albeit, this one was less subtle, more out in the open, due to James's condition. But he had never felt his own nerve endings as raw on the subject of his hidden life as they were now. Fleetingly, the unbidden thought of Regina came to him. The covetous, greedy look that he knew would be on James's face when he saw her in her regal splendor. The calculating look that would appear on other faces when he was seen with her on his arm, their silent calculations as to how long it would last, how long before they would have an opportunity to have her; how expensive would she be. St. John felt strangely unhappy at the prospect. He wanted to keep her to himself, all knowledge of their intimacies to himself. He would, he promised, if it meant never taking her out in public.

He looked up from these oddly unpleasant thoughts to see an intent face watching him from the depths of an armchair that faced the street. It was the last person he wanted to see, although only a few moments ago it was the very person he had wanted to gloat over. It was the blandly smiling Duke of Torquay.

"I see you have heard," he heard himself saying as he strolled over to a chair next to the Duke's.

"Heard what, Sinjin?" the Duke said in a rich whisper.

"The outcome of our wager, of course."

"No," Torquay said softly, his wide eyes losing nothing of their innocence, "I've heard nothing. Only when I heard of your posting to London with such haste, I too remembered some business in town. Country squires with eligible daughters can make the pleasantest holidays seem tedious, you know. Did you know, for example, Sinjin, that whereas the eldest was as beautiful as Athena, the youngest was as graceful as Terpsichore,

and the middle one was so lovely that she brought tears
to the eye? I confess I hadn't noticed it, but the Squire
is an honest man, so perhaps age had dimmed my eye.
Had you noticed their magnificence, Sinjin? I had myself been in the habit of identifying one by a rather
continuous giggle, another by an extremely tedious lisp,
and the third by the portly young man she seemed to
constantly wear, like a bracelet, upon her arm. It disturbs me that I might have missed such great beauty.
Now, had you noticed their beauty, Sinjin? For it occurred to me, much to my chagrin, of course, that if the
Squire could not net a Duke, he would be equally overcome by a Marquis."

St. John made a motion of a man brushing away a fly.

"It's too bad you didn't linger there longer, Torquay,
or you would have heard. I've won. I really have won,
you know. I'm here only to make arrangements for her.
She's chosen me, after all."

He hadn't really expected the Duke's reaction. It was
as sudden and as unexpected as a bright light blowing
out. The man recoiled as though he had been slapped.
The smiling eyes glazed over as if with a frost, the smile
was gone, leaving the face white and bereft of expression. "Ah," said the Duke with a sigh as if he had been
wounded in battle, "ah then.

"Where is she now?" he asked, almost involuntarily,
with none of the customary lilt to his voice.

"At Fairleigh, awaiting my message. Awaiting my
discretion," St. John replied carelessly, watching the
other man's expression.

But in that moment, the Duke had recovered himself,
and a new, strangely sad smile was posed unconvincingly upon the ashen face.

"Then I wish you well. I must confess that I am
strangely disappointed. In more ways than I can explain. In more than simply losing a wager. But then you
know, Sinjin, I was ever a poor loser. How did you do
it, I wonder? Prose on about the poetry of her instep
and her eyelashes? But I thought her impervious to
flattery. Offer her a goodly sum? But I thought her . . .
unimaginative about money. Make love to her? But I

thought her unacquainted with the art. I do grow old, Sinjin."

He paused and glanced down at his long white hands, which had gripped the arms of his chair till they were white-knuckled. He relaxed and flexed the fingers and then said softly,

"But I comfort myself with the expectation of watching the younger ones come to take my place. Perhaps I will then follow your ascendance with as much envy as any of the other novices to our arts. Perhaps I will become like poor James, and wait for your discard before I add her to my pack. Perhaps. . . . But I do go on. One of the disadvantages of age, Sinjin, this rambling on. I congratulate you, in any event. No," he said rising, "I more than congratulate you, you know. From the pinnacle of my five and thirty years, I salute you. I am lost in admiration." And, sweeping an elaborate bow that was a mockery, dredged up from some other lost generation of cavaliers, he made as if to go.

Some last vestige of vengefulness made St. John stop him.

"But what about the amount of our wager, Torquay?"

The Duke wheeled around, an ugly expression momentarily upon his face, before he said, sweetly,

"But how remiss of us. We never named it. Name it then, Sinjin. The game is yours, so the forfeit must be yours to decide. Name it."

St. John stood thinking for a moment. The Duke waited, standing rigidly still, then signaled for his coat.

When the footman came up to him, he bore both the long cape and a slip of paper on a silver salver. As he was assisted into the garment, the Duke rapidly scanned the message. His body stiffened for a moment, but then he crumpled the message into a tight ball in his fist and thrust his hand deep into his pocket. When he turned to St. John again, there was a sparkling light in his eyes, a dancing joy ill-contained in an otherwise impassive countenance.

"Name it," he said again, but St. John could scent his impatience, his newly fortified almost vaunting delight.

Some niggling fear at this rapid turnabout in the

midst of what he had thought was total victory made
him say, although even as he said it he was vaguely
ashamed of it:

"Oh nothing for me. But perhaps Regina would like
some trinket. Some bracelet, some token to remember
you by. For surely, it was you that brought us together,
after all."

"Done," said Torquay, with a disturbing sidewise look
at St. John. "Pardon my leaving with such unseemly
haste," he said over his shoulder as he walked to the
door, "but remember, I did admit that I was a poor
loser. A trinket, then." He laughed. "A token to remember me by. Oh certainly," he promised, and with
one more strangely illuminated look, he left.

It was some time before St. John recovered himself
enough to leave. He had sat, lost in thought, for hours
after Torquay had left. He suspected his rival's ambitions, but after all, he was, despite everything, a gentleman. No, he would not sink so low as to abduct
Regina now that she was spoken for. Now that the
wager was won. If he did, he would never be able to
show his face in any of their circles again. No, he was
not so lost in dishonor as to bring that fate down upon
his head. No matter what the impetus. He was too
conversant with the proprieties. And there was no doubt
that he had been badly stricken by his loss of the wager.
So that could not be in his mind. Still, something in his
affect had disturbed St. John.

But more than that had disturbed him. He sat in the
chair for long hours. Till it was too late to pay a polite
call upon the Wellsleys. Indeed, he felt he would defer
his visit to the Wellsleys. The girl would keep. Perhaps
it would be better to be settled with Regina before he
set up another establishment with Melissa Wellsley.
After all, a man could only do so much at one time. He
sat and rationalized, and thought, and was profoundly
disturbed. So that finally, when evening fell, he went
around to Madame Felice's, but found to his absolute
dismay that even the earnest blandishments of her newest recruit, a rosy-cheeked young simpleton from Sus-
sex, could not inspire him to anything remotely resem-

bling lust. He paid her anyway, and walked, lost in thought, all the way home.

But even in his own wide clean bed, the voices persisted. James's hoarsely imperative question, "Does she do the French?" whirled in his head, along with Maria's shrill screams about his lack of prowess as a lover. Torquay's maddening smile drifted over Maria's tear-stained face, and the dumbly questioning look of failure on the girl's face this night. He heard James repeat again and again his matrimonial advice, and heard Melissa's little brittle, "Oh la, Your Grace,' and throughout it all, always, in the background, was the sound of a soft, cultured voice, and the sight of two clear green questioning eyes. And lying sleepless, in the small hours, he wondered how it was that in winning, he felt such an abysmal sense of loss.

He thought of her then, living in that snug little house with the discreet address that he had been preparing for her. He saw her standing there, looking around her with incomprehension. He saw her on his arm, looking up at him in confusion, as all the others ogled and whispered about her. He saw then, as if for the first time, although he could have sworn he had never seen it, that briefly seen and suppressed look of hatred that she had flashed at him.

He felt her cool hand in his again, her lips against his, her laughter meeting his as it sometimes had when the same ridiculous thought had occurred to them both at the same time. He remembered why it was that she was such a poor player at cards, and why she had been so grateful to him for his role that he had played in her life. He saw what his motives had been, and were, and for the first time, saw clearly what they would eventually lead her to.

Until slowly, and with maddening certainty, he came to realize that in winning, he had indeed lost. Lost something of unclear, but inestimable value to himself. And rising from his bed and pacing, he began to put all the bits and pieces together, until he stopped short in the middle of the room and reached a startling conclusion. And though he felt at last a little light-headed, and

certainly a little mad, he also felt almost as a schoolboy
in his glee and relief.

And then he began to plan his way clear to winning.
Winning all, finally and with sureness, and with a sense
of honor.

XV

The attic bedroom was shabby, the furniture in it well
used, and the gabled ceiling was too full of chinks to
completely keep out the sharp wind, but still Regina
was as grateful for the room as if it were a palatial
chamber. She sat in a small chair that seemed to long to
tilt sideways and collapse under the accumulated weight
of its years, and in the dim morning light the little
window permitted, counted and recounted the small
hoard of coins of her purse.

"Walking about money," Uncle George had termed it
when he had pressed it into her hands while she had
laughingly protested his gesture. But now, she thought
wryly, that was exactly what it was turning out to be.
For if she did not husband it carefully, she would,
indeed, have to walk the rest of the way along her
journey.

There had only been enough to take her for a little
way along the coach route, that was, if she expected to
both eat and sleep along the way. She had been lucky
enough to encounter a farm family on their way to town
on the previous morning when she had let herself out of
the house at sunrise. If they had been curious about
her, they had soon forgotten all their questions when
she had begun to admire the youngest of their tow-
headed brood, and for the rest of the ride in their
wagon, she had been treated to stories about the virtues and escapades of their entire family. And since
they rejoiced in a family of nine children, there had

been enough conversation to last until they had finally
let her off at the posting house.

Again, she thought, she had been lucky in disembark-
ing here after a few stops, for the night.

For though the inn had been rather shabby and down
at the heels, the landlord's empty rooms had been enough
to convince him to admit the well-dressed lady, even
though she had no escort, no maid, and paltry luggage
with her. After a suspicious sniff, he had let her pay in
advance, and had given her shelter in this dreary room
under his ancient roof.

But now morning was come again. And her jot had
been paid for only the one night, and somehow she must
find a way to continue her travels. It was, she reasoned,
what she ought to have done in the first place. Although
Miss Bekins had never replied to her letters, she was
the one and only other human left on the earth who
could be trusted. All the niceties that she had worried
about, as to whether Miss Bekins could afford her presence, whether she could find a position at the school, or
would even be genuinely welcomed there, were forgotten now. There was no other place to go.

But how? she sighed, rising. There was only enough
money left for either a few more stops on the coach, or a
few more meals and nights' lodgings.

"An excellent game," she could almost hear that hoarse
voice laughing. Indeed excellent, Regina thought, rising
and taking up her traveling bag again. Oh yes, Your
Grace, an excellent game.

She asked only for coffee in the inn's main coffeeroom,
although the scent of good country ham and bread that
the few other travelers were indulging in caused her
nostrils to widen. While she sipped at it, she eyed the
others in the room. There were only four of them: two
solid looking country men, avidly eating and discussing
livestock in broad loudly interested tones; a morose
looking shabby pedlar who seemed lost in some internal revery; and one stout overly dressed old farmer,
obviously on some family business. They had all glanced
up at her when she had entered, with varying degrees
of curiosity, and then had lost interest in her. She was

clearly, their attitudes said, neither of their world or concern.

When the bored-looking young serving maid began to clear their now deserted tables, Regina rose and went over to her. "Excuse me," she said in a hushed tone, "but I wondered if you could be of some assistance to me."

The girl stopped her stacking of plates and looked at her with ill-concealed suspicion. Ladies of quality, her expression clearly read, did not stop to converse with kitchen wenches. Not when there was both a landlord and landlady, and fellow travelers to be approached. But Regina had been fearful of the sharp-eyed landlady, and had felt that perhaps only someone in similar financial circumstances would understand her request.

"I'm in rather . . . an awkward position," she began, quietly, for she did not want the only remaining patron, the old pedlar, to hear her. "It seems, due to circumstances that are too tedious to go into, that my funds are running low. Oh, I have enough, I assure you, to pay my way here, but . . . I shall need to find some sort of . . . employment, for a brief space, so that I can continue my journey. I have many miles to go. To Canterbury, as a matter of fact," she went on, dismayed at the girl's blank expression. Was it possible that the girl was a deaf-mute? "And I was wondering if you could tell me if there were any . . . positions available in this town, or the next along the route?"

"What sorta 'position'?" the girl asked in a loud, hostile voice, straightening and pushing back a lock of her lank hair.

"Well," said Regina desperately, "perhaps teaching, or . . . companion, or sewing, or. . . ."

But the girl laughed, flinging back her head and guffawing. "Teaching?" she laughed. "Not likely, and the onliest companions any of our folk might be looking for from you would be as a companion of the night, if you get my meaning. And why should anyone pay good money for a stranger to sew for 'em? This isn't London Town, my dear," she said in a mock accent, swinging her hips.

Regina flushed when she saw how quickly even the serving girl held her in contempt, and caught the pedlar's interested glance at her. She backed away in confusion.

"Hold on, Clary," called the pedlar, rising and coming toward them both. "Remember what the preacher says about Christian charity."

"I assure you," Regina stammered, aghast, "that I do not require charity."

"Naw, naw, you don't get my drift," the pedlar smiled, his long thin face showing animation. "Now Clary, my paw told me to cast bread upon the waters . . . specially if it don't cost nothing to do it. Listen, my whole business depends on good feelings. 'Good feelings'll sell more thread and gee-gaws than good prices,' he said, 'and don't forget it my lad.' Now," he said holding up two none-too-clean hands, "I don't need to hear your story, nor do I want to either—the less you know," he winked, "the less to regret. But my business is people, y'see, and I read people like the gentry reads books, and I say there's no harm in her, Clary. No harm atall. And if she were about the sort of business you mean, Clary, a guinea to your shilling she wouldn't be after asking you where to find it."

The girl flushed and ducked her head.

"Not that you're not a lovely little thing," the pedlar grinned to the sallow little maid, "but any fool can see that you're a good girl. But now listen, miss, it's a lucky thing you did run into us, Clary and me. For if it's work you're after, someone will have to set you straight, and Clary and me, why, we've worked all our lives, and likely will continue to do so, you're right to ask us. But no," he said, shaking his head, "no one hereabouts is going to be looking for a teacher, nor a companion . . . and even if they was," he added kindly, "they wouldn't be looking for one . . . off the street, if you get my drift. So you have to set your sights different-like. You see?"

"Now," he said, thinking, "Clary, what about Mrs. Stors in Witney? Didn't I hear that that wench of hers Gilly was coming to her time? And wouldn't she be needing another girl to serve in the taproom and main room? Why there's your opportunity, miss," he said, seeing Clary's little nod, "for Mrs. Stors is a good woman, she is that. And if you carry a tankard, and set down a plate, she can use you I reckon. Now the pay's not tremendous, mind, but there'll be good food, and lodging, and a good steady job for you. So if you can forget about all that teaching, and companioning, if you've got the stomach for real work, there's your chance."

"Witney?" Regina asked, thinking of her diminishing coins. "How far is that . . . on the coach, or can I walk to it?"

"Well," considered the pedlar, looking at her shrewdly, "I suppose I could advance you a few——"

"No, no, I assure you," Regina began, "that won't be necessary. It is only advice that I require now, please," she said gazing at him intently. "Only advice."

The pedlar sighed; she was such a beautiful girl, and he was a sentimental fool—he would not mind her being in his debt, even if he never saw her again, but he understood her look of horror. She was a lady, after all, and he took his hand out of his pocket again.

"Well," he said brusquely, "the stage ain't due for some hours yet, so if you take shanks' mare, strolling along under your own power, if you take my meaning, and walk straight along the road, you'll likely get to the next stop by late afternoon. Then it'll be only two more stops till Witney and the Crown and Gaiter. That's where Mrs. Stors will be. And tell her that Old Jack Potter sent you. That'll be recommendation enough. And good luck to you."

Regina thanked him and, picking up her case, put a few coins on the tabletop, and left.

Jack Potter watched her leave and, seeing her turn in the right direction, waved a farewell to her.

"You see, Clary girl," he sighed, "looks don't necessarily mean happiness. No, my old dad was right when he said that a beautiful woman attracts trouble like an old oak attracts lightning. So remember that the next time you wish you had big green eyes and a complexion like cream."

But Clary, who was scrubbing the tabletops with more vigor that she had shown in two years of work, did not find his advice comforting, at all.

It was late at night when the coach, with its customary flourishing of blowing horns and bustle, stopped in front of the Crown and Gaiter. The walk to the next stop along the coach line had left Regina weary beyond belief. Her slippers had not been made for a long tramp along a country road. But she had refused the offer of a ride from both a cat-calling group of young men in a farm cart and an overly hearty middle-aged man in a curricle. When she had seen any equipage approaching that looked well enough to contain any member of the gentry, she had quickly taken to the brush at the side of the road. She still wished to cover her traces.

But now she was lightheaded from hunger. When she had finally reached the next inn, she had splurged on a muffin and tea, and had been almost grateful that the coach was late so that she could sit and warm herself by the fire in the coffeeroom. She had been badly frightened by a slightly tipsy young man who had been ogling her, and who had looked as if he was gathering up enough courage to approach her, and had sat stiff and, she hoped, unapproachable looking until she had heard the clatter and rattle that signified the coach was approaching.

Once inside, she shut her eyes tightly and began to wonder, for the first time since she had begun her flight, what actually could happen to a young woman who had neither home, nor friends, nor family, nor trade. The thought had never really occurred to her before. There were, she knew, work houses for debtors, and poor houses for the old and destitute, but where they were located, and how one applied to them, she did not know. London, she reasoned, would be where they were found, but she could not go back there. But what did the friendless and homeless do in the countryside?

Women could work in trade, she knew, as milliners, market-mongers, and dressmakers, or in homes as serving girls, housekeepers, and servants. But one had to have skills or opportunities for the first, and references for even the meanest sort of employment in the second case. Even Belinda, her own maid in her uncle's house, had come with references. But she had neither a trade, nor friends in trade, nor references. She almost laughed to herself when she thought of what St. John's expression would have been had she asked him for references so that she could find employment as a parlor maid. But no, she soberly thought, she did not want to think of him at all. She had left Sinjin and Amelia and the Duke, and their whole world behind her.

Thus, when she saw the shingle with the Crown upon it swinging in the cold night breeze, she stepped out of the coach with mixed hopes for her future. It was late, she was cold, and she had only a few more coins between herself and whatever the unimaginable fate was for a homeless woman.

Mrs. Stors was a large broad elderly woman with a blunted face, whose skin clearly showed that at some time in her past she had been fortunate enough to live through an affliction of the smallpox. She listened to Regina impatiently as they spoke in the steamy kitchens. The inn was crowded to the doors. Today had been market day, and merchants, pedlars, farmers, and visitors from miles around the locality had crammed the inn full.

"Well," she said, staring at Regina sharply, "you don't look like a serving wench to me. But I do need an extra pair of hands tonight. And Jack Potter's a fair man. Still, I don't know what to make of you at all, I don't. You talk like a lady, you look like a lady, but your face and figure could get you a snugger bed than the one you'll have to share with Lucy, I can tell you. But I don't have time to jabber with you. So if you're not a thief, or a slut with a new game, I'll use you tonight, and we'll see what happens. But take off that fancy coat and put on one of Lucy's dresses, because I can tell you, my customers won't half believe you waiting on them with that Paris gown or whatever it is you're wearing. *Lucy!*" she bellowed.

A stout young smiling girl with black curls clustered

all around her broad red face appeared in the doorway, laden with tankards of ale.

"This here is Regina. Stop gawping. Take her to your room double quick and give her a dress to wear, and tell her the lay of the land. Quick. For she's to help you out tonight in the taproom. And be quick about it," she roared, and spinning on her heel, she rushed off into the kitchens.

Regina felt a bizarre sense of disbelief when she surveyed herself in the small mirror in Lucy's little room. The dress she had been given to wear was none too clean, and far too low cut and too short at the ankle.

Lucy's dress was an absurd costume for her. It was too brightly colored, of a cheap material, tight at the waist, and shockingly low at the neck. But a quick glance at Lucy's approving stare sank her hopes of crying off and donning her own severe blue walking dress again. Still, when she noticed with alarm how any little inhalation threatened the security of her precariously concealed breasts, she knew that she could never leave the room in it. But Lucy just grinned, and said, "Won't you be the sensation tonight," and after insisting that Regina unfasten the tight chignon she was wearing and "Fluff out yer hair a bit, love, so they won't think you're going to bite them," she left to the bellowing echoes of Mrs. Stors's "*Lucy!*" that rang through even the incredible hub-bub that rose from the inn.

Regina drew her hair back and tied it at the nape of her neck and, after resisting an impulse to tear off the dress and change back into her own clothes, she ruefully remembered the three coins that clung together for comfort in the bottom of her purse and, straightening her posture, she went wearily down the narrow flight of dark stairs and into the taproom.

It seemed to her that it was almost fantastic how the uproar seemed to quieten when she stepped into the room. The customers, a roiling sea of hearty countrymen, with a few rough-voiced women sprinkled among them, appeared to blur before her eyes. She looked down in confusion.

When she closed her eyes and waited for the earth to

swallow her up, the noise level began to rise again. She had no idea of how out of context she had looked, gliding into the crowded, smoky room, with her gleaming chestnut hair pulled back from her pale-finely featured face, her gently curved figure clearly delineated in the ill-fitting gown, her slender form hesitantly entering the room. But when she opened her wide green eyes, she saw the tables full of men beckoning, "Aye girl, some service," "Two bitters," "Some food here, Lass," and remembering Lucy's hurried instructions, she tried to place their faces and their orders correctly.

It seemed to be going well, it is not so difficult, she thought, when she could think, as she rushed from the tap to the tables, from the steaming kitchens to the uproarious tables. It was hot, there was a strong mixture of scents, of ale, of human sweat, of woodsmoke. But the patrons here were a casual lot, she thought. They were considerate enough, she thought, returning to the room with her eighth tray of small beer, for when she got an order wrong, they only laughed and handed the food about themselves. She could not distinguish one face from another, nor one voice from another in the uproar. But Lucy had passed her in her travels and had whispered, "Keep it going, love, you'll do fine."

The heat of the room had brought a pink flush to her cheeks, the drawn-back hair had escaped from its confines and drifted along her neck, and she was looking in confusion for the rightful recipient of her tray of beverages when she felt a strong arm clasp her around her waist and a merrily drunken voice slur, "Aye, here's the best thing I've seen in the market today."

She looked down in horror at the widely grinning man who had captured her and, trying to keep the liquids from tipping over, tried to escape his embrace. But a moment later he had risen and, taking her with his other arm, he held her still and pushed his sweaty, grinning face close to hers. "Give us a kiss, girl," he chortled. "Spice up the brew." A second later, she was swung away from him by another man, older and with the dirty face of a working farmer. "Don't be a pig, Harry," he laughed. "I did see her first, and I'm the one she's longing for," and with that, he captured her waist, groped at her buttocks with his free hand, and pressed her toward him for a kiss. As she felt his mouth upon her own, she gave a little shriek and tipped the tray, sending it splashing down on the table, and on all its occupants. Laughter rose up around her, and she pushed away from the man who had grasped her and, without thinking, swung her hand around and slapped him soundly on the face. The laughter rose even higher at that, and, tears in her eyes, she rushed from the room.

Mrs. Stors found her standing in the hallway, trembling. "It won't do," the woman said half regretfully. "It won't do at all. You don't have it in you, my girl. A serving wench can't behave like a debutante. There's no harm in the men, none at all. But they do expect a kiss and a tweak, or a cuddle and a saucy word with their victuals. Won't do to discourage trade. Oh they'll forget this soon enough, but you won't do. You'll never get used to it."

An unexpected light of sympathy came into the other woman's eyes.

"I don't know your game, and I don't want to. But there's a bed here for you tonight. And some victuals as well. And a few shillings for your night's work, but you'll have to be going in the morning. Try something else, my dear."

"No," said Regina stiffly. "Thank you for your efforts. But I don't deserve pay for this night. Nor will I disturb Lucy any further. If I may wait for the coach in your . . . parlor, I'll be gone in the morning."

The woman's face turned stony.

"Too much the fine lady for my charity, are you? Well suit yourself, but the private parlor's engaged by a gentleman. So if you don't want Lucy's bed, you'll wait in the street, my dear," and she turned and left.

Regina, regretting her rash words, went back to Lucy's room and, leaving the detested dress neatly upon the bed, dressed as warmly as she could.

Then, wrapping her cloak securely around herself, she quietly left the inn. She could see, in the fitful moonlight, that there was a place to sit on the side of the building, a long low bench there, she thought, for indigent coach travelers to rest upon. She sighed, grateful for the secluded spot, and settled down. Here, no one entering or leaving the inn could see her. She felt rather like a leper anyway, tonight. As she sat back and closed her eyes, the foolishness of her rash actions came to her. She was still hungry, still homeless, and still a long way from wherever her new home was to be. She would, she thought, take the coach however far she could still afford to go. And then she would have to see how she could fare. At least, she thought wearily, I shall finally know what exactly does happen to homeless young women.

And she closed her eyes and tried to doze until morning would bring the coach and the last leg of the journey that she could envision. So she did not see the slight cloaked figure leave the inn and, after a moment, walk quietly up behind her. Nor did she see the moment of hesitation, when it raised one hand to touch her shoulder, and then, after a pause, withdrew it. The figure stood, irresolute, while a cloud chased away from the moon only long enough to light the fair hair like a beacon. Then, with a small shrug, the figure turned and walked silently back into the Crown and Gaiter again, and with one last long glance at the shadowy recess where Regina sat, quietly closed the door again.

XVI

One more stop, Regina thought to herself as the coach bounced noisily through the morning mists. Only one more stop, time to linger in the warmth over one more cup of some hot liquid, before her purse emptied, and then she would have to do something. Only what, she still wondered.

She was now beyond hunger, beyond weariness, in that strange state of mind that exhaustion and deprivation brings. She felt enormously older and wiser than anyone else in her world, in that peculiarly exalted state of mind that extended sleeplessness can bring. She had not slept on the hard bench last night, rather she had sat awake as the night cold had seeped into her body until she embraced it as naturally as the warmth of a fire. She felt cold no more. And she could now review her future as dispassionately as if it were someone else's, with an Olympian detachment. Whatever else she did, she vowed, at last she would make no more pretense. At last she would be herself.

For, it had occurred to her during the long night, from the moment that her uncle had brought her to town, she had been untrue to herself. She had been living up to other people's expectations. First, she had pretended to be her uncle's cosseted and loved niece, when, if she had been honest, she would have realized that they scarcely knew each other. And she should have, she condemned herself, been setting about the task of finding her own place in the world. When Aunt Harriet had come, she should have been firm in her resolve; not for a moment should she have encouraged the woman to hope that she might eventually settle upon poor benighted Cousin Harry. She should not even have accepted his invitation to the theater simply for the expedient pleasure of being taken out for a night on the town. She should rather have taken the money that she was offered and fled to Miss Bekins, without standing on any ceremony.

In a veritable orgy of self-disgust, she had sat upon the hard bench in the inn courtyard and condemned herself like a prisoner in the dock. She should not have nodded dumbly and accepted the Duke's mad game plan. She should have forgotten about her dignity and screamed and shrieked and run free, without sitting like a fool and listening to his bizarre theories of self-respect and honor.

Indeed, in the case of the Duke, and her every encounter with him, she had been wrong. She had allowed herself to become caught in his web, to be fascinated by him, to almost welcome the verbal jousts she had with him, and, she realized with sinking heart, to enjoy other contacts with him as well. What arrogance she had had, she bitterly flailed herself, to think for a moment that she could deal with him as an equal. He had bested her every step of the way.

And then to cap it all, she should never, never have accepted the Marquis's protection. Never have pretended to be 'Lady Berry' simply for a safe harbor to rest in.

In all, she had pretended. In all, she had taken the easy way. She fairly hated herself now. And when she thought of those few moments in the frozen garden with Sinjin, how she allowed herself to be deluded into imagining he was going to make her an offer! Then the shame she felt when she remembered how she had rationalized her feelings in his embrace overrode all else. Even her appearance in poor Lucy's foolish little serving dress could not approach the self-disgust she felt at that. No, she had had enough of pretense. But, she thought, as the coach slowed at the gray stone inn, The Lion Crest, she had come to that particular conclusion too late.

When she stepped down and had her bag handed to her, she offered the coachman the next to last coins that she had. But he shook his head and declared loudly, much to the interest of the fellow passengers that were listening, that the sum wasn't enough. She had misunderstood, she thought sadly, and offered him the last coins in her purse, shaking her head to signify that there was naught else. He gave her a long hard look of regret. For, he declared in an undervoice, if he had known she hadn't the whole fare, he would have arranged some other way for her to pay him his due. But the objections of the passengers on the coach as to the delay merely caused him to drop the money into his pocket and sigh about lost opportunities. And the coach rattled off into the dim gray morning.

The mist was turning to a soft, sullen cold rain, and Regina turned to face the inn. She felt no further fear or trepidation. It seemed that there were few other depredations that she could suffer. She merely picked up her case and walked slowly, taking shelter under the overhanging eaves in front of the inn. She stood silently for a few moment, knowing that she could not go into the inn without the money for even a dish of tea. So she stood quietly, wondering with a strange sense of inappropriate laughter, about where she was to run to from here.

A moment later the door swung open, and the landlord, a huge bear of a man with bristling sideburns and a completely bald head, stepped out and looked at her with a welcoming smile. Yet he looked the sort of man who did not often smile, it was a forced expression for him. Regina was taken aback by the false welcome that seemed pasted onto his beefy face.

"Oh do come in, m'am," he said, bowing low. "I never thought you would just stand and wait outside in the rain."

She looked at him with amazement. What sort of new game was this?

"I'm afraid," she said quietly, "that you have mistaken me. I . . . I am simply waiting for the rain to let up before I continue down the road."

"Oh no," he said, picking up her traveling case. "I was expecting you, m'am."

"No," she said, seeking to get her case back as he turned toward the door. "I have no bookings here. You mistake me, I tell you."

But she had to follow him in as he simply walked off with her case of clothes.

He stood in the hallway and grinned at her. "If you'll permit me," he said, seeking to remove her dripping cloak.

"No," she said in exasperation, clutching the sodden garment to her, "I tell you I am the wrong woman."

"Oh no, m'am," he said pleasantly. "I was waiting for you to come off the coach from Witney."

Regina's numbed mind began to respond. Could it be possible that Mrs. Stors had regretted her harsh words and had contacted this man? Could there be a new position for her here? She followed the landlord as he led her to the back of the stairs to a private parlor. There, he paused and knocked softly on the door.

He opened it slowly and bowed her in.

"The lady you was waiting for, Your Grace," he said.

She stopped on the doorsill when she saw him. He was standing by the fire, and when he looked up, she found it hard to read the expression in his large blue eyes. But oddly, she felt only a vast sense of relief at seeing him. Seeing him, she thought irrationally, she felt a strange sense of homecoming.

He frowned, and came toward her.

"But you are frozen," he said, and taking the cloak from her, he led her to the fire. Once she was seated, he signaled to the landlord. "Some good hot soup, I think," he said imperatively, "and some other tempting foods."

"At once, Your Grace," the landlord replied, and bowing his way out, he closed the door behind him.

Regina lay her head back against the chair and relaxed. The fire was almost painful in its warmth. She felt a wave of tiredness sweep over her, but she opened her eyes to find him still frowning as he watched her. Somehow, he looked vaguely weary himself, she thought, the sensitive face looked paler, more thoughtful than usual, the cornflower eyes looked shadowed and were not lit with his usual inner humor.

"Yes," she breathed. "Yes, Your Grace, you were right. You do win. I have lost. I am a long way from Canterbury. A very long way indeed."

He did not reply, but stood close to her wordlessly until the landlord entered again with a full tray of dishes.

"First," he said, in his distinctive whisper, "eat and drink a few things. Then you can rail at me. I often find that vituperation is difficult on an empty stomach."

He guided her to the table, and she did eat some of the foods there, and drank some wine, at his insistence. But she found herself curiously lacking in appetite, and could not eat more than a few bites of any other of the array of foods before her. Then she sat back and looked at him again.

"I hope you haven't sickened, Regina," he said lightly, taking her hand and guiding her back to the chair by the fire.

"That would impair some of my plans, you know. It would be most inconsiderate of you. But you don't know how to take care of yourself, do you? Why did you turn down the offer of Lucy's bed? Foolish pride again?" he asked as he saw her eyes widen in surprise. "Or more of that sense of honor you do go on about? Oh yes, I was there. Snug as you can imagine, in the good lady's best parlor. But I imagined that if you refused poor innocent Lucy's bed, you could definitely refuse mine. And oh it was so warm and wide, but lonely, Regina. Alas, Lucy didn't tempt me at all. But I watched over you. I saw you wrapped in little else but your much discussed honor, sitting up all the cold night. I could have discovered myself to you then and there. But I decided, instead, to let you run your string out. And so you have, haven't you? For I know that you didn't even have enough money left to pay the coachman. You made quite an impression on Jack Potter, and he guessed truly enough that you, as he so succinctly put it, had hardly enough coins to jingle together. But I played it out to the end, that you can't argue. I waited to see if you could conjure up another Sinjin," he paused as he saw her wince, "or Lady Amelia, before I drew the final curtain.

"But now it is ended. It is over. Or have you any further protestations?"

"No," she said softly, "you are right. It is over."

"What," he asked gently, "no furious defense of virtue? No glowing plans for independence? No aspersions upon my character? I am disappointed. Truly. And here I looked forward to some superb operatic scenes. Perhaps you are too tired? Perhaps you would like to rest a while before you begin a tirade?"

"No," she said again. "No, I am beyond tired. But you have won."

He looked at her for another long moment. And she simply sat and gazed sadly back at him. He looked so complete, she thought, so elegant and in command. And so apart. His dark blue close-fitting jacket accentuated the fairness of his hair, the dazzling white of his neck-cloth showed the purity of his skin. A fallen angel, she thought again, amazed again at how none of his career was written upon that disturbing and clever face.

"Why?" he asked, turning to gaze into the fire and prodding a wayward log with his booted foot, "were you on your way to Canterbury?"

"I thought you knew all," she said.

"Why, so I do, but even I have some limitations. I knew all the facts, but there was no way of my guessing your intent."

"I was on my way to join Miss Bekins," she said. "But you knew that."

"But surely you received her message." He frowned, turning to face her. "I heard that it was glowing congratulations to you on having landed such an estimable position. She was so delighted to hear of your good fortune. Imagine, finding a position in a Duke's household.

"But, never fear, I was careful not to specify exactly what sort of position it was, and since I rejoice in having fathered one small (although sadly trampled) creature to carry on my noble line, her assumptions about your future duties were of the most benign. And she could hardly have withheld the news of the good fortune that had fallen her way."

Regina only looked up in stupefaction.

"I never received any message, she never replied to my letters at all. What good fortune?"

"Only that your estimable Miss Bekins is even now as we speak on her way to a marvelous job as a teacher in the New World, passage paid. Did you know that she always wanted to travel? A learned woman, your Miss Bekins, but a trifle too sober-sided for my tastes. A keen-edged hatchet mind like my own dear Miss Pickett is more to my taste. Still, she was adventuresome enough to leap at the chance to travel. You know, my love, it is an ill wind that blows no good at all. At least, my . . . arrangement with you resulted in some good. Miss Bekins would never have secured that exciting position in ah . . . Massachusetts, I believe, if it were not for certain intervention. And it was fortunate, imagine, she had only five hapless brow-beaten young ladies under her charge when I located her. No," he said, watching her closely, "I never did promise that I play a fair game. I do tend to try to cover all exits and entrances."

"But I never heard from her," Regina cried in a small voice.

He turned to the fire again and asked in a low voice, "Who posted your letters, my dear?"

"Why, I gave them all to Sinjin and he——" She stopped and closed her eyes.

"Ah well," he sighed. After a moment's silence, he spoke again in a livelier, mocking voice.

"So it's been out of the frying pan and into the fire for you, Regina, hasn't it? You changed your mind about Sinjin's vile offer, and escaped only to find yourself forced to comply with mine."

"He told you about that?" she asked.

"Why no," he answered, "rather I told him about it. It seems that St. John agreed to join our little game, to see if he could win you from me. Or from yourself. No matter, but it had become a three-sided venture. Did you not know? Then I imagine you made your choice out of affection alone. Whatever caused you to change your mind? The eternal fickleness of women? But you might have done better to stay with your original choice. He has a fine house in Curzon Street, you know. And I, well, I am erratic, I might just decide to incarcerate you in some pokey country abode, ringed around with daisies, far from the Opera, and balls and flash of the city. For I am very possessive, of my . . . possessions."

"I didn't change my mind," she said, rising and walking hesitantly toward him so that she might better read his expression. "I never chose Sinjin, you know."

He gave a little involuntary start. "No," he said, "I didn't know. Sinjin seemed to feel that you had, though."

"No," she said, "I gave him no answer at all. He took that for 'yes.' I suppose he couldn't understand my not saying 'yes.' "

"Neither can I," he said quietly.

"I told you. I told you that I would never sell myself. Although," she said, shaking her head, "I do see now that it was a foolish thing to say. You were right, I think. It is very easy to make claims, to say 'never,' when you don't really know hunger, or desolation, or fear. Then it is very simple to say 'never,' very difficult to mean it. You were right."

"No!" he exclaimed roughly, and swinging around, held her shoulders with his hands, seeming to have been shaken out of some rigid inner control. "No, Regina, I was not right. Not at all. I may be in control now. I may have the power, and the authority, and the facilities, but I do not have the right. Give up all else to me, but not that. I know full well that I do not have the right, and never did."

She did not shrink back from him, or avoid his blazing eyes, only swayed a little, and said firmly,

"No. You are wrong, Your Grace. I was such a pompous little fool that night in your carriage. 'I shall never sell myself, not for jewels, or comforts, or fine clothes. I shall not live a life of servitude.' I said that, didn't I? But I was wrong. I was, in the end, quite willing to sell myself—for security, for safety. You were right, you know."

"I see," he said, releasing his grip upon her, a look of infinite sadness upon his face, and turned from her again and remarked, in a hoarsely sorrowful voice, "So you do not come to me . . . precisely 'intact,' do you? What was it? I am surprised," he went on, wheeling around to face her and saying in a savagely mocking voice, "at Sinjin's ineptitude. Did he hurt you? Shock you? Have his tastes grown so bizarre that he put you off the idea of your new career entirely? It's really rather too bad, now I shall have the task of reeducating you. It can be very pleasant, you know, if it is done right."

"My Lord, Your Grace," she laughed, putting her hands to her head, really the food and the warmth were making her dizzy with weariness. "You do have a lovely picture of me, don't you? No, I'm sorry to disappoint you, Your Grace, but no, I did not . . . no, yours was the only lesson I received in . . . no, I am yet 'intact,' as you put it, in body. But, not in spirit. No, neither in principle."

"What are you talking about?" he whispered furiously.

"I was, in the end, willing to sell myself," she wept.

"Do you know, Your Grace, I was. I thought, now this is a jest you will appreciate, I actually thought, when he said he had an offer for me, that it was an Offer. I thought he was asking me to marry him! And even though I did not love him, or really even know him, I was willing to say yes. For all those reasons I discredited earlier. For comfort, for security," she wept openly now, "for safety."

"Ah Regina," he said, and gathered her close to him, and held her closely, and stroked her hair as she wept.

"But that is not," he spoke softly as he comforted her as a brother might, "such a terrible thing. No, rather that is the way of the world. That is very acceptable, you know. Why half of England would not be wed today if that were not such a normal thing. There was no crime in that.

"And," he said, holding her a little away from him and touching her teary cheeks, "every young woman has her heart broken at least once, you know. It makes you quite fashionable," he said with a sweetly sad smile.

"No," she smiled back—impossible, she thought, impossible not to smile back at him—"my heart was not touched. You do not understand. I did not love him. But my pride in myself, ah, that was broken. How could I have contemplated . . . allowing kisses, embraces . . . deceiving myself—all for only comforts and security?"

But he only gazed at her, his face unreadable, until he lowered his head and, holding her head between two hands, like a man holding a delicate cup, he kissed her long and longingly. "You learn quickly," he murmured in an unsteady voice, raising his lips from hers. "Is it that I am such an extraordinary teacher, or is that you are such an apt pupil?"

Regina could only stand and wonder at the emotions he could so swiftly raise in her. He kissed her again and then put her away from him reluctantly.

When he stepped back, his eyes were dark and solemn. He pulled himself away from her and, walking to the mantel, struck a pose, one leg negligently thrust out on a low stool in front of it, his head thrown back, and that damnable mocking smile again in place.

"I would wish," he began theatrically, "that at least there were a scribe here, or a witness. For I am about to do something so entirely noble, so full of lovingkindness and bravery, that I expect at any moment to hear a choir of heavenly angels. Or at least see a brilliant shaft of sunlight suddenly appear. My dear Pickett would swoon with rapture and anyone of my acquaintance would dine out on it for a year. For I am about to make an enormous sacrifice, you know, and no one, no one would believe it. Least of all myself. But you have quite turned me around. You have evidently magicked me."

"Regina," he said in a softer tone, "the bargain I made with you was an unfair one. An evil one, if you will. But I was rather like that Chinese emperor who proudly trotted about his kingdom stark naked until one day, one innocent little boy pointed out the fact that he wore no clothes. And only then did he feel shame. Not that I can feel shame, mind you, for I don't think I can call up that emotion at all, being a nobleman, you know. Yet I think I can still dimly perceive that elusive thing called 'Honor,' " he smiled. "For you turned down Sinjin's offer and mine as well, preferring to work at anything, even as a common kitchen wench, rather than accept our largesse for far less work, at least in our humble estimation. I did misjudge you, Regina, but then," he mused, "females such as yourself are not thick upon the ground, at least not in the circles I have been traveling in. And they have been circles, it seems, all coming around eventually to the same starting point."

He stared at her for one brief moment and then went on more briskly, "I did, I know, some quite unforgiveable things, but then I do not wish to be forgiven. I cannot say I'm sorry for what I've done. How can I feel remorse when I had not done it, you would not be here with me now? And I cannot turn back the clock. I can hardly go back to your aunt and Cousin Harry, and bow, and say, "By and by, I was lying, I have never touched Regina at all. I am, after all, only a blackguard." No, I cannot. And I don't think I would want to. You didn't belong with them, you know. And I can't stop Miss Bekins on the high seas and pirate her back to her pitiful little school in Canterbury. But I can make restitution. For you see, Regina, a good friend of mine," he paused and laughed and went on, "But I exaggerate even now. Rather say, my one good friend recently reminded me of another wager I once made. A wager in which the winning was far more bitter than the losing. I think I am done with wagers for a space. Regina, our game is canceled. I have not won, but neither have you lost. I shall give you a certain sum of money, and you may do as you please with it. You will be free. And somewhat wealthy. So you can finally discover what it is you want of life, and what it is life wants of you. There, it is done in a stroke. All done. But curiously, unlike what the preachers all say, I do not feel instantly cleansed, or one whit better. But it is done. I am the rulemaker of this game. And I have ended it as a draw. You can establish your own school, or travel and join your Miss Bekins. Or become a patron of lost causes. Or even go back and take over little Lucy's job. Whatever you wish. You will be completely free."

But Regina, looking at the pale and tormented face before her, only felt dizzy with the realization that had suddenly come to her. That all along she had felt drawn to him. That each time she encountered him she felt truly alive. That his mocking face had intruded on all her thoughts, awake or asleep, since she had met him.

She looked at him and wanted to be close in his arms again. She wanted to hear him rage, and mock, and discourse. She wanted to laugh and cry with him. He had entered her life and brought with him life, and she had the feeling that if he left now, he would take with him part of her life. She no more understood him than she understood herself, but now, in the heightened state of awareness that she had reached through turmoil and weariness, only her instincts still worked for her. And she knew that she did not want to leave him.

She walked close to him. "I do not want your money," she said slowly, "nor do I accept your charity. I consider that I have lost the game. I accept only that."

"Damn you!" he said savagely, and drew her close to him. "What are you trying to do to me, Regina? What other new defense are you breaching now? How far will you go before you destroy me entirely? You are leaving me nothing, you know," he breathed into her hair. She felt his body shudder, and then he spoke softly again.

"Then you will have to marry me, Regina. You could do worse, but I don't see how."

All her exhaustion suddenly vanished, and she pulled away from him.

"Marry you?" she cried.

"Yes, it is not Sinjin's 'offer,' you know. I make you a true offer. Marry me."

"So that you can complete your degradation!" she cried to his astounded look. "So that you can finally prove to all and sundry that you have no care for your rank or name? So that you can snap you fingers and say, 'See what I have done now? See how I am married to a nothing, to a no one, to a nonentity?' Oh no, you shall not use me thus."

"No, no, Regina," he said, his voice between laughter and tears. "What sort of nonsense is this? If I wished to marry for that reason, I assure you . . . oh, I assure you that there are others far more suitable to those purposes than you. Others of my much more intimate acquaintance, Regina."

"But I am not a lady," Regina protested.

"But you will be a Duchess," he smiled, "and if I wished to find someone unsuitable . . . oh Regina, you have no idea of how many unsuitable females I have managed to know. You, at least, can speak, and read, and write, and reason. You have not lived in the gutter. Oh, if I wanted to astound the world with a wife, I could do far better than you. But you are wrong, Regina, you *are* a lady, you know."

"But Sinjin said," she began, "that if I married . . . him, I would be sneered at, snubbed, avoided . . . it would be a scandal."

"Oh," he laughed, holding her close again and rocking her. "It will be a scandal, my love, to see how many, how very many will trip over themselves to become acquainted with you, to issue invitations, to include you in their every affair of consequence. For you will have a title, but more than that, you will have money and power. It is marvelous what a social equalizer that is. Oh you will be accepted. That is, if you wish to be. But I somehow doubt that it will be important to you. But if it is, you will have that. My birth, if not my worth, will give that to you, if you want it. And as for me, why I never cared about my acceptance and, strangely enough, neither has the world. And for those others who insist on being high sticklers, why, you wouldn't like them anyway. But for your children, love, why distance lends acceptability—they will be as acceptable socially as golden guineas, I assure you."

"Why do you ask me to marry you," she asked, holding him tightly, "when I have already agreed to your bargain?"

"Because it is best for you," he said, giving her a light kiss for each reply, "because I have a softness for green eyes, because you are lovely, because I wish to be envied, because I want to."

"No, why?" she asked again.

"Would you unman me entirely?" he smiled. "Would you win all, sweep up all the winnings and leave me without a cent in my pocket? Ah, Regina, you grow greedy."

"But I must know," she protested.

"First answer me," he said. "First give me your answer. For unlike Sinjin, I do not take your silence for 'yes.' Oh no, your silences are too loud for that. First answer—but know now," he said, "I do not offer you a marriage of convenience. I am too selfish for that. If you take me, you must take me completely. My money and my life, you little highwayman, for it would be a real marriage, of mind and body. Now answer, just one syllable, but answer," he said. And then prevented any answer by covering her lips with his own. She clung to him, staggered by her avid response to him, as though through no will of her own, as though her body had more wisdom than her brain. Here at last, she felt warm, protected, and at peace. Yet his lips, his clever hands, and the taut strength of his body brought her everything but peace. And then, when she felt she must

somehow get even closer to him although she did not
know how that could be achieved when she was locked
to him already, he raised his head suddenly, seemingly
to listen. He drew away from her, and walked to the
window and stood staring out. His shoulders seemed to
slump. She stood wavering, feeling bereft, as though a
part of herself had gone with him.

Now that he had left her and she could admit the
world again, she too heard the muted stampings of
horses, the rattle of a vehicle, the sound of voices, the
inn doors opening, the sounds of fresh activity.

"You are saved again," he said wearily, still looking
out of the window. "For see, enter the deus ex machina.
Comes the conquering hero. The shining knight. Again,
Regina, you are saved from me. Perhaps it is best," he
mused, almost to himself. "It was a mad idea at any
rate. It was not remotely noble. I was only taking
advantage again. It is poetic justice, it is deserved."

He swung about from the window.

"Come in, Sinjin," he called pleasantly as the knock
came upon the door, "We await your pleasure."

XVII

St. John stood in the doorway. He saw Regina immediately. Her pallor, her exhaustion, the state of her dress,
still crushed and damp from the rain and her travels,
and her wide green eyes a little frantic, struck him to
the heart. Ignoring the Duke's low bow, he strode to
her side.

"Regina," he said, "you are all right? You are safe?"

"Untouched," Torquay laughed. "Ah, but you arrive
in a good time. In but a moment more, she would have
been foully ravished. Cruelly used. Lancelot, you arrive
in time. In a good hour."

"I am well, Sinjin," Regina replied, and looked up at
him with disbelief. "Why did you follow me here?"

"But I had to," he said urgently. "I had to find you and speak with you. You were right, Regina. Right to leave when you did. It was the best thing you could have done. It . . . confirmed all that I felt about you. Regina, look at me, I must speak with you."

"But take off your coat, Sinjin," the Duke said lightly, "for you are dripping rain all over Regina, and I have only just dried her out."

"Leave us alone, Torquay," St. John said roughly, casting off his dripping cloak and staring down at Regina.

"So that I do not awaken love's young dream? Yes, I am *de trop* now, obviously," the Duke said, walking toward the door.

"No," cried Regina. "Do not leave, Your Grace, please, please stay here."

"But Regina," St. John said in a deep low voice, "I must speak with you . . . alone."

"His Grace has the right to hear anything that you might say to me. Is he not a player in your game?" Regina insisted with unfamiliar harshness. "Please stay," she asked again of the Duke, who stood by the door.

He smiled, and shrugged, and closed the door. He stationed himself by the window, watching her with a bemused expression.

"Regina," said St. John, taking both of her hands in his, "it was wrong of me to presume both upon your innocence and the situation that you found yourself in. When I read your note, I had already realized that fact. I came home from London to tell you so. I have been following your traces since you left us. I have inquired at every inn along the route. I have been frantic. Amelia is with me. She is just outside the door. She . . . she berated me too, Regina," he said, remembering the cold fury with which Amelia had greeted him, the contempt in her voice, the icy quiet that she had maintained throughout the days of their journey. And the curious thing that she had said when she had handed him the note Regina had left for him. "It was a cruel thing to do, St. John, no, more than cruel, it was unforgiveable. But at least I think you have set me free." But his search for Regina had been so desperate that he had not had time

to think further about Amelia's strange remark. "She
has come along with me so that you might be . . .
adequately chaperoned on our return trip. For you are
coming home with me, Regina. You are returning with
me. To be my wife. It cannot be otherwise."

"An embarrassment of riches," the Duke laughed from
his position at the window.

"You," St. John said through gritted teeth, "you are
the author of all these difficulties. You are in no position
to comment on this. No, Torquay, you shall not have
her."

"You are almost as bad a loser as I am," the Duke
said, "but you are right, I shall not have her. I only
mention the curious fact that she finds herself in the
unique position of being offered the name and fortune of
two noblemen within the hour. What a lovely pair she
has to choose from! A dissipated Duke, and a slightly
used Marquis. What a noble pair! And what a demand
there seems to be for your hand today, Regina. Are you
using a new scent? You see, Sinjin, I made her the same
offer myself, only moments ago."

"You?" St. John exclaimed, giving a short ugly laugh.
"You married to her? Must you try to contaminate everything you touch? Is there no thing you hold in honor?
No matter, Regina, you are safe now, from him, and
from me."

"Yet remember, Regina," the Duke said quickly, "I
did make you yet another offer, another choice. You can
go completely and the devil take the pair of us. You can
go completely free of us."

"Never free from me, I swear it," Sinjin said furiously.

Regina looked from one man to the other.

"But Sinjin," she asked, "what of the social suicide
that you spoke of? How can you now offer me what you
said was impossible before?"

"That is the news I bring you," Sinjin smiled, "for I
have discovered that it is easily enough solved. We can
get around it, Regina."

St. John took a packet of beribboned papers from his
pocket and spread them out on a table before her. They
were creased, and in some cases dirty and tattered

parchments, but he handled them with great care, as though they were priceless.

"I spent many long hours with my solicitor in London, before I came here. He is a canny and, surprisingly, very socially correct man. I confided in him, and I am glad of it. For he has devised a simple plan for us to win free of our problem, Regina. There are many émigrés now, from across the channel. People of birth and title and rank but who have been separated from their fortune and lands, penniless but considering themselves lucky to have not been separated from their heads, by Madame Guillotine. There are those willing to sell their titles, for a consideration. We will have papers—take your pick. Choose a name. Choose a rank. You can have any, or all." He laughed in delight.

"We will put it about that you are an émigré who has been educated in this country, that would explain your lack of an accent. No one has really ever known you, Regina. Even at the Squire's ball, you remained incognito. It will do. It will serve. You must see that."

"Oh I shall keep mum," the Duke drawled. "Never fear that I shall divulge the truth," he said, intercepting Regina's quick glance toward him. "It is a neat solution. Remember I told you, Regina, that most people will sell anything in order to find comfort in life, even their birthright."

"You must see," St. John said, his gray eyes pleading with her, "I need you, Regina. I will make a good husband to you. It will be only a little thing to do to ensure our happiness. What matter it what name you are known by? You will change your name when you marry me, anyway."

"But not myself, Sinjin," she said calmly. "I did tell you that I didn't love you, Sinjin. And I still do not."

"But you shall," he insisted, cursing the circumstances that led to Torquay's standing there, silhouetted against the window, for if he could only hold her, embrace her, he could convince her. He thought of his sick shock when, having made all his plans, he had returned to Fairleigh in triumph, only to find her gone. To find her note. Each word that she had written to him had caused him another stab of remorse. He wanted her now as his wife and mistress in one. He would not live in the double world of James, nor in the despised one of the Duke. With Regina, he saw, he could be complete. And he now saw how he could accomplish it. But there again was the omnipresent shadow of Torquay.

"If we were alone, I could convince you," he said huskily.

"How ungracious, Sinjin," the Duke said. "You are making me feel like an interloper, rather than another aspirant to her hand."

"Then leave," snarled the Marquis.

"Sinjin," Regina said rapidly, seeing him start toward the Duke with fists clenched, "I would never, no never consent to having my name changed in order to have my name changed. Berryman is no noble name. I have no title. But I am Regina Berryman. If I were to pretend, even if only for a little while, that I were a French countess, or lady, soon I would come to believe it. I would be living a lie. You too, Sinjin, would, in some small part of your mind, come to believe it. And somewhere in all the deception, I would lose track of my real self. It would not do. No, never. At least His Grace was willing to have me, common name and all."

" 'Love is not love which . . . alteration finds,' " the Duke quoted softly.

"Love!" St. John shouted. "What does he know of love? Is that the name he gives to all his pastimes? Don't be deceived by his glibness. If I could tell you, Regina, of what he has done in the name of his 'love.' " He stared down at her. "He is a byword for licentiousness. You are too young to understand what lengths he has gone to. How he has sullied his name and his body. What he has lain with . . . what women . . . what——"

"Creatures," the Duke put in in an oddly subdued voice. "Almost a bestiary full, in fact. Everything save for giraffes and donkeys. I fear he is right, Regina. I have ranged far. I have done things which, for all my honesty, I would rather you did not know of. I might say that it is all done. That I expect I could become an uncommonly dull husband. That I grow old, and weary, of such amusements, especially since they never did amuse me the way I expected them to. I might say that with such a wife, I would feel no need of them. I might say that you would leave no room in my admittedly small heart for any others. There simply would be no more room. That I yearn for some truth. Some end to this unending game I have played with my life. All that I might say. But he is right. Understand that completely. He is right. I can only offer you an unclean hand, and a slightly tattered title."

"But," she said, freeing her hands from St. John's grip and walking toward him, where he stood rigid, close to the window with a rigid smile upon his drawn face, "you offer it in honesty. Do you not?"

"That yes," he said seriously, for once unsmiling, cold, and curiously defenseless. "But Sinjin offers you a great deal more, Regina. Be aware of that. He offers youth, a name that is not half so shocking as mine, a title, and a fortune. It was not he who plunged you into this situation. It was not he who sent your Miss Bekins halfway across the world. It was not he who invented this cruel chase we both have led you. Yes, he became a player, he dealt himself in. At first, I believe, only to annoy me, but he soon played in earnest. But he did not invent the game. Remember, Regina, I abducted you. I harrassed you. I sought to corrupt you. I am the originator of the game, even though I was the one eventually captured by my own devices."

"Do you withdraw your offer, then?" she asked, her eyes searching his face.

"I do wish I could," he said regretfully. "But no. I am not, at last, so noble. I cannot change so much. It would not be possible. I still offer you, for whatever use you wish to put them to, my name, my fortune, myself."

"Why?" she insisted, in a choked voice. "Out of guilt? A sense of reparations? To compete with Sinjin? I must know why."

He put up both his hands in a gesture of defense, and smiling only with his lips, he said hoarsely,

"Will you play for such high stakes then? Will you leave me nothing? No little vestige of myself? I see you will not. Say then, because you are the most honorable creature I have ever found."

"Honor." She shook her head.

"Why do you wish to marry me, Sinjin?" she turned to ask.

"If only we were alone," he swore, "I should show you. But why? Because I love you, Regina. I must have you with me. I can speak with you. I can commune with you. I desire you. And need you." He tried to think of what else she would want him to say, and helplessly asked, "What else do you require of me?"

"Perhaps, honesty," she said. And turning again to the Duke, she asked, "Do you need me, Your Grace?"

"Your Grace?" He laughed. "It is a little late in the day for that, isn't it? At least let me hear 'Jason' from your lips, once."

"Jason, then," she said. "Leave off the game, I pray you. I must know. Do you need me? Why?"

"Have done," he sighed. "Who would not need you?"

"Do you?" she insisted.

St. John stood still and watched them incredulously, unwilling to believe the look he saw upon her face for Torquay. She never took her eyes from his face.

The Duke, at last, so pale that she feared for him, smiled once again, only this time with real humor and tenderness.

"I need you," he said quietly in his hoarse voice. "Indeed, more than any other man on earth could. And yes, I want you. And yes, damn it, I love you, insofar as I can understand the word. For I do not use it overmuch, as I am not sure I understand it altogether. But I am a selfish man, Regina. I think that if I really understood what love was, I would deny you. And insist that you leave at once, with Sinjin. I would renounce you. But I cannot. As I said, I am not a good man. But how foolish I am become. How can you wish to come with me, knowing what you do? I see your move now, Regina. Your victory is complete. Go to Sinjin, then. Collect all your winnings and go."

"I want to go with you, Jason," Regina said after a pause, hoping never again in her life to see that blanched

ick look upon his face, and wanting to erase it with her
ips or her words. She stepped toward him and looked
ull into his face. "Whatever you have been or done. I
lo not know either what love is. But, to begin, I like
ou, Jason. Even when you frightened me, I could not
lelp thinking of how much I could like you. I am happy
vith you when you cease to be on guard against me. I
hink of you constantly, and have done for weeks, it
eems. And for some reason, I only want to be with
ou. And yes," she said softly, forgetting St. John's
tanding so close to the two of them, seeing only her
vorld in the Duke's intent eyes, "I desire you, too. You
lid teach me what desire is, and I find I want only you
o teach me more. All of that. Is that love?"

"Let us attempt to find out," he said gravely, catch-
ng up her hand in his.

"You cannot do this, Regina," St. John choked. "You
o not know what you are doing."

"She is marrying me, Sinjin," Torquay said softly, his
aze never leaving Regina, his hold on her tightening.
That is what she is doing."

"No," St. John began, but Regina spoke swiftly, cut-
ing off his words.

"Yes," she said. "But Sinjin, do not grieve. For I
hink you have not lost anything. I think you do not
now yet what it was that you had asked of me, or
vhom it was that you asked it of. You wanted me to lie,
nd lie again, to myself and to you. You asked me to
narry into a lie. No. It is you who must yet discover
vhat love is. It is more than desire, I know. More than
ossession or passion, although I know that is a part of
.. It is rather, in the end, I think, a part of friendship.
ook to your friends for it," she said.

"Is Amelia just outside?" the Duke said softly. "Then
 must have a word with her. She must ride back with
s and stay for a while at Grace Hall. For I want you
ell chaperoned, Regina. At least, I will begin this
ight. And she will want to witness our marriage. I
now she will want to. But we shall invite a great many
eople, Regina. And you shall see how many will stum-
le over themselves to come to us."

He held her hand tightly and took her to the door with him, but she paused to look up at St. John.

He stood still, his finely chiseled face seemingly graven in stone.

"Some day you will find it, Sinjin," she said carefully, "but you were deceived. It was not I. No, never was it Regina Analise Berryman. For her, there was only desire. For 'Lady Berry,' there was love, and only for her. But that is . . . that was . . . never me."

St. John stood for a long while, only staring down at the hard-won papers he had brought with him. The names: Mme. de Roche, Mme. Vicare, Mme. Chambord, swam before him. He had lost, the thought kept repeating. Lost all.

The door opened and Torquay came in once again, moving with the noiseless grace he always appeared with. St. John felt a hand upon his arm. And a soft voice said:

"We would like you to come too, Sinjin. To wish us happy. Regina would like that very well. As I would. No, Sinjin, understand. You are yet young with a world of women ahead for you. Regina is the only woman in the world for me, indeed my only hope left for love . . . for honor, if you will. But understand, I do not gloat in triumph. I do not caper and fling your loss in your face. I, of all men, understand what a loss it is. I have long since ceased to regard this as a game. But you must pardon me for singing. For that is what I am doing, Sinjin. Forgive me. But I must sing," and as noiselessly as he had come, he left.

St. John heard, as from a distance, the sound of a carriage in front of the inn. He walked, dazed, to the window, and saw through the rain-misted little squares, that Amelia was entering the dark coach with the distinctive crest. A moment later, he saw Jason Edward Thomas, Duke of Torquay, his distinctive bright hair dewed with rain, drape his long cloak about a small figure that stood close to him, as if welded to his side, to shelter it from the downpour. He saw the bright head dip for a moment, down under the cape-draped arm, and for a long moment the figures clung together. And

en he handed her up into the coach. A moment later
e entered. And then the equipage took off, the horses
oving briskly down the darkened road.

But St. John Basil St. Charles, Marquis of Bessacarr,
ood at the window looking out into the deserted road,
me purple beribboned papers crushed in his hands,
s arm against the window, his head lowered on his
m, for a long while, a very long while, after the dark
ach had gone.

About the Author

Edith Layton has been writing since she was ten years old. She has worked as a freelance writer for newspapers and magazines, but has always been fascinated by English history, most particularly the Regency period. She lives on Long Island with her physician husband and three children, and collects antiques and large dogs.